Love Gone Wild

Amy Matayo

Love Gone Wild
Reality Show Series Book Two by Amy Matayo

This book is a work of fiction. Names, characters, places, and incidents are products of the author's imagination or are used fictitiously. Any resemblance to actual events or locations or persons living or dead is completely coincidental.

For my sisters, Tracy Steelman and Emily Mincks, for being the best friends I've ever had

And for my dad and mom, Hal and Jan Millsap, for raising us to love each other

Acknowledgements:

I would like to thank my readers for coming back for book two. It was a humbling and thrilling experience every time anyone bought my first book, *The Wedding Game*, especially when someone would take the time to give a nice review or send an encouraging email or make a sweet face-to-face comment. I appreciated each one, and I'm grateful for you.

A huge thank you to my fantastic agent, Jessica Kirkland. Without your guidance I would still be staring at a screen, wondering what the heck to do with the finished manuscript stored inside my computer. Thankfully you always know what comes next. You're savvy when I am clueless, sharp when I am dull, excited when I am lifeless, a marketing genius when I am not (which is always since I hate marketing). I'm eternally blessed by you.

Thank you to my editor, Julie Gwinn, for taking my very rough manuscript and turning it into something (hopefully) worth publishing. But more than that, thank you for believing in me and championing for me early on.

To Jenny B. Jones for being my friend and mentor from the very beginning. I don't know where I'd be without you—probably eating brownies at Panera and crying over what to do with my life. But thanks to you, there are rarely tears dripping on my chocolate frosting.

To Carla Laureano for commiserating with me every morning between the hours of 7:00 and 11:59, and every afternoon between 12:01 and midnight. You've talked me off the proverbial (and not so proverbial) cliff many times, and your words of encouragement mean everything to me.

To Stacy Henagan, Joy Francoeur, and Nicole Deese for reading this unedited manuscript and offering advice on how make the story better. As far as I know, you've never compared notes or made fun of my obvious lack of talent. At least not to my face.

To Alec Stockton for giving my family the chance to get to know you and for sharing my love for writing. You make life fun in all the ways that matter. Welcome to our lives, friend.

To my family—both the Millsap side and the Matayo side—for putting up with me when I'm writing under a deadline and going through last-minute freak-outs. Please forgive me for not answering my phone and forgetting to text back and rarely showing up on time and begging for food. Wait—never mind that last one. I still want food. Pizza, please. Or maybe tacos. Cake is good, too. And pie.

To my husband and kids for loving me even when I'm crazy and for bearing with me when I haven't slept for days and for putting up with me when I forget to make dinner. Next time that happens, call my mom. She's supposed to be making us tacos. And a cake.

And to Jesus Christ for saving my life. I'm messy and ridiculous and constantly screwing up, but your grace makes all the difference.

I love you all.

Prologue

They sat around a table at Anna's favorite restaurant, yet another sign in a long list of signals that her parents weren't happy with her. First, there was the spontaneous phone call asking her to join them for dinner at Carmine's. The suggestion alone chilled her, snaking an icy trail down her spine that still hadn't warmed hours later. Nervous, Anna twisted her thumb and shivered in place. Her parents hated this restaurant, hated Italian food—and the red sauce that so often made a mess of perfectly elegant attire. *No one should ever be caught slurping spaghetti in public*—a rule her mother lived by.

But Anna kept her thoughts to herself. As always, life was easier that way.

It took only a minute for the third sign—the real reason they were here—to make its appearance. Anna's rejection letter into Northwestern Law School lay on the table between them, but she had nothing to say, no valid reason to give them for her latest failure.

"So what are we going to do about this?" her father asked yet again, growing impatient at Anna's loss for words.

"Look on the bright side," Anna said. "I think we all knew law school was a stretch for me, so we should look at it as a blessing. America hardly needs one more Lloyd practicing law in this town. And just think, I'll be the subject of one less lawyer joke…"

She stopped talking when her father's face bloomed red, swallowed hard when her mother's went rigid and entirely devoid of humor. Anna shifted in her seat. *Her parents.* She knew they often wondered if she'd somehow been switched at birth—if possibly somewhere out there, their real academia-loving child was roaming the earth with a Trapper Keeper, a pocket protector, and a copy of *Harvard Review* tucked under one arm.

But instead—they had me. And that ambitious law graduate was nothing but her parent's dream.

"Listen here, young lady..." Alexander Lloyd began. Not since JFK had there been a man as well-esteemed in political circles as Anna's father. National magazines had devoted three-page spreads to their family—treating them as modern-day royalty in a world that no longer needed them. Kings and queens might be a thing of the past, but the role of Princess fell on Anna anyway. And with that title came every suffocating rule that could exist for a girl—and she resented them for it.

The only thing that could make things worse was if Alexander Lloyd decided to run for President, which would only be a matter of time. And her fate would be sealed forever—a secret service prison with the whole world watching.

"...The Lloyd line has been full of lawyers since the dawn of time, and no daughter of mine is going to break tradition." Anna suppressed another sigh, resisted the urge to point out that, at twenty-six she wasn't exactly young, and—for possibly the millionth time since she drew her first breath—cursed the fact that she was an only child.

Anna was a disappointment at almost everything she put her hands to. From her kindergarten piano recital to her five attempts to pass her driver's test, to her inability to get into Harvard Law School—hence the *Harvard Review* that she *didn't* have under her arm. Nothing had come easy for her. In fact, most things in life had never come at all.

And everyone seated around this table knew it. Two of them had a plan to fix it, and Anna would silently live with the fallout forever.

"The way I see it, you have two options," her father said. And I have a feeling you won't like either one."

Anna knew she wouldn't. Knew it in her bones before he said the options out loud. After all, it was the same path her parents had taken…the same one her grandparents and uncles and almost anyone with the last name Lloyd—with the exception of a distant cousin that no one had spoken to in over twelve years—had also taken.

One way or another, she would become a lawyer.

Or just like Catherine Zeta Jones in *Intolerable Cruelty*…

She would find herself one and marry him.

One year later:

<u>Chapter 1</u>

It was her last shot at adventure before real life set in permanently, and Anna Lloyd grabbed onto it with everything she had. She needed this. She wanted this. There were just two problems.

One, she had to fly to get to Alaska. More than anything in life, Anna hated to fly.

Somewhere between "We've been cleared for take-off" and two front tires going airborne, she found herself clutching the armrest in a white-knuckled death grip. Her breaths came in asthmatic gasps as she shot rapid-fire prayers toward heaven like a million bargains with God. *Get me on the ground safely, and I'll spend every second of the rest my life in church. Swear to, well...You.* And today would be no exception.

Which is why she decided to buy candy. She had to get through the torture of flight somehow, and Snickers seemed to be the best option.

"Can I help you, Ma'am?" The lady behind the counter looked at her with an air of suspicion, as though Anna's two minutes wandering around the store automatically meant she was looking to shoplift something.

"No thanks. I'm just killing a little time." Which she was. She still had over thirty minutes until boarding time, and waiting patiently wasn't her best attribute. Neither was her bra size, but that was another issue entirely.

"Well, let me know if I can help you," the woman said.

"Actually, I can't seem to find any—" and that's the last sentence Anna uttered before her world collapsed around her. Heart stopped. Mind shattered. Senses obliterated.

The last thought she had before her vision blurred red was...

How could I be so stupid?

***

Anna curled the tabloid in her lap and willed herself to calm down. The plane ascended above the clouds, situated outside her window like mounds of dollar-store cotton balls. But instead of being frightened like she expected to be, Anna was too shell shocked and angry to care.

"The way I see it, Anna, you have two options..." Her father's long-ago words played in her head like a call to arms while she sat and stared at the image of option one smiling from the front page of the newspaper in front of her. Ryan Lance—son of Chicago's most high-powered fundraiser and her lawyer boyfriend of ten months—kissing a B-list Hollywood actress whose last movie barely made the Hallmark Channel, and it was one of the cheesiest ones at that. But the actress wasn't the main story.

Anna was. The article outlined in graphic detail why the boyfriend of America's next First Daughter would be cheating in a seedy nightclub on the same night Anna was leaving on an extended trip. Was he bored? Was he sad? Was it his way to cope with Anna's selfish decision to audition for a reality show and leave town for five weeks?

They didn't know it was his idea.

"You would never survive a show like that," Ryan had said several months ago while Anna watched last season's finale of *The Alaskan Wild* in her parent's living room. It was her mother's fiftieth birthday, and the family had gathered with a few local celebrities and Chicago

news anchors to celebrate with a garden party in the back yard. Needing a break from all the back-slapping and general suck-upping that happened around America's probable First Family, Anna had escaped inside the house to catch the end of the show. She was tired of the charade. Plus, she'd watched the entire season and didn't want to miss the end.

"Wanna bet?" Anna had always loved the outdoors and had spent most of the season foolishly wishing she could participate. But the odds of making the cut were slim. The odds of getting her parents to agree were even slimmer. But suddenly she'd decided to try. It usually resulted in failure, but she knew for a fact that casting calls were being held the next week and she didn't usually back down from a challenge. She raised an eyebrow in Ryan's direction, her meaning clear.

The laughter died down instantly. Her mother's gaze turned steely, though Anna could have sworn she saw a flicker of a smile. "Anna, you can't be serious."

"I am serious. I'm going to audition." When no one said another word, she had an idea. "If I win, I'll donate the money to charity. A million dollars to the organization of dad's choice would be a nice photo op for his campaign. Just think of the publicity it would garner."

Anna felt dirty saying the words, but she was desperate.

"Anna, come on," Ryan said with an eye roll and a glance in her dad's direction. "You're not going to audition, and you know it. You have absolutely no survival instinct. You'd never make it."

But her father's gaze flickered with interest. Her mother stood stock still, not moving and—more than likely—not breathing. Ryan just looked at her. Then swallowed. Then shifted in place. The son of one of the country's most prominent political fund raisers suddenly had nothing to say. Nothing but—

"All right, then. Try out. Donating the money to charity is a great idea, especially if it's timed to happen right before the election. A million dollars handed to a bunch of unfortunate kids should garner all kinds of sympathy votes."

Suddenly, Anna wanted a shower.

Surprisingly, everyone had agreed. But no one really expected her to make it onto the show. Truthfully, neither did she. But four months later, here she was. A seriously out-of-place girl landing in the Alaskan wilderness to join a team of ten players with absolutely no idea what she was doing. The prospect both thrilled and frightened her, because in twenty-six years of living she'd never been allowed to do something this crazy.

Anna tucked the tabloid inside her bag and looked out the window, blinking away the memory, trying to ignore the hurt stealing her breaths and leaving her lightheaded.

She only hoped *crazy* wouldn't kill her. That she could survive without completely humiliating herself. Ryan, her parents—no one would let her forget it if she didn't come out a winner. Or at the very least, a strong contender. As for her relationship with Ryan, it would stay intact without a doubt. It had to. No matter what she'd seen on the tabloid, Anna wasn't about to fail at it, too. Her father's political future...*her* future...depended on it. Ryan's family had deep pockets, and her father needed this to work—needed his daughter to not ruin things for a change. Because if she didn't—then he could kiss his political future goodbye.

She'd never felt so trapped before. Even the prospect of getting lost in the wilderness didn't compare to thoughts of life with a cheater, no matter how much she still loved him.

"Ma'am, can you please pull your seat upright?" The flight attendant asked in a clipped voice. *Ma'am.* Not even twenty-six, and she'd been called that name twice already today. But at least the woman didn't recognize her. Today of all days, Anna didn't want to deal with having to paste on a smile and play nice with an overeager celebrity stalker.

Not that Anna was *that* famous, but she almost always got recognized by someone.

Relieved, she straightened in her seat and glanced out the window, fighting back a wave of unwelcome tears. The clouds below broke momentarily, giving her a brief glimpse of the Alaskan forest below them. In twenty short minutes, they would land and begin this crazy journey. It would be her last taste of freedom for the foreseeable future, reluctantly agreed to in a half-hearted attempt by her family to amuse her sense of adventure.

Hopefully it wouldn't be the biggest mistake of her life.

But even if it was, in light of today's events, Anna no longer had anything to go home to, anyway.

***

The flight attendant might not know who the woman was, but Jay Maddox knew. He knew, and it irked him in more ways than he could count. Every reality show had a token celebrity—everyone knew that. He just never expected this show's celebrity to be someone so ill-equipped to handle what was coming. An athlete maybe. Or a chef. A dancer, even. But a politician's daughter? A woman who just might be America's next First Daughter? The woman had probably never lifted a finger in her life...more than likely had servants and chauffeurs at her beck and call like a spoiled Kennedy.

Not to mention Secret Service. Jay looked around the plane, but didn't see any sign of a telltale earpiece on anyone. Maybe candidate's kids didn't require round-the-clock supervision when adulthood came into play.

No matter. He gave her two days out here. Three tops. Although her clothes looked even less equipped for this than she did, so the time should probably be cut in half. Who wore designer jeans and an Armani top to an Alaskan survival show, anyway? She would be begging for rescue by nightfall the first evening, of that he was certain.

Never mind how he knew her shirt was Armani.

"Are you excited to be here?" The chick to his right—Heidi, if he remembered correctly—leaned lightly on his shoulder in a pitiful attempt to peer out the window, though something told him she was more concerned with having a reason to press against him than actually seeing the sights. The leftover mint from her gum filled his senses, though she ruined what might have been a pleasant experience by popping it loudly in his ear. Jay shifted in his seat and looked around, hoping no one stared in their direction. He dropped his voice to a whisper and silently willed the girl to quit being so openly flirtatious. Of course he was flattered, but come on.

"I guess so. I've never actually flown this far, so I'm not quite sure what to expect," he said as casually as he could manage. He looked over his shoulder and set his sights on Anna Lloyd once again. She sat diagonal from him, flipping through the latest issue of *People* magazine, looking like she didn't have a care in the world. Probably accurate considering she came from money. Those kinds of people rarely worried about anything.

Must be nice.

Jay looked out the window, growing increasingly irritated but unsure why. Maybe it was his own challenging upbringing and the fact that nothing in life had ever come easy. Jay hadn't had a real family in years, not since his dad was killed and his mom subsequently went crazy. Since then, he'd been in charge of keeping the remnants of his leftover family together against the most difficult odds, whether he wanted to or not.

He cleared his throat, uncomfortable with the direction his mind had traveled and thankful for the distraction brought on by the plane's solid landing. It taxied on the runway as the screech of brakes drowned out his thoughts and ushered in a small wave of excitement. Nothing could dampen his mood now, not with snow-covered mountains in the distance and the promise of adventure looming in front of him.

The girl named Heidi craned her neck toward the window while Jay stood to retrieve his bag—a duffel he bought back in high school. Across from him, Anna Lloyd struggled to pry a ridiculously large Louis Vuitton bag free from the overhead compartment. She pulled, then pulled again with no success. Jay rolled his eyes. The lady needed help, and just his luck, he was the only person around who noticed.

"Here, let me get that," he said, reaching for the obscenely expensive bag as he attempted to ease it from its spot above her head. He didn't want to scratch the two-thousand-dollar leather. It took a little work, but after a moment the bag broke free. With a slight groan, he hoisted it up and over and set in on the seat in front of her.

"Thank you," she said. The soft inflection of her voice was unexpected, as was the weird way it tripped his pulse. Stupid. "In hindsight, I probably shouldn't have brought this thing. It looks completely out of place." The way she barely looked him in the eye roused his curiosity, as did the moisture he thought he spotted just below her lashes. *Had she been crying?* Jay had to admit that despite her choice in luggage, she didn't *seem* arrogant...though he knew from experience that looks could be deceiving.

Jay eyed the Louis Vuitton in front of her. "Yeah, cheap nylon might have been a little smarter considering we're going to be trekking through mud for a month."

To his surprise, Anna laughed—her eyes brightening with unshed moisture—before catching herself with a press of her lips. She looked instantly worried, like she had broken some secret code of conduct that only the rich and well-respected knew about. "I'll remember not to be so dumb next time." The easy admission impressed him, though he wasn't sure why he should feel anything at all. Jay cleared his throat.

"Need anything else?" he asked in an effort to be polite. He needed to get back to his own bags. He glanced back toward his seat in time to see Heidi, sitting on her knees with her face pressed into the glass. He rolled his eyes; he'd never made that move so much in his life.

"No, I'm good. But thank you." This time her smile turned warmer…the kind of smile that conveyed both familiarity and pleasure in a simple gesture. It wasn't the first time he had seen it. After all, his sister subscribed to *People* magazine, so occasionally Jay read it by default.

Still, he had to admit the smile looked good on her.

"Okay, then I'll see you later." Jay rubbed his hands together and turned to go, then remembered his manners. "Sorry, I guess I should've introduced myself. Name's Jay." He held out his hand, which Anna Lloyd shyly shook.

"Anna." She cleared her throat. "My name's Anna."

"Nice to meet you, Anna." With a nod, he turned to leave, shaking off a strange desire to go back and talk a little longer.

But Anna what's-her-name wasn't his problem.

In order to prove it, he forced himself not to turn around as he walked off the plane into the cold Alaskan air.

Chapter 2

"I'm Dean Passmore, and welcome to season three of *The Alaskan Wild!*" The announcer stood in full-bodied camo—looking ridiculous—in front of a dense array of towering spruce trees. Even his hat blended with the scenery. The only thing that didn't blend was the guy's face. It's hard to fade into the background when you're wrinkle-free and spray tanned to brown-sugared perfection. Especially disturbing since the guy looked barely thirty and temperatures were frigid. Jay shivered and crossed his arms. Alaska in April was supposed to be warmer than this, right?

The guy smiled wide, his white teeth were like fresh snow on a mound of mud. "As you undoubtedly know, four years ago, the premier of The Wedding Game helped to put RealTime on the map when it became one of the top ten most watched shows in prime time." He clasped his hands together. "Of course, then it was rocked by a scandal and folded after only two seasons." He rested his chin on manicured fingernails. "Anyway, this show has fared better—so far, it's been controversy-free." Dean laughed as though they were actually being filmed.

He quickly glanced around their group of ten. Almost everyone stood rigid and scared, airplane propellers slowing to a stop behind them as nerves intensified, including his own. They were here. This was it. The long-awaited promise of adventure was suddenly one big, fat reality. Jay could cut through the tension in the air. If he had a knife— which he didn't because of stupid airline regulations. He tried not to think about the marble Swiss Army blade his grandfather gave him confiscated by airline security, then stuffed haphazardly in an envelope with a promise to be mailed to his home address in Dallas. Instead, he forced himself to focus on the group.

"So as I was saying," the announcer continued, "I'd like for each of you to introduce yourselves—give us your names and ages, where you're from, and anything else you'd like to share. Just don't take more than thirty seconds or so." He gave a small laugh, high-pitched and fake.

Jay listened as everyone gave their answers. Eric, Patti, Nico...and another four contestants. Then they came to Anna whom—he wasn't all that surprised to discover—worked as an aide to her father as a communications director. Her boyfriend Ryan, he knew, worked as an attorney for WGN News, the largest station in Chicago and one of the biggest in the country. His father was the chief fundraiser for Alexander Lloyd's presidential campaign.

In Anna's family, it seemed money and opportunity went hand in hand.

"Jay," the girl next to him whispered. "He keeps talking to you. Do you want to answer?"

He shook his head to clear it. "Um...no. Sorry. I'm Jay Maddox, and I'm from Dallas. I'm twenty-four and work for a construction firm that specializes in stadiums and high rises." He went on to give a few details about his job, careful to leave out the most important. Some things needed to stay private, away from the prying eyes of television. This Heidi chick, though—she hadn't taken her eyes off of him. Flattering maybe, except her attention was starting to verge on embarrassing.

"My name is Heidi. I'm nineteen and really looking forward to getting to know everyone here." Her gaze settled directly on Jay for this before it swept the contestants again. "I attend Texas A&M, but I haven't decided on a major yet," she piped up, her southern drawl poured on thick. "But I'm thinking about criminal justice or something." Jay heard someone snicker, but Heidi seemed oblivious as she twirled her ponytail around a finger.

The announcer's grin stretched across his taut face. "Well, Heidi, clearly you're the youngest person here. I guess time will tell if that's a detriment, or an asset…"

"Oh, I'm sure it will be a good thing because I'm full of energy and stuff."

Jay glanced at Anna just in time to see her bite her lip on a smile.

***

"Okay, so on to the important information" Dean Passmore said a few minutes later. "For the next four days, survivalist expert Dr. Mark Callahan will be with us. He's lived exclusively in Alaska for the past twelve years. He's even braved this terrain a few times himself. Hasn't died yet." Dean laughed. Doctor what's-his-name didn't crack a smile. "Anyway, he's going to teach you the basic skills you'll need to know before our trek begins—how to build a fire and keep it going, what edible plants to look for, how to kill and cook wildlife…"

Involuntarily, Anna made a face. Not once, not *once* in this entire process did it occur to her she might have to do this. Not that she was opposed to eating a hamburger or the occasional steak. She just never imagined having to kill a cow to do it. How did one go about killing a cow, anyway? Did they even have cows in Alaska? And if not cows, what animals *did* they have? Elk? Deer? Antelope? All of a sudden, she remembered watching an episode of *Survivor* years ago— one where everyone was starving, and they had to eat live scorpions as part of their challenge. There was no way she would eat a scorpion, no matter who dared her to. She'd die of hunger, swear on her life.

"Is there a problem, Ms. Lloyd?"

Anna blinked at the announcer's question. "Um...no. I was just, just..." She hated being in the spotlight all by herself.

"I'm pretty sure she was trying to think of the best way to slaughter a cow," Jay spoke up, causing all eyes to shift toward him.

Everyone laughed except Anna. Was he making fun of her? More importantly, how did he know? Anna stared at him for a long moment before looking away.

"Well, aside from the obvious—that there are no cows in the Alaskan wilderness—" The announcer looked right at her and smirked, "does anyone have any questions? Thirty days is a long time to spend roughing this terrain, so I'm sure you're bound to have some." He rubbed his hands together and waited a gratuitous three seconds. When no one immediately spoke up, he continued. "Well then, we should probably get started. I want each of you to get in pairs and we'll assign you to your stations. We have a lot to cover in the next four days."

***

Two days later, Anna walked toward the medical trailer, muttering a few choice words as she went. Even though she'd only been attempting this fire-making thing for an hour, blisters had bubbled and broken on her fingertips and palms, and scratches sliced her wrists. Stupid Girl Scouts. No matter what they sang, it did *not* only take a spark to get a fire going. It took friction and energy and determination—all of which she was fresh out of.

Blood, however, she had in abundance.

She pressed her hand against the door and winced as the metal connected with the tender, ripped flesh of her fingers. Biting back a cry, she stepped inside, the sterile scent of alcohol and antiseptic filling her senses.

"Is there any way I can get some Band-Aids or something for—"

She sputtered to a halt at the sight of the guy who'd helped her with her luggage—Jay, if she remembered right—sitting on the table in front of her, a large cut on his side.

Completely shirtless.

Fire shot up her neck. "I'm sorry, I—"

"Just have a seat right there," the nurse said, gesturing to an empty chair directly in front of the table, "and I'll be right with you."

Despite an intense desire to leave, Anna had no choice. With her pulse hammering in her throat, she inched herself toward the chair and sat down. In a room the size of a small closet, there was nowhere to look. Still, she tried to find something—the sterile paneling, the gray carpet, the nurse's white coat—to focus on.

And then she saw the oddest thing...

"Are you an actress?" Anna asked the nurse before thinking the better of the intrusive question.

"Excuse me?" The woman shot a look in Anna's direction.

"Your script." She nodded toward the counter next to her. "At least it looks like a script lying on the table right here." She cleared her throat. "I think it would be so cool to audition for a play or movie. I've always dreamed of being a character actress. They always seem to get the best lines."

"No, I'm not an actress. And that isn't a script." The nurse reached for the stapled paper and tucked it inside a drawer. "It's a study on the dangers of bacteria found among the uncontained wildlife in rural Alaska. I needed to brush up, you know, in case something goes wrong out here."

Anna frowned. The explanation made sense in the most disturbing way. What kinds of diseases could they contract out here? And what if they didn't have the correct medication to stop a dangerous infection?

"What happened to your hands?" Jay asked, breaking her train of thought, forcing her to acknowledge him. Feeling her face slowly burn, she glanced up.

"Over an hour of rubbing sticks together." She held them out. He didn't try to hide his grimace.

"Well, did you at least start a fire?"

She blew a strand of hair off her forehead, trying not to notice the appeal of his slow southern accent. "No. For all my work, I didn't get so much as a plume of smoke. It never even *smelled* like flames, not even for a second." The nurse unrolled a strip of gauze and cut it, then pressed it to his side. The wound looked painful, but Jay only watched, uninterested.

"That's too bad. Heidi had a fire going in ten minutes, and I still can't figure out how she did it. She beat my time by five."

Anna suppressed an eye roll. Of course she did. The perky, blonde, supermodel-lookalike sounded like an airhead, but then it was the airheads that always fooled you. Every single time.

It was the politician's daughters—who tried hard by themselves and still couldn't manage to accomplish much—that were the most predictable.

"That figures." She didn't mean to say it out loud, but instead of the hostility she feared, Jay grinned.

"That girl's a firecracker. She goes about things in some strange ways, but she seems to be a girl who gets things done. During target practice she—"

"What happened to your side?" Anna was sure whatever stories he told about Heidi would be simply fascinating, but right now she didn't feel like hearing them. That is, unless Jay what's-his-name wanted her to start dry-heaving over his feet. If there was anything she hated more than her own personal failures, it was listening to other people's effortless successes. Maybe that made her heartless. Maybe it made her jealous. Maybe she didn't care.

"Oh…" Jay shifted in his seat, looking uncomfortable for the first time despite the angry-looking gash running four inches long just under his ribcage. "Um, once the fire started, Heidi turned around with the flaming stick and burned me."

Her mouth fell open. "She *burned* you? That looks more like a knife wound."

He closed his eyes. "Well, she didn't move the stick right away, so it seared into me pretty deep…"

Anna shouldn't have giggled—she'd probably hate herself for it later—but it escaped anyway. She couldn't be sure, but she thought she heard the nurse snicker too, as she ripped off some tape and secured it to Jay's wound.

"I can't believe she burned you," Anna said. "If I were you, I'd watch myself while we're in the wilderness. It would be a sad day if she mistook you for a bear while holding a shotgun—"

This time, the nurse definitely laughed. Jay, however, didn't.

He hopped off the table and reached for his shirt. "I'm glad you find this funny, seeing that you haven't even managed a fire. What do you plan to contribute to the team, Anna? Top notch stick gathering? I'm sure that will impress the heck out of your parents and boyfriend. Ryan, isn't that his name?"

Anna sucked in a breath—how dare he talk to her like that; besides, she didn't want to talk about Ryan, her stupid cheater boyfriend and all the ways he'd broken her heart only days ago. She opened her mouth tell him so, but of course Jay chose that moment to stand up right in front of her, all muscle and tanned skin and man. She tried to avert her eyes—hard to do when his biceps flexed while tugging the shirt over his head.

Man, the guy was built.

And he had the most interesting tattoo right above his heart…

Anna looked away and tried to remember his snide remark. It took some effort. "Yes, it's Ryan." What were they talking about? Her voice sounded pinched, breathy. Too late she realized she should be angry with him, so she did her best to recover. "And I think they'll be proud that I came here at all. It isn't every day that a woman like me signs up for a show like this." There. That sounded confident, right?

And what *was* that tattoo?

Jay tugged his shirt around his waist, much to Anna's disappointment. "A woman like you…" He shook his head. "A little proud, don't you think?" His voice dripped with judgment as he ambled toward the door. Just before he opened it, he threw her a look, one that raked her up and down. "Good luck. You're gonna need it.

So much for confidence.

Chapter 3

Jay rifled through the gear they'd just been assigned by the show and berated himself for the thousandth time. No matter how he twisted and turned the scenarios in his mind, he couldn't justify the way he'd talked to that Anna chick back at the medical station. Top notch stick gathering? He might as well have called her worthless. That she would contribute nothing significant to the team. What kind of man talked that way to a woman?

Not him. Definitely not him.

He stood up to go find her when Heidi's squeal stopped him.

"Jay, look at this!" She held up a shiny silver object like she'd discovered the Holy Grail itself. "Is this what I think it is?"

Jay suppressed a sigh and nodded. "Looks like a lighter." He bent down to retrieve it from her hands and then spotted another one like it just inside the bag. "It looks like you have two of them, in fact." An odd thing, considering—

"Then I wonder why they had us working so hard to build a fire if they were gonna give us these? This is so awesome!" Her eyes lit up like a kid at Christmastime. "Do you think they packed any candles for us to use? Just think how cool it would be if we could use candles at night in the wilderness! It would almost be like we were in the movies. Like *Sahara*! Have you seen that movie…?"

But before he could answer, she busied herself back inside the bag. He watched in puzzlement for a long moment as she excitedly flipped past a fishing net and rags and bandages and pliers—all items the show deemed necessary for survival. Heidi was…interesting. Flirty. And definitely attracted to him. So why couldn't he muster up anything but indifference?

And why did his mind keep drifting to that Anna chick?

Jay sighed and stood up, unable to turn that thought into anything coherent. More and more lately, he found himself wondering about life. He felt anxious. Restless. But he couldn't pinpoint the reason for it. All he knew was he was tired of drifting, tired of living an existence that hadn't felt settled in nearly a decade. He had prayed all winter that this trip would give him some clarity. It had to. He needed a breakthrough.

But for now, he needed to find Anna.

It was time to apologize.

***

Anna's bad day had just gotten worse.

"What the heck is this?" she muttered under her breath.

She wasn't talking to anyone in particular, but she got an answer anyway. One she didn't expect.

"Pretty sure it's a lighter."

Her head snapped up to see Jay standing above her. She glared, doing her best to look irritated—hard to do while staring into direct sunlight. She blinked against the glare and studied her pack again.

"I know it's a lighter, Texas," she answered. *Was* he from Texas? She seemed to remember him saying so. "But why is it here? I spent hours and hours trying to start a fire with nothing but toothpicks—which is impossible, by the way, no matter what you and your girlfriend say."

"She's not my girlfriend," he quickly said.

"Whatever." She waved him off. "But they have the nerve to stick a lighter in here?" Her voice had risen, and people were starting to stare. She huffed out a breath and crossed her arms.

"Speaking of Heidi, she seemed pretty happy about it a second ago."

"I don't see why when, according to you, she's able to start raging fires with just two fingers and a wish. What does she need a lighter for?" Anna knew she sounded jealous, but it couldn't be helped.

Jay's smile only made her more irritated. "It took a little more effort than that, but—"

"What's next?" she interrupted. "Are they going to bring in catered meals every day?"

"Heidi seems to think so. Plus the bubble baths she's talking about taking at the end of each day," Jay said.

Anna just looked at him. "You're kidding, right?" The darn water would probably bubble and foam on her command.

But something in the expression on Jay's face told her he wasn't. He almost sounded...annoyed. Maybe he didn't like her nearly as much as she liked him. "Of course I am," he said. "Look, I just—"

But Anna tuned him out and dove inside the bag again. "Nice. We have a net..." She held it up. "But no hooks. Do they expect us to just catch fish when they swim by?" She raised an eyebrow. "Kind of hard to do for someone with hands like mine, right?" Without checking for his reaction, she tossed the net aside and reached for a leather pouch.

"Why are you so upset about this stuff? The way I see it, a lighter will make things easier," he said. "And besides, if this proves to be too much for you, you could always push the button. You'd be out of here in five minutes." Earlier that afternoon, each contestant had been outfitted with a GPS tracking device attached to their packs. Fashioned with a red emergency button, if any contestant chose to withdraw, they simply pressed the alert to summon a helicopter to their location. It would take a dire situation to get him to concede defeat, he just hoped the rest of his teammates were as determined.

"Heck no," Anna said, breaking into his thoughts. "I came this far. I'm in it to the end, even if it kills me. I just think lighters are stupid." She looked up at him. "Is there a reason you walked all the way over here? Shouldn't you be with your girlfriend getting burned on your other side? Hurry, Jay, maybe you can have *two* scars before the sun goes down."

He knelt down beside her. "I came over here to say I'm sorry for the way I acted earlier in the trailer. I wasn't nice, and I want to apologize." Jay held out his hand offering her a truce.

She studied him for a long moment before finally shaking it in agreement. "Fine, apology accepted," she sputtered out with a sigh. "I'll see you in a few hours."

If I'm lucky.

The thought came from nowhere and bothered him all afternoon.

Chapter 4

Anna tore her eyes away from the ring of contestants and focused on the announcer, feeling the pulse in her throat ratchet up several notches, especially when she saw the red light from the camera trained on her face. They were on-air. The four training days had come to an end, and as of now everything she did for the next thirty days would be captured for America to watch.

"As I was saying, an hour from now, each of these contestants will be led by guides to their starting points," the announcer spoke into the camera, explaining the show to viewers at home. "They'll be equipped with maps, supplies, Go-Pro Action Cameras, and little else. And they'll be entrusted with one task: survive the wild, and hopefully win the game." He cocked an eyebrow into the camera.

"However…" the announcer continued, "We decided to make *The Alaskan Wild* a little different this season. The truth is—for everyone here— surviving the terrain might be a little tougher than it's been in previous seasons of the show. Because here's the thing, America—the surprise part of this competition, if you will. The twist that neither you at home, nor the men and women standing here, know about." He gestured dramatically toward each of the contestants, a lopsided grin tilting his lips as the beginnings of what could only be called an evil twinkle glimmered in his eyes. Anna blinked at him, at the camera, at each of the other contestants that suddenly looked as startled as her. Jay briefly caught her eye. He obviously hated surprises as much as she did.

More than airplane flights and thoughts of starvation, surprises left her feeling cold and clammy, drenched in a cold sweat. Needing an anchor to steady herself, she clasped her hands together and began to twist her thumb.

And then she saw it. Anna's gaze fell on a little wooden bowl the announcer held in front of him. He'd been clutching it the whole time, but all of a sudden it seemed threatening. As though all the answers to this suddenly twisted game were contained inside that tiny brown sphere. What was inside that bowl?

"I'm sure you're all wondering what this is," the announcer said.

Anna nodded as a murmur skittered through the contestants. Each couple stood side by side in a single row. The announcer paced the length of them, while the air buzzed with unease and a fair amount of fear. Call it instinct or a simple foreboding, but everyone knew something catastrophic was pending. Anna shouldn't have been surprised—disaster followed her everywhere.

Holding his hands in front of him, the announcer looked into the camera. "We all know these contestants came here separately. To test themselves. To prove to one another and the entire country that if they could survive the wilderness of Alaska, they could survive anything life throws at them. And of course, they came to win some money." His soft laugh carried with the wind.

"These individuals…" the announcer continued, "…they wanted a challenge to push themselves to the next level. So they came to us: the creators of *The Alaskan Wild*. And they begged us to help them escape their mundane lives."

Anna's eyebrows slammed together. She wouldn't exactly call it begging.

"So to everyone represented here…" He turned to face them. "We heard your cry. And we are determined to give you the fight you so desperately wished for."

Maybe she was mistaken, but Anna thought she saw the guy smirk. The blood in her head whooshed between her ears.

"So contestants, I need you to do something for me." He made a tent with his index fingers, resting his chin on the tips. "Women, please take two steps forward and turn to face the men." At their looks of bewilderment, he gave a slight laugh, seeming to enjoy this bit of drama. "I know this part wasn't discussed with you before now, but surprise is part of the competition. This show is all about pushing you to the limits. It's about finding out just how committed you are. It's about being able to answer the all-important question…the question each one of you came here hoping to solve."

And it's about ratings, Anna thought. *Bombshell twists only happen when numbers are down. She'd watched Sing America long enough to know that.*

The announcer hesitated. Anna could almost hear the producers shouting directives into the monitor tucked inside Dean Passmore's ear. *Now pause for dramatic effect. Now swipe at a fake tear threatening to fall from your eye. Now look meaningfully at the contestants. Make sure you lock eyes with each one for at least two seconds before moving on.* When the charade was over, he turned his pitiful attempt at a smoldering gaze toward the lens again.

"Just how deep is your desire to win?"

Deep. It's deep. With her pulse pounding in her ears, Anna gripped her thumb like a vise and turned and squeezed.

"Let's find out, shall we? I have in my hand a bowl. In it, the names of every man in this competition have been written down."

"Ladies, I'm going to pass this bowl to each of you. One by one, I want you to withdraw a slip of paper. But don't open it. Not yet." He wagged a finger at them as though they were a group of naughty, over-eager children.

No one looked eager.

She watched as the bowl made its way down the line. To Rain...to Desiree...to Heidi...to Patti. And then it was Anna's turn. Swallowing, she reached into the bowl and pulled out the last folded rectangle, feeling the crispness of the parchment as it shook in her hand.

"So ladies, when I count to three, I want you to open your papers. Ready?"

Anna clenched her hands, willing the shaking to stop.

"One..."

Why am I so nervous?

"Two..."

Because surprises never work out for me.

"Three..."

Oh no oh no oh no.

She opened the paper, staring in confusion at the name written on it.

"Ladies, look at the name in front of you," he said. "Take a really good look."

"You wanted a challenge. You wanted to push yourselves to the limits and see how far you could go. Well, what better way to be absolutely certain—or uncertain—about your strengths and abilities than this? What better way to find the answers you're looking for than to face thirty days of the ultimate test?"

"Unlike past seasons, this year's show won't revolve around a large group of contestants. This year, we're pairing you up and switching things around. So welcome to the all-new *The Alaskan Wild!*"

All new? Anna frowned.

"Now ladies, for this season's show, the name written in front of you is the name of your new partner."

She blinked in horror as the paper slipped from her fingers and floated to the ground. *What in the world would her parents think now?*

Chapter 5

All his excitement about this trip had vanished along with his ability to appreciate the scenery he'd been so eager to see. The rugged Alaskan terrain morphed into an ugly mass of brown, green, and gray as Jay stomped through it, kicking anything in his path out of the way. Whatever. He was ticked. They'd been duped. He was stuck in the middle of nowhere for thirty days with a complete stranger...a stranger who'd teased him *twice* about his burn and done nothing but sniff and sigh in the hour they'd been walking.

That burn still stung. Jay clinched his jaw to ease the pain.

Neither one of them had spoken a word since the announcer declared them partners. Jay felt bad for his silence, but what was he supposed to say? *Hey, I know we just met and you seem like a nice enough person, but why the heck am I stuck with you?* He never would have agreed to come here had he known the producers would yank him away from a team environment and force him to spend thirty days alone with this uppity chick.

Jay adjusted his backpack and marched forward, trudging uphill. He wasn't sure they were headed the right way. What's more, he didn't care. Pushing a low branch to the side, he moved around it, realizing too late it might snap back in Anna's face.

"Ow!" Right on target. "Can you be a little more careful next time?"

"I'll try, but I can't promise anything." He kept going and stepped around an exposed tree root. Fallen leaves crunched underneath his hiking boots.

Behind him, Anna sighed loudly. Again. "You know, I'm not happy about this either. You're not the only one whose life got turned upside down this morning. And now we're stuck together, and I'm not even sure we can handle—"

"I can handle it, even if you can't." He sent a rock sailing with his foot, unwilling to admit he had the same doubts. "But you'd better figure out a way, Anna. I'm not losing this thing because of you." As soon as he said it, he felt bad. But nothing like the way he felt when Anna said her next words.

"Because of me? Please. If we lose, it'll be because your temper got the best of you and got us into trouble." Her voice sounded steely. "Besides, you're just mad they didn't stick you with Heidi."

A laugh burst from Jay's lips before he had time to stop it. "Now that you mention it, we might have been an interesting pairing. If you know what I mean." He wasn't usually this crass, but something about this girl got under his skin.

She blew out some air. "I know what you mean, and she's not that pretty."

"If you say so. Though your standards and mine might be a little different."

Heidi was blonde, reed thin, and voluptuous. Everything Anna wasn't. Not that she wasn't pretty—she was. Some people thought she was exotic looking, with dark eyes, full lips, and flowing dark hair that draped across her shoulders like a rich cashmere blanket. The kind of blanket a guy like him could curl up with on cold winter nights in Alaska. *Wait, what is wrong with me?*

"We have totally different standards, obviously," Anna said. "I haven't found Barbie dolls all that attractive since I was six years old. About the time I discovered they're rigid, made of plastic, and completely brainless." She marched around him, and Jay caught himself fighting back a grin. This girl was feisty. Tough. A little jealous, maybe?

And possibly the future President's daughter.

"Don't you have, like, Secret Service men who should be following you right now? I could be a serial killer for all you know."

She made an unflattering noise. "What are you going to do? Kill me and roast me over a fire pit with America watching? I'll take my chances." She tossed him a look over her shoulder. "No, I don't have Secret Service following me. I would hate that."

"But isn't your father running for President? Isn't that what happens to the kids?"

"First of all, I'm twenty-six—hardly a kid. Second of all, he's *running* for President, he isn't President yet. They don't dole out secret service to every candidate running for office. Do you have any idea how much that would cost the taxpayers?"

Why did he feel like he was getting a history lesson here? A snooty, You're-An-Idiot lesson delivered by what appeared to be the most pretentious individual he'd ever met?

"I know he's not President." He spoke slowly. "But your grandfather was. Doesn't that entitle you to some sort of protection? Like a bodyguard? A police escort? Someone to protect you from guys who might murder you and leave your body in the Alaskan wilderness?"

She gave him a look. "Oh, you're really scaring me," she deadpanned. "Besides, why would they feel a need to plunk down good money just for my protection? I'm sure the powers that be are breathing easier knowing I'm being watched over by you."

He rolled his eyes. Pretentious. And bratty.

Just then the shadow of a bird glided across her feet. They both looked up, then at each other, clearly wondering the same thing. *Should they shoot it? And if they didn't, would they see another one soon?* Jay shielded his eyes, frowning as it flew away. On cue his stomach growled, but the idea of killing their dinner still seemed so foreign to him. He shopped at Kroger. Bought frozen pizzas. What was he supposed to do with a fully feathered bird?

"I don't want to shoot one either," she said, surprising him. Something about her tone eased the tension in the air, and he smiled. But when she closed her eyes and muttered, *Toto, we're not in Kansas anymore*—he couldn't contain his laughter. She looked over at him. "How are we supposed to spend the next thirty days shooting things out of the air? The last chicken I ate was of the fried variety and came from Chicken Little's on east 35th."

"I hate to break it to you, Anna. But I'm pretty sure chickens aren't an option in the forests of Alaska." He started walking again. She stepped up beside him as they hiked a twenty-five degree incline. Not steep, but the trek grew increasingly tough considering everything they carried.

"What do you think will be the worst thing we have to eat on this trip?" she asked.

Jay shoved a hand in his pocket. "I don't know. Maybe that." He nodded toward a mouse as it skittered in front of them. Its tail flipped back and forth, sliding underneath a patch of underbrush before it disappeared altogether.

"I am *not* eating that."

"Famous last words," Jay said. "You'll probably be the one to skin it." When she said nothing in response, he changed the subject. "Are we going the right way? I haven't even looked at the map, and I bet we've walked a mile already." Before they began their trek, the teams were given individual maps and dropped off at different starting points, each two miles apart. Cameras were fastened to their vests with instructions to interview one another at various points throughout the day. With each day's hike stretching five miles or so, at the end of forty-eight hours the teams would set up camp together, meeting at checkpoints along the way to regroup, restock supplies, and be filmed as a group. On the off days, they were responsible for finding their own place to rest. Which meant tonight, Jay and Anna were on their own.

Anna pulled the map from her bag and opened it, chewing her bottom lip. "We've gone one-point-three miles, I think. And yes, we're going the right way. I think."

"Your confidence is overwhelming." Jay came up behind her and plucked the map from her hands just as a breeze picked up. It fluttered through her hair and sent a hint of her perfume wafting around him. Trying to ignore it, he scanned the map. "We have three-and-a-half miles to go today, give or take." He tucked the map back inside her bag and scanned the sky. "Think we can make it before dark?"

"Oh, we'll make it," she said. "As long as you'll quit dragging your feet and pick up the pace." She smirked and turned to go, but her foot caught on a patch of undergrowth. She tripped, the weight of her backpack sending her reeling. Jay jumped forward to catch her, but she landed on her knees with a thud, looking a bit like a turtle.

He laughed before he could stop himself. "Now, what was that about dragging my feet?" It was the wrong thing to say. With a groan, Anna reached out and shoved his leg. Just like that, he landed on his butt beside her. Soon they were both laughing, rolling around like two crazy people in the dirt. It was weird, but at least some of the tension in the air dissipated. Hopefully, with time, all of it would.

Anna pulled herself to a sitting position. "What are we doing out here?" Her words came out on a laugh mixed in with a little whine.

"I mean, one minute I'm on my way to an adventure to prove myself to my overbearing family and boyfriend—and then, wham!—I'm partnered up and walking around Alaska with a strange man. No offense."

Jay ran a hand through his hair. "None taken. Trust me, I feel the same way."

Anna shoved his arm. "At least we can be miserable together, I guess." She pushed her hair off her forehead and leaned forward with her head in her hands. "This whole thing is seriously screwed up."

He studied her for a long moment, feeling something different than he'd felt a moment ago. "Oh, it's not that bad." He shrugged. "It could be worse, you know."

Her fingers opened. She looked at him through the slits. "How?"

He grinned. "I *could* be stuck out here with Heidi. And she actually could be looking for a place to light some candles and settle in for a bath."

Her hands fell as she gave him a straight-faced stare. "Knowing her, she'd probably find a boiling stream somewhere. A full-on sauna made just for her."

"I'm sure she would. But honestly, I'm glad I'm here with you instead." And strangely enough—he meant it.

Chapter 6

Five hours later, Anna couldn't remember the last time she was so cold.

The sun had made a pass across the sky, but it still shone far in the distance. Not as brightly as before, but in muted, peachy-orange hues that reminded her of the soft glow of a Girl Scout campfire. She would kill for the warmth of a blaze right now. Her legs were still moving, but she could no longer feel them. In just one afternoon, keeping herself warm had turned into a full-time job.

"I'm s…s..sorry, but I'm f…f..freezing. Can we stop for a second so that I can g…g..grab another jacket of out my pack?"

"Sure. Hand me the map while you do it. I want to see how much farther we have."

She gave it to him and shrugged out of her pack. "Not far, but it might as well be miles."

She'd been studying the map for hours, calling off orders to *make a right, veer left, watch out for the stream that should be coming up shortly.* There was no stream. No water. Even worse, the only animal they'd seen was the bird earlier that morning. So either she was the world's worst map-reader or something was wrong. Getting lost on the first day would be the worst possible scenario. She came here to prove something to herself—that she was strong, capable, *not* the girl who dented her father's new Audi Q7 by hitting it with a golf club on the first day he bought it. *Not* the girl who forgot her lines on opening night of A Midsummer Night's Dream in high school, and subsequently ran off the stage in tears. N*ot* the girl who avoided her parent's angry stares as the class valedictorian delivered the most motivational speech in graduation history.

Definitely not a serial failure.

But if she couldn't do something as simple as read a freaking map, the only thing she would prove is her incompetence. As if she needed another reminder.

She pulled a down jacket from the bottom of her backpack and tugged it on—grateful for the protection it gave her from the wind. Her skin immediately warmed. She unscrewed the cap from her water bottle and took another sip. Her stomach growled in response. The liquid felt good going down but left her wanting more.

Jay lowered the map and scanned the area, then studied the paper once again. "Okay, so..." His hesitant words made her stomach drop. She knew it. Somehow she'd gone and gotten them lost.

"I read it wrong, didn't I?" Her words caught as emotion filled her throat. She was so tired. So hungry. She'd been on this little adventure for a whopping half-day, and already she had failed her teammate. "I knew I should have let you lead. How bad did I mess up? How lost are we?" She scratched her neck, then latched onto her thumb and twisted it back and forth until it popped—a stupid childhood habit she'd never been able to break. "How could I be so stupid?"

"Wow." Surprised by his tone, she reluctantly looked up to see Jay frowning at her. "You're pretty quick to jump to the worst case scenario." He studied her a bit longer before turning back to the map. "I was going to say that I think we made a wrong turn about two hundred yards back..."

Can't you do anything right? She closed her eyes to the memory of her father's words berating her.

"Quit being so hard on yourself." Jay tapped her foot with his boot. "It's a couple hundred yards, not miles. We can double back and be on track in fifteen minutes. Maybe ten. Just put on your pack and let's go." He shrugged into his own coat and zipped it, then flung his pack over his shoulders. "I think there might be a stream in the next mile or so, and I for one want to go fishing. I'm starving."

With a groan, she plunged her arms through her pack, thinking the thing had gained weight in the last few minutes. Jay stepped forward and lifted it onto her back. When his hands stayed on her shoulder, she glanced back at him and found herself staring into the bluest eyes she'd ever seen before.

His gaze softened as he looked at her. "It was an innocent mistake, Anna. No big deal at all." Jay chucked her chin. Anna's insides jumbled together at his look...at the way he spoke straight to her, as if he recognized every insecurity she'd ever had about herself. "Understand?"

With him so close...Anna couldn't speak. So she nodded.

"Good." Jay took off walking, completely clueless to the fact that he left her speechless for once.

***

"I think we need to make a deal," Jay said, turning around to face her. They were almost there; she could hear water rushing by in the distance.

"What deal? Maybe I don't want to make one." Earlier, she'd realized she could spar with him without worrying about it. "Something tells me I'll get suckered into it somehow, anyway."

"Ah, Anna, you of little trust." He hooked a hand in his pocket.

"It's faith. The line is faith. And you're right—I don't have any."

"That's just sad." He shook his head at the ground before looking back up at her. "Do you want to know my deal or not?"

"Not. But something tells me I don't have a choice, since we're the only two out here and I have a feeling you're going to keep talking." She would never speak to Ryan or her father or anyone that way, but Jay seemed to find it amusing. It was nice to be free to be herself. To just...be.

Anna looked up at the darkening sky for a moment, enjoying the peacefulness. She reached overhead and tried to stretch, not easy to do with the backpack obstructing her movements. Finally, she gave up and surrendered to a yawn. When she finally tore her eyes away from the sky, she looked over at Jay. Maybe she imagined it, but his eyes seemed to linger on her mid-section, where her coat had risen to reveal a little skin. When he shook his head and met her gaze—cool and detached—she knew she was being ridiculous. She heard him sigh, long and slow.

"Now that you're done stretching like a cat—"

"I don't like cats," she said, having no idea why she felt the need to clarify it.

"Good. Then if we see one out here, you should have no qualms about shooting it for dinner. I'll build the fire."

"That's disgusting, Jay!"

He grinned. A nice grin, really. It went well with his nice hair and nice skin and ridiculously nice physique. She gave herself a mental slap. They'd only been out here one day. Why on earth was she thinking about the way he looked?

"Anyway, as I was saying, it occurs to me that we both have a particular set of skills..." Jay said.

Anna sucked in a breath, more than a little thrilled at his movie reference. Without knowing it, he had set a game in motion—a little game she'd played with herself since she was young that involved inserting movie quotes into conversations at opportune, and occasionally inopportune, times. Her parent's hated it and rarely participated; in ten months, Ryan had never once tried.

She worked to bite back a grin. "*Taken?*" she asked. "Liam Neissen?"

Jay winked. "The first one. The second was crap." Her grin escaped, because he was right.

Still, they were getting off track. "So what about this deal?"

"Well, you have something I want, and I have something you want, and I think we might be able to help each other out."

Her eyes narrowed. "Forget it, Junior." Seriously, they'd only just met.

He laughed. "First Texas, now Junior. Is there no end to the nicknames?"

"I'm older than you by a year," she shrugged. "The name fits."

Just then the media helicopter appeared overhead. It hovered above them, cameras trained on their figures as they moved like field mice through the rocky terrain.

They both glanced up, only giving it a passing thought. "What I was going to say is this, you're going to quit worrying about me getting angry, you're going to stop putting yourself down, you're going to stop apologizing, and you're going to be in charge of the map. Because I actually believe that you're capable of getting us where we need to go."

"*That's* our deal? Sounds a little one-sided to me. You didn't mention anything about yourself, so what do I get out of this deal—what are you going to do for *me*?"

She immediately regretted her words when a slow, lazy grin stole over his face. Thankfully, he didn't make the obvious comment. "When we set up camp, I'm going to catch us some fish. That's my part of our deal—keep you from starving to death and becoming a pitiful E-News headline. Deal?"

A smile crept onto her lips as relief washed over her. "Deal."

Chapter 7

"You suck at keeping your part of our deal."

"And you know this after only forty-five minutes?"

Jay looked over at her, resisting the urge to ball up the stupid fishing net and haul it at her head. He still remembered that awkward moment when she caught him staring earlier. But her jacket had risen up, and her bare midriff was *right there* in front of him. What red-blooded American male wouldn't stare?

One that knew she had a boyfriend, that's who.

Jay forced himself to focus. Fishing. He was fishing. And hungry. And he wasn't the only one.

"You know, you could stop complaining and help me." He dropped the net into the water for what felt like the four-hundredth time.

"That wasn't our deal. I'm supposed to shut up and you're supposed to catch dinner, remember? Though, as I said already, you're not doing the best job."

Jay glanced up as Anna resituated herself on the bank and examined her fingernails, looking comfortably cute in her hiking boots and weatherproof jacket.

He returned his focus to the water. "Except you're failing at the shutting up part."

She sighed and stood up. "Fine, I'll help you."

The relief he felt was palpable. Normally, the lack of food wouldn't bother him. He'd gone with much less at various times in his twenty-four years. But he was soaking wet and the only thing not freezing was his head—only because it was covered in the world's ugliest camouflage cap. So much for the sixty-degree selling-point they'd been given by the producers. With ninety-mile winds and head-to-toe wetness, it might as well be forty-below.

He and Anna had just hiked five of the worst miles he'd ever trekked in his life, and the walk had taken nearly nine hours. It would be even more grueling tomorrow. Somehow, some way, he had to provide them with something to eat. Otherwise, he shuddered to think of what they might face.

He repositioned the net and moved closer to Anna, who had snapped a branch from a tree and was busy trying to spear a fish with the pointed end.

"Forty-five minutes is all I need to figure out there's not a dang thing in this water. I haven't seen even a minnow float by." He looked deeper into the knee-deep liquid.

"I saw a snake earlier, but it swam away," she said.

He glanced up at her. "I wish you had told me. We could have eaten it."

She made a face at him. "Gross, no. Maybe I'll change my mind if this keeps up a few more days, but for now, forget it." She jammed the spear in the water, muttering to herself when it came up empty. "Do you think the others are having more luck than we are?"

"I'm not sure. There's literally nothing out here, so I can't imagine we're the only ones struggling."

"We'd better not be, because if I find out tomorrow that Nico and Heidi ate a bunch of Salmon for dinner, I'm gonna be so ticked."

In spite of his sour mood, Jay laughed. "She probably already caught three with her bare hands."

"No doubt they swam right to her and jumped into her arms." Anna piped up.

"She probably rocked them and sang a lullaby before taking a knife to their heads." She laughed then, and he watched her out of the corner of his eye, enjoying the way her whole face lit up when she smiled. He swallowed hard, trying to concentrate on the fish he wasn't catching.

Tomorrow all the couples would meet at a checkpoint seven miles from here. All he and Anna had to do was make the punishing hike to find it. It sounded about as fun as plucking their fingernails out one by one, but they had no choice. The place would provide shelter and supplies, a small amount of food, and a halfway decent place to sleep. They would spend two days there before heading off on their separate journeys again.

Jay was relieved to join the rest of the group, but he had to admit his time with Anna was more enjoyable than he expected.

He stole another glance at her standing across from him and holding that spear in the air. He didn't know her well—how much could you learn about a person in five days?—but she seemed different out here. During the training period, he'd seen a girl driven to build a fire, driven to shoot on-target, driven to be…perfect. Whether for herself or for some other force he couldn't see. For Ryan? For her family? He couldn't be sure.

The only thing he knew was that out here, with him, she seemed relaxed. Normal. Though no matter how many times he turned it over in his mind, he had a rough time sizing up what 'normal' was for Anna Lloyd.

Jay had seen the magazine articles, the newspaper clippings of Anna at political functions, fashion shows, even a handful of Hollywood parties. She was beautiful. Wealthy. Polished and poised. Groomed for high-society life and all the glamour that came with it.

But in person, she seemed comfortable in dirty jeans and an army-green down jacket. Seemed to enjoy lobbing insults and fishing with a stick in an obviously empty stream. And had a weird habit of forcing her thumb all different directions when she was nervous. He'd have to ask her about that one eventually.

But undeniably, in one day Anna had managed to undo every assumption he'd ever held about her.

"Can I ask you a question?" he asked. Maybe he shouldn't, but he wanted to know.

"Sure. Unless it's about why I still haven't caught anything."

He grinned into the water. "It isn't. Just…what made you try out for this show? Not that it's any of my business, but it doesn't seem as though someone like you would—"

"Rough it like this?" She finished his thought. She picked some algae off the stick and tossed it into the water. "You want the honest answer, or the nicely packaged, rehearsed one I gave the producers?"

He raised an eyebrow. "You mean you lied?"

"Not *exactly* a lie." She bit her lip. "I told them I needed to prove something to myself, to see what I'm made of. That's the truth, but I also did it because sometimes I get sick of living in the spotlight. My family is a bit notorious, if you haven't noticed." *Have you seen the tabloids? There's a great picture of my boyfriend on the front cover this week kissing an ugly chick who probably charged a thousand bucks an hour.* "I guess a big part of me just wanted to disappear for awhile."

He understood the need to hide, but he was surprised she picked this place. "So you chose a TV show in Alaska for that? You know, Anna, plenty of people manage to hide out in Hawaii. Or Fiji."

She smiled. "That's true. But Hawaii doesn't have all this." She held up the empty stick and gestured to the freezing water lapping around them. "I love nature. I love getting dirty and working with my hands. I love adventure and proving that I am not, in fact, a failure at everything I try. I do not, however, love the temperature of this water."

He gave a small smile, but couldn't ignore something she'd said. "You're not a failure."

She shrugged. "Several people would say differently. There's law school, my ACT, my freaking driver's test." She counted off the supposed shortcomings on her fingers. "And that's only the beginning. There's the failed beauty pageant I entered and got kicked out of at age nine—"

"Kid pageants are ridiculous," Jay interrupted.

She raised an eyebrow. "Tell that to my mother. Anyway, my parent's like the spotlight; it's important for my father's career. They do *not* appreciate my affection for mud and nature and roughing it, however."

A knowing grin crossed his mouth. "So being the devious daughter you are, you convinced him of the merits of a TV show that lets you do everything you want to do, while at the same time, keeping the family in the spotlight." He shook his head. "All you have to do is fly to Alaska and win some money. Kill two birds with one stone. Am I right?"

She looked up at him and grinned. "Busted. One day with me, and you've already managed to see through my little scheme."

"You're more transparent than you think," he said. Score one for her. "And your father was that easy to convince? Why does that surprise me?"

For some reason, she blushed. "Well, there might have been the matter that I promised he could donate my winnings—if I win, that is—to charity right before the election. Use it as a photo op."

He just stared at her. "I'm guessing small children will be involved." When she didn't disagree, his eyebrows rose in mock outrage. "That is the most pathetic thing I've ever heard. How do you live with yourself?"

She rolled her eyes. "It worked, didn't it? I'm here."

For a long moment they just looked at each other. And then Jay winked. This girl was something else.

"Yes you are, and I, for one, am glad. Now we're just going to have to make sure we win. I'd hate to miss the fun of seeing you at this heartwarming photo op." He picked up the net. Empty again. "If I'm invited, that is."

She grinned. "Oh, you're invited. Consider yourself my date."

***

"Your date, huh?" he heard himself say into the darkness.

The question had played through Jay's mind at least a hundred times since they gave up fishing an hour ago and settled down for the night. Exhausted, they'd both collapsed in a heap beside each other. Jay's eyes had fallen closed almost instantly. Now, he was surprised to find himself awake.

"If you want to be," Anna whispered. She lay in her bag next to him, the pull of sleep making her eyelids heavy. "I'd love it if you came with me." The small smile she gave him almost seemed drugged, as if exhaustion made anything more than a lazy grin impossible.

"I'll go with you." He smiled back at her as a shudder ricocheted down his spine. Whether from the cold or her angelic expression was anyone's guess. He decided the former was safer. "It's chilly out here," he said, strong-arming his thoughts into neutral territory. Anna shifted onto an elbow and faced him. In that moment her hair seemed richer than normal, her eyes a deeper shade of blue.

They glistened in the moonlight, matching the smile that turned intimate. Seductive. "Maybe you should move closer. They say it's the best way to generate heat."

Just two sentences, but his pulse slammed against his neck at the implication in her words. She'd just issued an invitation, and Jay wasn't foolish enough to turn it down. Fighting the urge to scramble out of his bag, he slowly stood and made his way toward her, nearly stumbling when she moved backwards an inch to make room. With his heart racing, Jay peeled back the blanket and joined her inside her sleeping bag. She was right; heat shot through him in an instant, nearly consuming him in its intensity. Their bodies fit perfectly, every inch of them connected. Her hands traveled up his arms, fingertips dancing up his neck and winding through his hair. He ignited, a flame raging and burning until he thought he might die from it.

"Kiss me." Her words were so soft he almost didn't hear them. Her breath on his neck so light, he almost didn't feel it.

"Anna—"

"Kiss me, Jay."

A bitter, howling wind rushed over them, but he barely noticed it as his mouth found hers. She responded, her lips parting to let him in...tasting...testing...roaming over his tongue, his chin, his neck, his collarbone. Her hands tugged at his shirt, her rapid breaths feathering against his neck. He'd never been with someone who made him feel like this...so perfect, so right. She fit against him so well.

He wanted nothing between them.

But just as he moved on top of her, she abruptly stopped kissing him, pulled back to look him in the eyes.

"You know this isn't real, right?"

He blinked at her, confused by her words. She didn't make sense. The only thing that made sense was kissing her again, feeling the curve of her hips under his, tracing the fullness of her lips with his own. He cupped the back of her neck and leaned toward her, only to feel her hands push him back.

She shoved hard.

Knocking him off her.

Jolting him awake.

Awake.

Jay lay there in the dark, breathing hard, still in his own bag and shivering from the cold. He glanced over at Anna, curled on her side sound asleep. She snored softly, her lips slack, parted as her breaths surged in and out in a relaxed, rhythmic pattern. He'd tasted those lips on his. Remembered the feel of them molded and pliable against his only moments ago.

He couldn't believe it had been a dream. A stupid, stupid dream.

Jay dragged a hand over his face and closed his eyes, praying sleep would yank him away from this embarrassing nightmare.

Sleep never came.

Chapter 8

The sound of gunfire exploded in the distance, and Anna stopped walking. Her stomach clenched and dropped at the sound, knowing it meant one thing: someone had shot an animal. Assuming they hit it, one of the other teams would soon be eating lunch.

Jealousy burned her insides like acid.

"It's no use feeling sorry for ourselves," Jay said. "Hopefully we'll stumble on something soon." He readjusted his wool beanie, leaving his hands behind his head as he studied her. "You okay?"

No. I hate this. I want to be rescued and dropped off at McDonald's. She shrugged. "I've been better."

A hint of a smile pulled at Jay's lips, the first she'd seen from him all day. He had been jumpy. Moody. Unusually short with her. It was really starting to tick her off. Maybe now he would get back to normal.

He began to walk again, taking a few hesitant steps until she moved in beside him. "Me too. Like, last week when I went out for pizza with friends to celebrate the start of this show. That was definitely better. And the cake they brought out later..." He pointed a finger at her. "Also better. And the next morning on the way to the airport when I drove through—"

"Shut up, Jay." Anna sent him a searing look, secretly relieved to see him looking her in the eye. From the moment they woke up, he'd avoided her, instead focusing on the scenery or packing up the campsite. She sighed, thankful his moodiness had passed. "I just thought of something to add to our deal. We're not allowed to talk about food, ever. Especially you."

He bent over and picked up a long stick. "Why especially me?"

She eyed him. "Because pizza is my absolute favorite food, and I haven't had it in two months."

He used the stick to slap at a dangling leaf in front of him. "Two months? Why not?"

"Because I was trying to eat smarter."

"Pizza isn't that bad for you. In fact, some might argue that—wait." He looked over at her. "Don't tell me you were on a diet."

She glared at him. "Not a diet. Just...I was trying to lose a little weight."

Jay rolled his eyes. "Because you were going on a television show and wanted to look better," he deadpanned. "You know, a show where you don't eat anything for a month and have to scrape by just to survive. Makes sense to me." He was making fun of her. But dang it, he was right.

"Okay, fine. We both agree it was stupid." She snatched up her own stick and copied his movements, slapping and pushing aside the untamed landscape as they walked. She pulled her jacket tighter, a chill traveling down her already frozen spine. Much colder and hypothermia might set in.

"Tell you what, I'll make you a deal," he said.

She sighed. "Another deal? You haven't even made good on the last one yet."

"It's like salt on a wound. Quit bringing it up." He gave her a look. "I was going to say that when we win—after you selflessly donate your millions to the suffering children of the world—I'll take you to Golden Corral and buy you anything you want on the menu."

"I hate Golden Corral." She shuddered.

"Golden Corral *and* cats? Are you even American?" He gave her a look that made her stomach flutter. "That settles it. We can't be friends anymore. My cat Fluffy and I eat the Golden Corral buffet every Thursday night. They have the coolest sneeze guards and all-you-can-eat lobster…"

"Please tell me you're kidding."

"I'm kidding, but it got your mind off pizza." He squinted at the overhead sun beating down on them, but strangely offering no semblance of warmth. "You could always press the button. If you did, we could be at Dominos by this time tomorrow." His countenance sobered slightly.

She shook her head. "I'm not pressing the button. I don't care how bad it gets, I didn't come here to quit."

Jay reached out and squeezed the back of her neck. Her insides flipped a little, and without thinking, she moved in a little closer to him. "That's what I like to hear," he said, leaving his hand in place. "I'm not quitting either."

***

"Jay, how much further do we have until we reach the checkpoint?"

He kept walking. "Probably another hour at least," he said. "I can't imagine we'd make it there before night—" He turned, surprised by the look on her face. "Anna, what's wrong?"

"Nothing, just…" She frowned in front of her. Jay followed her gaze toward a dense grouping of trees where a ramshackle cabin sat tucked deep inside. Constructed mostly of different sized logs and mud, it was covered with a bright blue tarp, it couldn't be more than two hundred yards ahead of them. "Do you think that's it?"

"I really hope not." He studied the structure, trying to picture their group of ten staying there for the next eighteen hours. The place looked abandoned, as if someone had built the shoddy house years ago in a hurry to escape the elements, then deserted it when the immediate need for shelter had passed. If this was the checkpoint, the sleeping arrangements would be miserable. "Surely they wouldn't make us stay there."

In an answer that made thoughts of a warm bed and hot shower disappear into the cold Alaskan air, a thin plume of smoke rose from the metal pipe jutting from above the tarp. Someone had built a fire.

"It looks pretty rough, like maybe it's—" She stopped talking when a tall, blonde-headed bombshell in blue pants rounded the corner of the cabin. She held a bundle of twigs in front of her to add to the already growing fire.

Heidi.

For the first time in nearly forty-eight hours, both of them picked up the pace, a renewed burst of energy propelling them forward. They'd found the checkpoint. Relief joined them like a third team member.

When they got close, Heidi smiled at him like she was seeing a long lost friend for the first time in years.

And then she completely ignored Anna. *This was going to be interesting.*

Chapter 9

Anna was tired. Wanted to crawl into her bag and sleep for days. As it stood, she sat barely upright, fighting the pull of sleep and feigning interest in another one of Josiah's nature stories. He'd been telling them for nearly an hour, completely unconcerned that everyone around him was nodding off as slumber yanked them downward. They'd all trekked the same rugged terrain, all fought the same harsh elements. Nothing about this was new...or interesting.

He cleared his throat once again and kept talking.

"And then she fell headfirst into the river, and before we knew it, half our supplies were floating away," Josiah continued, pointing out a list of Desiree's shortcomings. The woman should be outraged, but she leaned against the cabin wall with an amused smile on her face, listening as though his was the most interesting story in the world. "It took almost an hour to gather up everything. Even still, we never found her net. I thought fishing with only one net might be a problem, but we somehow managed to catch three anyway." He rolled his eyes, remembering. "Still, those were the best fish I've ever eaten."

"Probably better than tonight's meal, for sure," Heidi piped up in an annoying voice that reminded Anna of that ridiculous character in Legally Blonde. High-pitched. Perky. *Gag.* Plus there was the fact that Anna had done the cooking—a dinner that consisted of rabbit, rice, water, and an unnoticeable amount of salt. Anna waited, but no one commended her meal—not even Jay.

"Although," Heidi continued, "I was *starving* earlier, so I barely tasted what Anna cooked. It might have been gourmet for all I noticed." She waved her hand. "After all, going four hours without eating when you're hiking all this way is super, super hard."

At that, Anna's mouth fell open. *Four hours?* She glanced at Nico—Heidi's partner—and waited for him to dispute the claim. He didn't. *Four freaking hours?*

She glanced at Jay, wondering if he was as outraged about this as she was. But he simply sat on the ground, legs propped up, head leaned back against the cabin wall. The guy looked as confident and unruffled as a GQ model—assured of himself and his place in this game. And why shouldn't he be? He was gorgeous. Charming. Funny. Even though she hated to admit it. Why did it bother her so much to admit it? *Maybe because he is everything Ryan isn't.* The thought brought a wave of nausea over her stomach. She'd tried to put the tabloid report out of her mind, but it was there—nagging at her. *How could he do that to me? To us?*

Anna rolled her eyes toward the night sky at the injustice of it all. When her gaze settled back on the group, she found Jay staring straight at her. Heat spread up her neck at his intense gaze. But then he grinned. Made a face. And let his head hang to the side as he pretended to fall asleep.

Anna suppressed a laugh. He was as annoyed with these stories as she was. She looked out across the open space and sighed. Except for the continuing drone of Josiah's voice, the night was peaceful. Intimate. Natural in its best form—despite the cameras aimed straight at her face.

Gigantic lenses surrounded them, stationed at various intervals across the landscape to film the contestants for the next two days. From the moment the adventure began, media helicopters hovered overhead and mini-cameras were attached to their backpacks, but she hadn't been prepared for the mega-lenses situated around the cabin. In two short days, aside from the mini cameras strapped to their backpacks, she had almost forgotten they were taping a show. As it stood now, Eric and Patti were busy giving interviews. Anna and Jay had already taken a turn, a five-minute reiteration of how hard the journey was and how treacherous she found the terrain. Anna hated the way she'd had to force some extra tension into her voice, but rating mattered.

"So Anna," Heidi began, "tell me about your awesome boyfriend. Of course I've seen the pictures, but is he as handsome in person as he is on the cover of People Magazine? Because I, for one, think he's hot."

Anna blinked, a little taken aback by the comment. Of all the things she could think to say about Heidi, shy wasn't on the list.

"Um, I guess he's as handsome in person. Then again, I try not to pay much attention to the tabloids." Something caught her eye as it fell from Heidi's lap and landed on the ground. Anna couldn't be sure, but it looked like a Snickers wrapper. Confused, she leaned forward for a closer look when Heidi spoke up again.

"You mean to tell me you didn't see the magazines at the airport, the ones that showed him—?"

Jay cleared his throat. "Any other questions, Heidi?" He sounded bored, not at all interested. His reaction only seemed to fuel her sudden feistiness.

"Yes, actually." She sent a pointed look toward Jay, and then settled her gaze on Anna again. "A little birdie told me coming on this show was your idea. That if you win, your dad's campaign stands to benefit nicely."

Anna blinked at Heidi, then glared daggers in Jay's direction, caught off guard at being called out in front of everyone. "Um, yeah, I guess it was. Though I haven't really decided what will happen to the money if we win." She continued to stare at him, hoping for some backup. But Mr. Gorgeous, cool, and not at all guilty-looking just sat there offering no help at all. She decided to nudge him a little. "I guess it would be up to Jay, at least partly. And he already said he wanted to use his half to help feed starving children in Africa. That, and take you on a date."

"Really?" Heidi said.

At Heidi's flirtatious smile, Jay's cool demeanor heated fast. After a quick glance toward the camera, he nailed Anna with a look.

"I believe you're the one who wants to help save the children. In such a selfless way, I might add." He shifted in place. "As for dates, I can get my own without your help."

"We could take a trip to Vegas," Heidi offered with a hand on his knee, which only intensified Jay's glare.

"I'll give that some thought," Jay said back to her. "Right after Anna and I feed those kids." He rolled his eyes in her direction.

Anna looked away to keep from smiling.

***

Jay rubbed the back of his neck, not because of an actual ache, but because of the tension caused by this increasingly uncomfortable group. Everyone had made it back—even the tree-hugging-chick and her unfortunate metrosexual-looking partner, who casually walked up two hours after everyone else. The poor guy wore a look of perpetual confusion, as if he'd seen something in the forest too traumatic to talk about.

But despite Earth girl's weirdness, Jay felt better. Amazing how something as simple as a roof over his head and a fire giving off heat could turn his outlook around so quickly. But Anna...he might kill her for suggesting that date with Heidi. And he would, too, if he didn't find her so darn attractive. He'd replayed that dream in his mind a thousand times in the last twenty-four hours.

Jay stifled a groan, wishing the memory would end.

Sort of.

He leaned back, using his backpack as a chair of sorts—bulky and uncomfortable, but offering a little support for his tired muscles. He settled into it and eyed her across the campfire. She sat across from him, the firelight framing her body in a hazy glow of orange. Her legs were pulled up in front of her, her head resting on them as she gazed almost trance-like into the flames. The ends of her hair shone like melted chocolate, and he found himself imagining its softness sliding through his fingers.

He'd always had a thing for brunettes.

Jay removed his hat and tunneled his hands through his sandy hair, gazing up at the starry night sky. The beauty failed to capture him, so it didn't take long for his gaze to drift over Anna again. She'd been fighting sleep for hours, and once again her eyes drifted to a close and popped open as she struggled to stay awake. No wonder. She'd barely slept the night before.

While he had failed to sleep on their impossibly hard bed of twigs and rocks, she tossed and turned, often groaning out in frustration. Once she even kicked at a nearby tree, cursing under her breath as though it were responsible for their entire foodless, sleepless existence. In spite of his misery, it had taken all kinds of self-control to keep from laughing. Watching her now, the lack of sleep was taking a toll.

His gaze bore into her through the rising embers, imploring her to look at him. After what felt like forever, she jerked awake and caught his eye. A yawn followed, chased by an embarrassed grin.

Go to bed, he mouthed, a slow smile crossing his lips.

She frowned, nodding toward the group to say, *I don't want to be rude.*

Jay nailed her with a stern look. *Go to bed*, he mouthed again. He snapped his gaze toward the cabin, letting her know he meant business. Catching him completely off guard, she stuck out her tongue. His burst of laughter that followed was out before he could stop it. Funny how his anger had completely dissipated.

"What's so funny?" Heidi leaned toward him, a look of fascination on her face.

"Oh nothing. I was just thinking about something that happened yesterday…" he lied.

"Well maybe you could share it with me inside the cabin," she offered, her invitation clear. Another time, another place, he might have taken her up on it.

"Maybe tomorrow," he lied. "I'm a little tired right now." He reached for his canteen and took a long drink to appear nonchalant.

But when Anna stood up across from him, his heart sputtered unexpectedly. "I'm going to bed," she said to the group. "I can't keep my eyes open any longer." She picked up her boots and moved around the circle toward her backpack. Shoulders sagging, she grabbed her pack and walked toward the cabin, catching Jay's eye just outside the doorway.

Jay winked at her, determining something then. They were a team, would be for the next month. And she shouldn't be alone. He waited until she walked through the doorway, hesitated a moment, then stood and brushed the dirt off his pants. With nerves rattling his gut, he followed her inside. She was busy unrolling her bag, situating it in front of the cabin's only window.

"Need help?" He heard the timidity in his own voice, heard the wobble, heard the fear of rejection. He cleared his throat to shake it away.

"I think I'm okay. What are you doing in here already?" She glanced over her shoulder at him. It only took a second for his pulse to race.

"I'm tired, and that conversation was getting old. Have you noticed that no one seems to be having a hard time with this yet?"

"Yes, and if Heidi had said one more negative thing about my cooking..." Anna climbed inside her bag and stretched out on her side, tucking an arm underneath her head to look up at him. "She's lucky I didn't grab my bowl and pummel her with it."

Jay laughed at her unusual burst of temper. "A catfight at the first checkpoint. *That* I would have loved to see."

Anna rolled her eyes at him. Blue eyes. Eyes a guy could swim in and not even notice he was drowning. "You would have been disappointed," she said. He forced himself to concentrate. "There wouldn't have been any Jell-O or wet T-shirts involved."

That got his attention. Biting back a smile, he flipped open his bag and stretched it out beside Anna's, then climbed inside to face her. He looked her in the eye. "I don't even like Jell-O."

His heart gave a little fist pump when she laughed. "But the wet tees aren't a problem for you?"

He clutched his chest in surrender. "I suppose I could endure them if I had to. Maybe we should go ahead and pencil in a date for this fight, just so I can get the miserable experience over with?"

He laughed when her arm landed across his chest, followed by a tiny burst of fake outrage. "Go to sleep, Jay."

He shifted onto his back and closed his eyes, unable to shake his smile when he realized her arm still lay against him and showed no sign of moving.

Chapter 10

That morning, they awoke to a major drop in temperatures. Though the tight sleeping quarters left everyone feeling toasty—albeit somewhat cramped—inside their sleeping bags, the warmth was fleeting. The first crack of the door escorted in a blast of cold air and delivered a warning. It was time to get moving. They had breakfast to eat, a campsite to clean up, and new provisions to add to their already heavy backpacks. Anna filled their canteens, using the fresh water provided by the show. Water was plentiful, but food was scarce. Other than the meal supplied the evening before and the two loaves of bread set out this morning, the teams were on their own. The survival aspect of the show was genuine.

Saying goodbye to everyone had been…weird. Problematic for sure, because there were safety in numbers. But she had to admit she enjoyed her time with Jay, and for the next twenty-six days she wanted to embrace it. Within minutes, they came to a wide clearing. Jay stopped walking and stood still, a transfixed expression crossing his features. She came up beside him, inhaling brisk air and the woodsy scent of pine. Alaska was beautiful in April. She closed her eyes for a moment and let the breeze erase the tension building in her neck, sighing when a peacefulness took its place. "Wow. I was starting to think this state was made up of nothing but trees."

Jay shielded his eyes. "This is amazing." He quietly took in the view, mesmerized by it. "Have you ever seen anything so pretty?"

"No, I haven't. Not since—" Anna stopped abruptly as three black spots moved in the distance. Just like that, the tension was back. "Jay, what are those? They look just like—

"Bears. A mother and two cubs, probably." Neither of them moved. Judging by the way Jay's shoulders went rigid, she knew he was worried. Which left her stunned when he began to walk straight toward them.

She lurched for his arm. "What are you doing?"

He shrugged. "I'm following the map." He flipped it open and scanned it before turning it toward her. "It says that we need to walk two miles this way. At that point, we should run into a stream. Of course we'll have to cross it, but hopefully we'll be able to catch some fish first..."

"And if they charge toward us? If they attack? If they try to eat us alive and leave our bones here to rot?" Okay, maybe that last part was a little overdramatic, but where was the outrage? Where was the fear?

Nowhere in the vicinity of Jay. He just stared at her. "Then I'll shoot them, and we'll have a nice dinner." He made a tiny X over his heart and held up two fingers. "I swear."

Her jaw dropped. "And you have a lot of experience shooting bears, do you?"

He adjusted his backpack and held onto the shoulder straps, looking bored with her line of questioning. "Not bears. But I've killed a few mountain lions in my time. It's really not a big deal."

Wait. What?

"Mountain Lions?" Was he for real? "I thought you worked on a farm in Texas."

He nodded, tilted his head as he studied her. "Not on it. For it. Still, I've shot a few animals in my time."

She just looked at him. "Jay." She spoke slowly. "I have a feeling I don't really know that much about you. Just what is it that you do for a living?"

"Well, it might be a little different than what you think..."

***

"The name of the game is *Spill It*, Anna," Jay said. "If you refuse to answer the question, you're not playing it right."

She shook her head. "It's not that I don't want to answer, it's just that I don't think you've known me long enough to ask personal things like that."

Jay wasn't buying her explanation. He yawned, hoping to give off a whole *your excuse is lame* vibe. "It was a simple question, Anna. Now either answer it, or lose the game." He rolled his eyes. "You will officially be the first girl I've ever played with who lost on the second question..." he muttered, cutting his eyes toward her to see her reaction. Just then a large heron sailed overhead, the first they had seen all day. He groaned in frustration when it disappeared before he could dislodge his gun. Checking the safety, he walked with the rifle aimed at the ground. That kind of unpreparedness wouldn't happen again.

"There went dinner again," Anna quipped, looking in the empty space where the bird had been. "You need to remember our deal."

"You need to remember our game," he tossed back at her. "Because you're about to lose. Besides, I answered your questions. Both of them."

"I asked the first one before we started playing this dumb game. It doesn't count."

"It counts," he said with a nod. "Believe me, it counts."

Okay, so maybe saying he worked on a farm had been a bit of an understatement. In actuality, he worked on a ranch. A fifteen hundred acre spread on the outskirts of Dallas. And okay, maybe the word *worked* was also a stretch. Actually, he managed it, and along with his management duties, he oversaw the daily tasks of thirty-two employees. He had, however, shot a couple of mountain lions trying to attack their cattle once. That part was true. But he'd never shot a bear and wasn't entirely sure he could pull that off. Thankfully he hadn't needed to find out. They wandered off before he and Anna had gotten close enough.

His frantic, silent, gut-busting pleas with God had seriously paid off. He swiped a thick layer of sweat off his upper lip before Anna had time to question it.

Of course, with explaining his job to her, he had to admit to that the management job was, in reality, an indefinite assignment to help prepare him for the much more daunting task of taking over Manhattan Construction, the second largest commercial construction company in Texas. Owned by the rancher he worked for, the company had been in charge of building the new Cowboy stadium, the single most acclaimed project in Texas history. Dozens of companies fought for that job, but Manhattan's reputation superseded them, and they came out with the bid. No expense was spared, giving the company free reign to be creative. The experience Jay garnered from observing the monstrous project was invaluable.

Anna had listened to his words with growing interest. He knew she was surprised to learn his story—it was plastered all over her face. Obviously her expectations of him had been low, and he tried not to let it annoy him. After all, he understood her reaction. Not many twenty-five-year-olds had his kind of background. Then again, not a lot of men his age had been saddled with so much responsibility.

The more he shared, the more she peppered him with questions. *How long have you been working there? Where did you get your degree? What goes into running a ranch? Have you ever milked a cow? Shoveled manure?* The last two questions made him laugh. And the answer was a resounding *no freakin' way.* He answered each question with a mixture of what he hoped was patience and honesty. Until the last one.

Does your father work there, too? That one, he glossed over, mumbling something about student loans and a sick uncle and a bunch of other half-truths that were the only off-the-cuff excuses he could come up with. Avoidance. He'd become a pro at it for years now. Maybe one day he would be comfortable enough to share that part of his story with her, but he doubted it. His siblings had come up with the game, *Spill It,* a game he had played with them during their growing up years. Jay couldn't remember who came up with the title—only that it wasn't him—but it offered a welcome distraction from the crap called Their Lives. If one of them was having a hard day, someone would think of the most outrageous question and ask it at random. The rules were simple: answer the question, or lose the game. And if anyone refused, they couldn't re-enter until all members had bowed out. To this day, they kept the game going when they were together. In fact, in nearly a decade, not once had anyone refused a question.

Until Anna. But Jay wouldn't give up easily. Out here, he wanted to talk, especially to her. More than anything right now, he wanted to know more.

"So are you going to spill it, or not?" he asked, bumping her arm with his elbow. "It can't be that bad."

She bumped back and huffed out a sigh. He caught his grin, knowing he had her in five, four, three, two...

"No, he isn't." She scowled at him. "Are you happy now?"

Jay raised an eyebrow, pleased with this bit of information. "He isn't? If not him, then who?"

She answered with a longsuffering sigh, but he didn't care. The point of the game was honesty, and it wasn't his fault that her current boyfriend wasn't the greatest kisser. He would, however, take credit for being happy about it.

"The guy who took me to prom junior year. His name was Noah, and he was a senior. When he drove me home afterward..." Her voice trailed off onto a winding path of memories. Pleasant ones, judging from the wistful smile playing about her lips. Jay gave her a moment to recall them. After all, a week rarely went by that he didn't think of Lydia from math class, and that memory involved slightly more than just a kiss.

"That good, huh?"

Anna blinked, her face blooming a pretty shade of pink. "Um...it wasn't bad. But Ryan is really great too."

"You're backtracking on your answer."

"I have a right to change my mind, don't I?" she snapped. But her mind wasn't changed. The unwavering scrunch of her eyebrows conveyed every syllable of doubt in that claim.

"Sure. Consider me convinced." Jay didn't even attempt to hide the sarcasm.

Anna shot him a look. "Okay, now it's my turn, and I'm going to think of a good one. Something even more embarrassing than the question you just asked me." She stumbled over a large rock directly in her path and landed on her hands, cursing loudly enough for him to hear. He lurched forward to help her up, one hand landing on her waist, the other...a little lower than he meant it to.

"Wow. Don't hold back your words on my account," he said, quickly letting go.

She gave him a look. "Next time you want to help, try not to grope me quite as much." Jay grinned as she picked bits of leaves off her gloves. "Where's the fun in that?"

She rewarded him with a kick on his behind. *She has a boyfriend,* he quickly scolded himself. As he expected, no guilt materialized.

As they walked, an unfamiliar sound began to drift in their direction. Louder than the usual noises out here, the noise competed with the rushing wind to capture their attention. Jay looked at Anna, noting the alarm that widened her eyes. He imagined the same emotion was reflected in his own.

Something was up ahead, and it didn't sound good.

Chapter 11

The river rushed past and slapped at the banks, water shooting upward as it crashed onto the rocky shoreline. Jay and Anna stared between it and the rusty kayak supposedly left here for them to float across, dumfounded. Overhead cameras captured the scene—the swell of the river as it roared to life, angry, twice is previous size, issuing a warning to anyone daring to approach its depths. Which is exactly what Jay and Anna needed to do. Approach it and cross over. Somehow. Without drowning. Because this poor excuse for a boat had a dime-sized hole on the side, which made filling up with water a near certainty. How much was anyone's guess.

And Anna couldn't swim.

Despite her wealthy upbringing, lessons hadn't been high on the list of must-haves in her early life. Designer clothes? Check. Exclusive private schools? Check, check. A BMW for high school graduation to impress the fellow classmates and parents? Check, check, and triple check.

Swimming lessons to save oneself from death on national television? Not a priority.

Fear lodged in Anna's throat and stuck there. There was no way she could cross that thing, not even in a kayak. No way she would survive, not even if Jay personally carried her on his shoulders. Plus, she was freezing, and living through the torment of ice forming on her already cold skin didn't seem all that appealing.

Jay had other ideas.

"Well, I guess there's only one thing we can do," he said, a sigh of resignation emanating from his words. "Help me flip this thing over."

Her hand clamped down on his arm when he took a step forward. "Think of something else, because I'm not crossing that water. Especially not in *that*." Was she the only one who noticed it was a guaranteed death trap? She might as well be staring at an iceberg and climbing aboard the Titanic anyway for all the sense it made. Her voice shook, from fear or cold. Maybe both. Jay didn't seem to notice. Or care.

"According to the map, we have to cross here to remain on the right path," he said. "And if we veer off the course the map has provided—"

"The map, the map, the map," she said, mimicking him with a huge eye roll. "You sound just like that character on Dora the Explorer. Enough with the map. I'm not crossing."

His eyebrow rose. "How do you know Dora the Explorer?"

Anna shrugged, staring at the rapidly moving water. "I watch cartoons."

Jay blinked at her, something she couldn't read written in his expression. "Huh. Imagine that."

She flicked him a glance. "Imagine what?" She scratched her neck, pulled on her thumb, twisting...turning...cracking...as her heart rate spiked.

A ghost of a smile slanted his lips. "I just never pictured you as a cartoon-watching girl."

"I guess you find out something new every day. And here's another something new for you: I'm not crossing this water. End of story." She started to walk away. Maybe she could find another path around. How far could this river possibly stretch, anyway? She checked upstream and found her answer. A mad rush of winding, sparkling spring water lay in front of them as far as the eye could see. Her heart practically landed inside her toes. Her breaths came in tiny gasps, faster and faster until she thought she might faint.

"You can't swim, can you?"

"What makes you say that?"

"Oh, I don't know. The hyperventilating maybe? The black spots I can practically see floating across your eyes. The way you're gripping my arm with the gentleness of a pair of forceps. It's a toss-up, really," he said.

"There are not black spots—" she began indignantly, then said, "Wait, forceps?"

Jay shrugged. "I have a niece. And when she was born she got stuck in the birth canal, so in order to get her out they had to insert forceps up in the—"

"I got it, Jay," Anna said, a look of disgust crossing her face. "I know what they're used for. I was just a little surprised you did."

"There are many things you don't know about me, Anna. So many..." He shrugged out of his backpack and pulled out a pair of pants. He tied the legs together at the ankles, and then with a snap, dragged the pants through the air and rolled them at the waist. In seconds, they filled like a balloon. She had never seen anything so fascinating before.

"How did you do that? She eyed them, then Jay, then the pants again, trying to replay his movements in her head.

"Boy Scouts as a kid." He shrugged. "It's a floatation device, in case anything goes wrong." I want you to slip it around your waist, like this." He indicated for her to drop her pack. She shrugged out of it, then held her arms up over her head while he lifted the inflated pants and tugged them down around her. She should have been relieved.

Grateful even. But the only thing her senses could comprehend was how nice his hands felt on her arms, her waist, the top of her hips. By the time his hands adjusted the ring against her and fell away, she was reduced to nothing but a scattered mass of skipping heartbeats and broken breaths.

"There. Now you're safe."

But Anna knew she wasn't safe. Where Jay was concerned, safe wasn't worth the time it took to say the word.

"So, are you going to help me flip this boat?"

"Uh huh." The stupid sound was out before she realized she'd opened her mouth. And now she had agreed. Agreed to climb on that floating hand grenade and risk all hope of a long life. She blew out some air and stomped toward the so-called raft.

"Fine, let's flip it. But you're right, I can't swim. If this boat sinks, I'm counting on you to save my life. And just so you know, I'll be really mad if I wind up dead."

"Sweetheart, we can't afford to sink. If you're dead, how am I supposed to win?" His grin was way too playful for her taste.

"You know, this might be a joke to you, but the thought of winding up in that water terrifies me. What if I fall and can't get up?" She latched on to the pants like they were a lifeline. Which they were.

"Then I'll regret my hasty decision to leave my life alert bracelet at home…"

She made an unflattering sound. "Not funny, Jay." This was *not* the time for corny commercial references. "What if I get swept away and drown? Or worse, what if I get tossed over a waterfall and land on a rock? Or what if I—"

Surprising her, Jay reached out and touched his finger to her lips. If he meant to shut her up, it worked. Her words evaporated, disappearing with her mind as all senses focused on that one warm spot where his finger pressed against her mouth. Her limbs turned to liquid and her heart pounded hard, and neither had anything to do with a fear of water.

"You're not going to drown. And you're not going to slide down a waterfall." A lazy grin stole over his face. "And you're definitely not going to be fish food. Just hang on to me and you won't get hurt. Deal?"

She nodded, clutching his wrist with both hands. They pushed the kayak into the water and stepped inside, one foot at a time. Jay reached for the only set of oars and began to paddle. Against the strong current, progress was nearly non-existent. Within a minute, a slow trickle of water bubbled around Anna's shoes. Trying to keep panic at bay, she searched for something, anything to say. "You know, this deal of ours keeps growing. Every time I turn around, you're adding to it."

"I have to, because your expectations are so dang high. First, you want me to kill dinner. Then, you want me to save your life."

"Save my life? I just don't feel like drowning. Is that too much to ask?"

"It depends on how heavy you are. Not sure I can hold your weight."

He laughed when Anna smacked him on the arm.

***

"Anna, stop moving around! If we sink, it won't have anything to do with the water in this boat. It'll be because you tip us over. So unless you want to land head first into the water—you've got to keep your butt still and quit looking over the side." They were almost to the opposite bank, but Anna was so afraid that progress was slow-going. He couldn't blame her. Heck, he was a better-than-average swimmer—competed for three years on his high school team—but this raging current was dangerously close to overpowering them. Lapping around the bottom of the boat in icy tentacles, the speed it traveled and pain it inflicted when it splashed upward and onto their hands and faces was almost unbearable.

"I can't help it," she protested, folding her arms in front of her. "I'm trying to see how close the water is to rushing in over the top of the boat. And from my estimation, we only have about three inches left. Are we going to make it before we sink another inch, Jay? Because in another inch we might drown." She sounded like a parrot—an inch an inch and inch!—and glared at him like a four year old, but he didn't feel irritated or even impatient with her. It's hard to feel irritated when you're inexplicably turned on at the same time.

Which begged a question: why was he turned on right now? Right now, when they face possible frostbite and a particularly uncomfortable drowning? Women had it right—men were pigs. Anna might as well hang him upside down and carve him into a pound of bacon.

"We're not going to drown. Just sit there for a second and let me think of the best way to get us the rest of the way across, okay?" Jay gave another stroke of the paddles, cringing when a fresh burst of water entered the boat.

"Paddle faster," Anna said, her voice raising an octave. "There's an idea."

Jay shot her a look but didn't bother with a response. She was scared, and apparently scared made her sarcastic and whiny. Besides, if he were being truthful, he was a little afraid, too. They were close to the bank, but the water was still deep in this spot. If the kayak tipped, they would both be forced under water. In the freezing temperatures, they would wind up with hypothermia. Or worse.

His feet were already numb from the icy water, even through two pairs of socks and thick hiking boots. He shuddered to think about what his face might feel like if it became submerged for even a second.

"Okay, here's what I want you to do," he said. He was stalling for time, making things up, had no idea what to say next. But he had to say something to keep this chick from falling apart. "While I paddle, I want you to try to get some of this water out of the boat. Use your hands or your boot or—"

"The pan we use for cooking?"

Jay just looked at her. Men were pigs, and men were also stupid, it seemed. "Sure, the pan. That's probably the best option."

He didn't miss the way she smirked at him. It wasn't exactly a smile, but it was far enough removed from panic to make him think they were making progress. She unstrapped the pan from her backpack.

"Okay, ready?" When she nodded he said, "Then start bailing."

Progress was slow going, and Anna might as well have been sucking the water out through a juice-box straw for all the difference it seemed to make, but within five minutes they managed to make it to the other side tired, soaked, and irritated.

As they emerged from the kayak, slime-covered rocks and loose silt stirred with the rapid flow of the lake. Jay halted his footsteps for a moment, tugging on Anna's arm to keep her steady until he felt assured of his steps. Dragging the boat behind them, slowly they approached the bank. Jay reached for a low-hanging branch from a large river oak and held on tight. Using the tree as an anchor, Anna climbed out of the water, sloshing and huffing as she stepped onto dry land. Jay followed her upward, oblivious to a branch hanging askew in front of them. He winced as it ripped across his cheek with the force of a pocket knife, his face pounding from the force of the laceration.

Anna dropped her backpack and flung herself on a slab of dry ground. Jay hoisted himself up and flopped down beside her, breathing in and out from the exertion of the last fifteen minutes. That might have been the single worst moment of his life—and God knew he'd had lots of them.

He swiped a hand over his cheek and drew it back. Blood stained three of his fingers. Pushing away thoughts of infection and lack of basic first aid supplies, he wiped his hand on a nearby rock.

"So that was fun," he said, blinking up at the misty late-afternoon sky. Water seeped into the ground around his head, both a discomfort and a relief. At least it was wicking off his thoroughly soaked legs.

"That was *not* fun," Anna countered, her lips shivering so violently she could barely get the words out. Jay wished he could think of a way to help, but aside from lying here to dry beside her, there wasn't much he could do.

He took a shuddering breath, inwardly commanding himself to stop convulsing. Three or four deep breaths later, and he hadn't made much progress.

The sun indicated the passing of the day—not dark, but definitely altering the feel of the afternoon. They'd walked five, maybe six hours since leaving the checkpoint. Jay guessed the time to be somewhere between four and five in the afternoon. He would give himself ten more minutes to thaw, and then force himself to get up. Someone needed to fish, and he wouldn't have Anna do it. They'd made a deal, and even though she'd been joking, she was right—he was slacking off on his end of it.

"I'm sorry I complained so much," Anna said.

"Oh, don't worry about it." He glanced at her. Her lips had slowed to a soft quiver and she stared up at the sky. "If you'd really started to bother me, I was prepared to push you into the water." One side of his mouth turned up when her lips pressed together.

Even though he looked right at her, he wasn't prepared for the way her arm landed across his stomach. "You would not have pushed—" She looked at him and gasped. "Jay! You're bleeding!"

"I know, but it's not that bad." He frowned at the look on her face. "Is it?"

"Your cheek looks like a sketch of the Red River, and we need to clean it up." She pushed herself to a standing position. "Do you want to come with me to the water, or should I just wet a rag and bring it here?"

Jay sighed. "I'll come with you." He slowly stood, putting on a show of acting inconvenienced. But the truth was a different story.

He kind of liked the idea of Anna's hands on his face.

Chapter 12

"You think it'll leave a scar? Dang it, woman! Stop pressing so hard."

He'd been griping like that the whole time. "Stop complaining, it isn't *that* deep. Now hold still while I—Jay! Quit moving around so much. If you're not careful, you're going to pitch us both back in the water."

"I might throw you in on purpose if you don't stop jabbing at my face."

"Try it and you'll be walking funny tomorrow."

Jay grinned. "Cheers?"

Anna's mouth twitched. "Diane and Jack, circa 1982." She inched closer to the edge and scooped up a little more water in the palm of her hand. Rubbing it on his cheek, she watched as blood washed away, then rose to the surface in a crimson stripe. She moved a little closer to get a better view, their faces only inches apart. Jay needed stitches. Even now, despite frigid temperatures that should work like ice to clot the bleeding, his blood flowed. But she didn't have a needle and the closest doctor's office was a thousand miles away.

"So how does it look? Give it to me straight," he said. His breath landed on her neck, sending a shudder down her already cold neck. Ignoring it, she worked her lower lip as she attempted to repair the jagged tear. The sight of blood normally made her queasy; today was no exception. .

She tried to dismiss the feeling and focus on the task at hand. "It looks a little…rough. And you probably *will* have a scar. But you know what they say about men with scars…"

He flicked her a glance without moving his head. His look turned teasing, seductive. "No, what do they say? Fill me in, Anna."

"Well…I…" she stammered and palmed more water, uneasiness in full bloom. "I don't exactly know what they say. I just know that scars are supposed to make men look more handsome, is all." She felt a stupid blush creep up her neck and purposely took longer than necessary, letting water run through her fingers before cupping more.

"So tell me, Anna." Jay said as she spilled it over his cheek again. "Is it true? Has this cut turned me into the sexiest thing you've ever seen?"

You already were. Her face burned like fire. "Oh, please. You're bleeding all over me. Sexy is hardly the word I would use." She turned to rinse her fingers again, closing her eyes until she felt in control. That man was way too handsome for his own good. Or hers.

She took a deep breath and slipped off a glove, wetting one of the fabric fingers and handing it to him. She sat down next to him. "Hold this against the cut and maybe it will stop bleeding in a minute."

The concern in his eyes tugged at her heart. "It's bad, isn't it?"

She blew into her icy hand. "It isn't *not* bad, if that's what you're asking."

"That's the biggest non-answer I've ever heard." Jay winked at her as he walked toward their supplies. Keeping her glove pressed against his face, he reached for the fishing net. "Do you think you could try this time?"

"Let me have it." She gathered the net in a ball and walked toward the water, remembering the times she used to fish with her father. It was one of the rare things they did as a twosome, though it didn't happen often. They'd gone exactly twice during her childhood. Always with a rod and hooks, but surely she could manage.

Just before she stepped into the water, an idea occurred to her. One she couldn't believe she hadn't thought of until now. She spun to face him.

"Jay, I have earrings in my bag!"

Midway through running a hand through his hair, he stopped to look at her. His raised eyebrow implied she was crazy. His turned up mouth confirmed it.

"You know, you can get dressed up if you want to, but normally I find the fish don't mind if you show up looking awful..."

She made an exasperated sound. "That's not what I—wait, I look awful?" She touched the ends of her hair before shaking her head. "That's not the point. The point is I have earrings. We need to get them!"

He just stood there. "What for?"

She rolled her eyes. That man could be so dense. "Because earrings have hooks. And hooks..." She waited for him to catch on. When he did, she swore an actual light switch flicked inside his head.

"Catch fish!" They both lunged for her bag, giving each other an awkward high-five that caught mostly air. Whatever. This would work. It had to. Jay's hand emerged with a small diamond teardrop that dangled from a solid gold hoop. Without hesitating, Anna snatched it and twisted the hook until it snapped.

"I hope you weren't planning on wearing those again."

She waved a hand in the air. "Who cares?" I'm more interested in eating than looking good."

"That's obvious—"

She cut him off with a glare. "I suggest you don't finish that thought. Now we just need to find a string…" Anna looked around, then eyed the drawstring hanging from Jay's coat collar. With a flick of her wrist, she whipped it free.

"Hey!" he protested.

"Do you have any better ideas?" She drew the hook through the braided fabric, twisting until it was secure. "Now we need worms or something to use as bait." She turned to scan the mossy area behind them, then grabbed a knife and bent low to dig through the hard earth.

Jay rolled his eyes and knelt down beside her. "Seems like you've done this before," he said, overturning leaves and sticks in a quest to find something living.

"I've been camping before. Nothing like this, but I know how to find a worm."

"Did you go often with your family?" Jay pitched a rock into a nearby bush.

There was no way to answer without sounding pathetic. "No. My parents sent me to camp. In Missouri." She took a deep breath and dug harder.

"Cool. I used to go for a couple weeks in the summer."

Awesome. She used to go every summer, for the entire summer, from the time she was five. When she was nine, a flu epidemic spread across the campsite three weeks into the session, forcing all the campers to be sent home. Her parents were vacationing in Italy and had to cut their vacation short to come get her. They were livid. She had ruined their plans. There she was, an only child, and her parents had no idea what to do with her without the comforts of school, nannies, and sleepaway camp.

Anna swallowed. "I went for the whole summer, starting when I was five."

Jay paused and looked over at her. "Five years old?" When she nodded, he sat back on his heels, knife dangling between his fingers as he studied her. "For three months?"

"Sometimes four, depending on the year." Their willingness to be away from her back then still hurt, even now. She shoved it down at the same time the earth wiggled. "Look, I found one!" Honesty was great, but only in small doses.

Jay studied her, seeming to understand her need to change the subject without even asking. After a few seconds, he turned back to the ground. Grinning softly, he jammed his knife into the hard soil.

"You know, you're putting me to shame here. Give me five minutes, and I'll take that worm of yours and raise you by ten."

A corner of Anna's mouth turned up in relief. For his willingness to play along...to move on to a safer topic...she was grateful. "Keep dreaming, Junior. Keep dreaming."

Searching the ground, they worked side by side in a quiet camaraderie, racing like two kids with a shiny gold trophy at stake. It was silly, but she found herself smiling. Because Jay made things fun. Because he didn't push her. Because he knew when to move on.

And because she knew that somehow in the wilderness of Alaska, she'd managed to find a friend.

***

"Yes, it *is* my turn. Now answer the question," Jay said.

"No it isn't. It's mine. *I* get to ask the next one," Anna said back. She just looked at him, her full lips tilted downward as she dropped the hook in the water again. But he'd been keeping track, and it was definitely his turn.

"You asked *me* what my favorite breakfast food is," he said, holding up a finger, "and I told you it was poached eggs with avocado and tomatoes. Then I asked *you* about your middle name…" He shrugged. "And really, Margaret isn't all that bad. And then—"

"You asked me about my summer camping trips," Anna interrupted. "So there you have it—it's my turn. But…poached eggs and avocados?" She made a face. "That's just gross. Now answer the question."

Jay's mouth hung open. "The one about summer camp doesn't count. We weren't playing the game when I asked that question."

She gave an overly loud laugh. "Oh, like we weren't playing when I asked about your job? When I said the same thing, you said it…" she held up her fingers like quote marks "…totally counted." She lowered her hands and flung the empty hook back into the water.

Jay was stuck, because she was right. Crap. It was her turn, and he felt sick. Because in all his years of playing this game—*whose stupid idea was it to play, anyway?*—no one had ever asked him this one. Granted, he'd only played with his siblings. And granted, it was a basic question. Silly, even. But it was quite possibly the most embarrassing, personal fact about him, and he'd never shared it with anyone. And here was this…this…*stranger*, standing in front of him all innocent and beautiful and expectant, and he had to come clean. He swallowed to keep from retching into the water, feeling his heartbeat take off in a sprint.

He flung the net with more force than necessary, refusing to look in her direction. "Eighteen. I was eighteen."

Her head snapped around to look at him. "What?" Laughter escaped, followed by a cough. *Here it comes,* he thought. "Are you kidding? Not until you were eighteen?"

He shifted impatiently to the other hip. "No, I'm not kidding. I was eighteen. You happy now?"

So much for holding back. She burst out laughing. "Are you telling me that Mr. *I'm Sexy*...was eighteen before he kissed a girl? Seriously?" She threw her head back and howled.

He had no defense except to call her on it. "Go ahead and laugh, but I think we've already established you think I'm hot."

All at once, her laughter fizzled, replaced by a scarlet red stain that bloomed along her neckline. She palmed some water and threw it on him. It landed on his neck like liquid ice cubes. "You are so full of yourself. Well, listen here, Mr. Ego, why don't you take your hot self and work on catching—"

The string gave a tug. Both of them gasped as they stared at it, at each other, and back. Finally, Jay moved toward her and they switched. He took the string, she opened the net, hands bumping and tangling together as excitement took over. Their breaths held as he slowly wound the line around his finger and Anna glided the net underneath the thrashing fish. Excitement shot through him, adrenaline pumping so hard it practically bounced off Anna. This fish was large. Three, maybe four pounds. They couldn't afford to lose it.

"Go slow, and tell me when you have it secured," he said. He kept rolling the line, the weight of the fish cutting the circulation in his finger. But he wouldn't let a little thing like a severed limb stand in his way. They would land this thing, no matter what.

"Okay, I think...hold on..." Her shoulders shuddered as she stretched the net and slowly brought up the sides, her arms weaving back and forth to keep the fish contained. Jay paused to watch the way she took over, as if she'd done this a hundred times before. She brought the ends of the net together and slipped her finger through the gill of the fish, rendering it helpless, completely unfazed by its size. A triumphant grin spread wide and full as she pulled the fish—net and all—out of the water for his inspection. He approved. He definitely approved. In fact, as he remembered their earlier conversation…as he looked at Anna holding that fish like a trophy earned from a hard-fought battle.

The word *hot* flashed through his mind like a neon sign at midnight.

***

"So, how old were you?"

Anna stopped chewing and looked at him, firelight accentuating the roundness in her eyes. She averted her gaze. *Interesting*, Jay thought. She was all over the question when she'd tossed it at him earlier. But now, she didn't want to answer.

They sat on sleeping bags on opposite sides of the fire. Both exhausted, sore, and hungry, they decided to abandon the map and set up camp for the night. They were only a mile from their intended stopping point, and the river had grown calm enough to attempt fishing again in the morning.

Thanks to the lighter—a gift from God, really—Anna had a fire built and blazing in just a few minutes. While Jay cleaned the fish, she gathered wood and set it aflame, never once complaining about not getting to rub sticks together. When he pointed out the fact to her, she flung a stick at his head, missing him by an inch.

"What do you mean?" She blinked and tried to look innocent.

"Give me a break, Anna. You know what I'm asking. How old were you when you had your first kiss? I fessed up. Now, it's your turn."

She sighed. "Okay, I was thirteen."

Jay's mouth tilted on a grin. "Ah, a young one. Let me guess. This super-awkward kiss took place either at the obligatory middle school dance where no one actually dances but instead stands around looking at each other all night, boys trying to figure out how to steal a kiss from a girl they haven't even attempted to talk too and girls all hoping to get a kiss from the exact same guy—the tall kid with the sweet smile despite his braces who makes all the points at the basketball game and is just *so cute*."

"Football. He played football," Anna said.

Jay gave her a pointed look. "That bit of information doesn't help you become less of a cliché."

"Is there an either/or in this scenario?" Anna glared at him.

"Of course there is." Jay smirked at her. "So it was either at this dance, or it involved a party, a locked closet, and a very uncomfortable two minutes in heaven or hell, depending on your perspective."

A slow grin filled Anna's face. "The best two minutes of that boy's life. I called it heaven. I guarantee he did." She winked at him.

"Oh really?" Jay pulsed tripped. "You honestly think you were that good back then?"

"I *know* I was that good back then. And you know what they say about age..." Her words trailed off, but the implication stood stock still and right in front of him, begging him to challenge her. But of course he wouldn't. He wasn't that stupid.

"Care to put your money where your mouth is?" It took a moment for the functioning part of his brain to catch up to the clearly dead part of his brain that he had, in fact, just challenged her. And he'd just used a cliché to do it, despite the fact that he had called her a cliché only seconds ago.

"Are you questioning my kissing ability, Jay?" She shifted in her seat. It didn't escape his notice that she had managed to move closer.

"I'm questioning your claim that a single kiss from you was the best moment in that boy's life. Frankly, I don't believe you."

She moved closer still. "Frankly, I'm going to prove you wrong. Drop that fish, Jay, and get over here."

He worked hard to keep his eyes from going wide when she moved onto her knees and crawled toward him. "Anna, it was just a joke. You don't have to prove yourself to me. Besides, it's cold and I'm tired and I'm..." *having trouble not picturing you undressed and inside my bag, just like the dream I haven't been able to get out of my head for three days.*

"You scared, Jay?" Anna stopped right in front of him, all ready and willing and not backing down. "Because I don't believe in walking away from a challenge."

Jay tossed his bowl aside. To heck with it. If she wanted a kiss, he'd give her a kiss. One she wouldn't forget. One that would scrape that acne-covered middle school boy right out of her fondest memory and replace it with him. A kiss she would remember long after this competition was over and would make her wish she could come back to this day, this place, this campfire, and this moment.

To him.

He inched forward until they were eye to eye, face to face, Anna still on her knees and him balanced on one hand as the other hand lifted to graze her chin, cup her cheek, splay against the back of her neck.

Just like the dream.

"This better be good or I'm going to tell everyone how bad you are at one's of life's most basic skills." His words sounded bold, but he barely heard them through the *throb throb throb* of the pulse in his neck.

"Oh, it'll be good," she teased, her soft smile lighting up the sky and warming the temperatures and turning all the dead colors around them vibrant shades of green and blues and blacks.

Somehow, Jay knew it would be.

And somehow, the blasted helicopter knew he was about to get what he'd been thinking about forever, because it chose that exact moment to appear from nowhere and hover right over their heads. Jay could feel the presence of invasive cameras even before Anna pulled back and looked up. He followed suit, trying not to care that somehow this felt like the biggest injustice he had ever been dealt.

"Why does it seem like that thing is always only following us?" he grumbled.

Anna, on the other hand, just shrugged. "Oh well, I guess you'll just have to believe me. Too bad for you, because I meant what I said. It would have been good." She slid him another wink and scooted back toward her bag, then climbed inside and stretched out on her back. Jay sat there a moment longer vacillating between the desire to cuss, throw something, or shake his fist at that pitiful excuse for a plane.

Pride won out, and he sat back onto his own bag.

"You know what?" she asked. Her airy voice managed to lighten the moment, and Jay welcomed the change.

Thinking she had the right idea, he lay back with a groan, glad to feel his disappointment subside. Every muscle in his body ached, some he didn't know existed. "What?"

"I'm stuffed. For the first time in days, I literally can't eat another bite." She said that last part with a British accent. Jay grinned and came up on an elbow. No way.

"Did you just quote Monty Python? *The Meaning of Life?*"

Anna bit her lip on a smile and rolled her head to look at him. She deepened her accent and rattled off another line. "There's no *s* in Burt Bacharach."

Holy crap, the woman was freaking awesome. She liked Monty Python. He had *never* met a girl who liked Monty Python. Now he *really* wanted to kiss her. "Or in Hal David," Jay added, sounding like a very drunk Russell Brand.

"Who's Hal David?" she tossed back at him.

"He writes the lyrics, Burt just writes the tunes, only now he's married to Carole Bayer Sager." Russell Brand would be proud.

"Waiter! This conversation isn't very good!" Anna finished in a fit of giggles.

They laughed in the semi-darkness, then intensified their accents and kept quoting lines…moving on to other movies…for the good part of the next hour. Just when Jay thought she was asleep, she hit him with one from *The Holy Grail*. Her voice was soft, barely registered above the crackling sound of the leftover embers.

"Jay? Did you know that a swallow can't carry a coconut?"

He closed his eyes, enjoying the sound of her voice and trying to convince himself that he hadn't just fallen for her. It didn't work all that well. Because even in the midst of this sometimes boring, sometimes treacherous game, this well-to-do girl managed to make life fun.

He released a satisfied breath and answered her question.

"I wish it would carry one over here now and drop it on our heads." A Hugh Grant-like timbre took over his sleepy words. "Might make eating a lot less work in the morning."

He felt—more than saw—Anna smile. "Good night, Jay."

"Good night, Anna."

Chapter 13

A few hours later Anna was awakened from a vivid dream, but she wasn't sure why. Heart pounding, she looked around and patted her arms, chest, and legs in sleepy confusion as she took in their surroundings. The fire was out, the water once again roared next to them, the sun hung at a different angle in the sky, and Jay was tucked inside his bag.

But.

Why was her head wet?

She blinked at the sky just as a raindrop landed in her eye. She gasped, the water so cold it burned. Then, as though the clouds had been awaiting her acknowledgment, icy raindrops the size of quarters unleashed around them, landing on her hair, her shoulders, her bag, their supplies. Lightening cracked in the distance, followed by a low rumble of thunder. The sound pulled Jay from his slumber.

He sat up, looking every bit as disoriented as she had moments ago. "What…what *is* that?" Jay scrubbed at the raindrops pummeling his face and scowled. "Get out of my face!" His beanie had slipped off in the night, so he snatched it and tugged it over his messy hair. "What is going on?"

"It's raining!" With water beginning to drip down her forehead, Anna scrambled out of her sleeping bag and gathered it in an awkward bundle. "Cold…*freezing* rain. And I think it's going to dump all over us if we don't move."

He climbed out of his bag and copied her movements, balling his bag in front of him. "Now what?" He looked blankly at her like a little boy in need of direction.

Anna rolled her eyes. The guy was barely awake and completely out of it. It was cute—it was freakin' adorable—but *come on!* The water felt like tiny droplets of dry ice searing into her face and neck. For the hundredth time, she wondered why on earth Alaska had ever sounded like a good idea.

"Grab your backpack and follow me," she said.

"Where are we going?" He yawned, but he still didn't move.

Anna rubbed her forehead for a moment, resisting the urge to snap him awake with a slap on the cheek. He just stood there like getting hit with frigid drops—fully dressed, in the middle of nowhere—was an everyday occurrence.

"I don't know where we're going, but would you please hurry up? I'm getting soaked here."

Water dripped from her eyebrows and slid down her lashes, making visibility nearly impossible. Lightening cracked again, closer this time. The threat of impending danger seemed to finally shock Jay to awareness. He looked up at the clouds, then snatched up his backpack and latched onto her hand, practically dragging them both up the side of the hill, dodging rough underbrush and pointy branches in a rush to find shelter. The rain pelted them so violently it physically hurt, while the increasing wind threatened to knock them both off their feet.

"Where are we going?" Anna's voice was barely audible over the racket.

"When we were fishing last night, I looked up the hill and saw what looked like a cave." He glanced back at her. "Just a few more yards and we'll be there." He clutched her hand and ran the remaining distance. Everything clung to them with uncomfortable stickiness as they slipped along the rain-slicked ground. Finally, with one last tug, Jay flung her inside a shallow cave, landing in a heap beside her. Only fifteen feet deep at most, it still managed to keep the elements at bay. Plus, a large rock jutted over the opening, its span helping to keep the rain away from them as the storm raged all around.

Anna shoved back her matted hair and took in their surroundings, concentrating on breathing in and out, clenching her jaw to keep the inevitable chattering at bay. A failed effort. Within seconds, her entire body began to shake violently. She closed her eyes and prayed for the shivering to stop, unable to open them even when she heard Jay rustling around beside her. The sound of a zipper filled her ears, followed by the *whoosh* of supplies as he removed them from his pack.

"Try to breathe slower, Anna," Jay said as he tucked something soft around her body. "When this blanket is secure, I want you to take off your coat and boots. And anything else that's especially wet. It's the only way I know to get your body temperature up." He pulled the blanket around her shoulders, taking care to fit it tight across her.

With her head vibrating against the rock, she cracked an eyelid to look at him. "Is this the part where we're supposed to strip and cuddle? Because you can bury that dream right now, Texas."

For some weird reason, a blush crept up his neck and he swallowed. "Dream? Trust me, lady, that's the last thing on my mind." An eyebrow inched upward. "Unless…"

"Forget it."

Jay laughed. "Looking under that blanket hadn't crossed my mind. I can't even feel my legs, much less my…eyes." He rummaged through his bag. Now Anna's neck was on fire.

With trembling hands, Jay pulled a blue tarp from his pack. Unfurling it with a snap, he used rope to tie one side to a jagged shard of rock, the other side to a dying plant that managed to grow through a crack. He retrieved two stakes and anchored both bottom corners, then dropped down beside her, breathing heavily from the exertion.

Thunder filled the hillside, but they were closed off from the elements. Their enclosed space was shrouded in near darkness. Tiny ribbons of muted light came in from both sides.

"Thank you," Anna whispered.

"You're welcome." Jay let out a sigh, long and deep. "Did you take them off?"

"Yes." She kicked her wayward boots from under the blanket to show him. Her coat was gone too, along with her sweatpants, both safely tucked beside her. She now wore a fleece pullover and thermal leggings that were only slightly damp, but at least she was covered. "I'm not sure how shedding clothes helps, but I'm starting to feel better."

"Good. Now it's my turn." Jay pulled a blanket from his bag and tucked it around him, his mouth twitching when he caught her staring. "You might want to look away. You know, in case this blanket slips."

Her eyes went wide. "You're not taking off everything under there, are you?"

Out came one shoe, then another. "Wouldn't you like to know?" he said with a wink.

Jay yelped when she rammed him hard in the ribs.

***

Several hours later, the storm hadn't waned at all. If anything, it had only gathered strength. Their top layer of wet clothes lay in a heap at Jay's feet. He'd moved them away from Anna early on to ease her shivering, worried that if she couldn't warm up, she might catch a cold, or worse. They couldn't afford to get sick out here.

She shifted positions, her soft snore filling their intimate little space. Despite the less-than-appealing conditions, he smiled at the sound and fingered her hair, smoothing the now-dried strands away from her face. Earlier, he made a makeshift pillow for her out of his half-emptied backpack, rolling it and tucking it until it looked somewhat comfortable. It didn't take much convincing for her to lay her head in his lap. He was thankful she could sleep...grateful that one of them was able.

He reached behind him for a rock that had settled into his spine, careful not to move around too much and risk waking her. Grabbing hold of it, he tossed it to the side and eased back into place. Anna stirred, then stopped when he placed his hand on her head. Something about the gesture relaxed her every time.

Jay leaned his head back and moved his fingers through her hair again. Smooth like melted chocolate—his assumption was dead-on.

Shortly after they made this place a temporary home—they'd been here much longer than he expected already—lightning struck close by. Too close. Anna had already drifted off and managed to sleep through it, but Jay sat wide-awake. He hadn't looked out to check, but he knew what they would find.

A tree blocked their exit. A deafening roar sounded when it uprooted. The ground shook from the force of the landing. The end of a branch brushed his toe on impact.

And it hadn't sounded small. From all he could observe, they were trapped inside this cave.

***

An entire day. They'd been stuck inside this cave for twenty-four hours. Digging out was going to be problematic, and he knew it. They were both growing weaker already. Though Anna hadn't said anything, he could see her cargo pants falling lower around her hips. Her shoulder blades protruded slightly from underneath her thermal shirt, and even through her coat, she managed to look thinner. What would happen by day seven? Or day seventeen? They should have reached their check-point over twenty-four hours ago. By now, everyone would be gone. By now, he wondered if they might be worried, or if anyone was looking for them. More than likely no one would notice their absence until they didn't show up at the next one.

Those thoughts had plagued him all morning.

Along with a few others.

He looked down at Anna's sleeping form. Her hair was glorious, shiny and soft even without the benefit of a recent washing. A beautiful shade of chestnut mixed with a hint of auburn, the strands felt like silk between his fingers. A ghost of a smile played about his lips as he watched her. In three days, she had made him laugh more times than he could remember. She was fast-thinking, quick-witted, sarcastic, and stronger than she knew. Unafraid of a challenge and quick to put him in his place.

The woman liked Monty Python, for heaven's sake.

When he looked at Anna, all he wanted was her. And she was taken. More than taken; she was unattainable. The most he could hope for was an enjoyable next twenty days, and maybe a win in the process.

He was even more certain of this now, considering what he had seen and heard no more than ten minutes ago while he sat here with his back against the wall.

He knew the sound before he peered through the tarp. He was used to having a red and black media helicopter following them around. From the first moments of the competition, the faint hum of its engine had hovered overhead as a near constant presence, by the hour on the hour for at least ten minutes a stretch. But this sound was different. Louder. Choppier. As though the machine were operated by twin-engines instead of one… as though the fan blades stretched across more airspace as they cut circles through the sky.

Sure enough, when he reached for a nearby stick to peel back the tarp, he spotted it. A helicopter. A white one. With the words *Rescue* emblazoned on the side.

Two people had just quit the game.

Chapter 14

Jay swung his knife at the fallen log that trapped them in place and licked his lower lip, taking an extra second to press the flesh into his teeth. They had hacked at this log for hours to no avail, and the pile of shavings looked like something you'd find inside a wall-mounted pencil sharpener at an elementary school. Next to nothing. Barely enough to start a small fire.

A fire much smaller than the intense burn rolling through his insides right now.

Anna's arm brushed against his, sending the faint scent of pine straight to his head as his arm buzzed with the contact. Six days in the wilderness, and she still managed to smell good. Jay plunged the knife into the wood to distract himself, then yanked it out again, trying not to notice Anna's fluid movements beside him.

It wasn't working. He'd stared at her too long while she slept. Held her too close. Fantasized too wildly about things they shouldn't be doing out here all alone. It hadn't helped matters when she wrapped her arms around his waist and nuzzled into his side, mumbling something about him warming her up. That's when his internal fire started. And getting angry with her was the only way he could think of to put it out.

"So do you think we are getting out of here today?" Anna asked.

"Nope." He accidentally growled, but he was so tired of answering this question. So tired of thinking about this woman when she was obviously taken. He kept forgetting that part.

"You don't think there's even a small chance?"

"Zero." He swallowed his irritation. With himself. With his attraction to her. With his mind that kept traveling to places that involved him kissing her...pushing her up against this rock wall...letting his hands dig into her hips...

"Well, you're real encouraging," Anna bit out.

He planted both hands on his knees and turned to look at her. "Do you *see* the size of this tree? Am I the only one aware of how enormous it is? We've been cutting away at it forever, so unless you develop some sort of super-human strength and miraculously shove it out of the way..." He tilted his head at her. "I guess we're stuck here for awhile. Probably won't make it out." He turned, but not before he saw the way her eyes narrowed.

"Why don't you shove it, Jay?" She pushed his arm out of the way and began to hack at the log again. "You'd better move back, Junior, so I don't accidently whack off your hand. I'd hate to see you bleed to death out here, especially in this small space. I'd hate to get any of it on me."

"Stop calling me Junior. I hate that stupid nickname, and I'm so sick of hearing it."

"Then quit acting like a baby."

"I might be younger, but it seems to me the one acting like a spoiled brat right now is you. If you were my kid, I'd give you an old-fashioned spanking."

"I'd like to see you try it."

"Bend over and I will."

She nailed him with a look, then elbowed her way into his personal space. He nearly fell backward, scraping himself with the knife in the process.

"What is your problem?" He whipped his hand around to check out the wound. No deeper than a paper cut, but that wasn't the point. She was half-crazy and totally hot. *That* was the point.

She slammed the blade inside the tree trunk with both hands. "You're my problem. This tree is my problem. This whole stupid competition is my problem. I am not going to fail at this. I won't fail at it. Not with my parents and Ryan waiting around at home for their precious Anna to screw one more thing up in their perfect little world. I can just see it now—'Anna Lloyd has to be rescued from her Reality TV show after getting trapped in a cave by a freaking twig!' They can stick that article right next to the one about her boyfriend who got caught kissing another woman in an L.A. nightclub!" Wood chips flew over her head. A few landed in her hair.

"If I'm such a problem for you, then push the button."

"I'm not pushing the button."

"Push the button, Anna."

"I said *no*, Jay. Though I'm sure you'd like me to do that, wouldn't you?"

He narrowed his eyes. "What's that supposed to mean?"

"You want to know what it means, Jay? It means that if I push my button, you'll finally get to go to the press and tell them all about what a failure I am, and then you can laugh with Heidi about what a joke this whole competition has been for you. I can hear it now. She'll tell you all about how she broke a nail while plucking the feathers off the turkey she killed with her bare hands, and how she built a fire by simply sneezing on two sticks." She mimicked Heidi's high-pitched drawl. "Meanwhile, you can laugh about how I couldn't even hack into a log, and then you can spend the next twenty years reminiscing about a dumb television show you once did called *The Alaskan Wild* and how it was quite possibly the stupidest thing you ever did. And then you can ask yourself—*whatever happened to that girl? You know, the crazy lady who lost it one afternoon inside a cave.* She fell back with a thud, landing hard on her rear. "So no, Jay. If it's alright with you, I'm not going to push the button. But if you want to push it, be my guest." She dropped her knife as a long, excruciating sigh escaped her quivering lips.

Wow. Just…wow.

Jay was speechless, and now she was going to cry. Watching her, the fire inside him turned over and faded into embers. Messy, powdery ones. He shifted in place, lowered the knife, and leaned against the wall to catch his breath, vaguely aware that his mouth hung open. He knew how to get a woman to talk, but he'd never had one completely unload on him. To top it off, he was completely blindsided by one thing she said. One thing that stunned him more than anything else and left him with an irrational desire to come to her rescue. He set his own knife aside.

"What did you mean, 'kissing another woman at a nightclub?'"

She rolled her eyes sniffed loudly. "I didn't say that."

"Yes, you did. Word for word." He sat back and looked at her. "Anna, did Ryan cheat on you?"

"Why would he do that?" The question was meant to sound outraged, but Jay heard the self-questioning, the self-doubt, the hurt that someone she loved wouldn't find her good enough to remain faithful. A tear fell, one that she roughly brushed away. Jay wanted to reach out and catch the others he knew would follow, but he remained still, letting her have her moment. His heart cracked a little from the sadness reflected on her face.

"Because he's a selfish jerk who doesn't know how great he has it." He lowered his head to look her in the eyes. "Anna, look at me." After a couple of breaths, she did. "I don't know why he would cheat on you, Anna. If I were in his place...if I had the pleasure of dating you, you can bet I would stay faithful. How did you find out?"

"A picture of the two of them was on the front cover of a tabloid at the airport. I have the magazine in my bag. Want to see it? The rest of the world certainly has." She laughed, rough and without humor.

Jay's heart sank. "I'll take your word for it." He picked away a sliver of wood clinging to the tree. "So you found out right before we boarded the plane?"

Her eyes met his, round and dejected. "It was the last thing I saw before sliding into seat 14B. A fun way to start a new adventure, don't you think?"

Jay remembered her sad expression, the way she sat and stared out the window during the majority of the flight. He also remembered resenting her presence as a part of the group, the way he assumed her to be a spoiled celebrity who had somehow bought her way onto the show.

"Actually, I think that sucks." Her small smile did little to ease the guilt he now felt.

"I couldn't get into law school, Jay." It wasn't a statement. It was a death sentence. And the words were so random, he didn't know what to say. "My family is made up of lawyers. Every single person." She looked at him then. "Except me."

He just looked at her. "I don't understand what—"

"It's just one more thing."

He waited, but she didn't elaborate. He blinked at her a moment longer. Still nothing.

"It's just one more thing, what? I don't get what not getting into law school has to do with—"

She made an unflattering noise as if he were the densest person in the world. Maybe he was. "It's one more thing, Jay. One more thing I can't do right. One more failure to add to my long, long list."

It was Jay's turn to sigh. "You think a cheating boyfriend is somehow *your* failure? Are you serious? Anna, anyone who cheats on you is a jerk. *He's* the jerk, and his bad choices in no way reflect on you."

She shook her head. "My parent's won't see it that way."

"Then someone needs to set your parents straight."

She rolled her eyes. "I didn't expect you to understand. She sat forward and picked up her knife again, then jammed it into the tree.

Conversation over.

He could push, he could make demands, and maybe he would later. For now, he decided to let it go. He picked up his blade and resumed cutting the limb, but the only thing he could think was that Anna was defending a guy who didn't deserve it.

"You're a good guy, you know it?" she surprised him by saying.

"Well, thank you." He set the knife on the ground and leaned against the rock wall. "Though I've heard that a million times before."

She laughed, breathy and musical—the first time he'd heard the sound all day. He realized then how much he'd come to depend on it. Nothing made this journey endurable like the sweet ring of her laughter. After a moment, it faded into silence.

"Spill it, Anna."

One side of her mouth tipped up. "Spill what? You didn't ask me anything."

"Spill whatever's on your mind. Clearly you're thinking about something."

She sighed. "Just that I'm sorry I said you would go to the press. I don't even know where that came from, and I don't believe for one second that you'd do that." Anna pulled off her cap and smoothed out her hair, twisting the ends into a loose side braid. They locked eyes for a moment before Anna looked away. "Anyway, I'm sorry."

"Don't be." Jay glanced at the fallen tree, then back at her. "But you're right. I wouldn't."

She shrugged. "I know."

He smiled. "Unless a lot of money was involved. Then I'd sell you to the highest bidder."

She laughed. "I knew you didn't like me."

He kept sawing at the log, waiting for the moment her words would click into place and ring with truth. They didn't. Which told him everything he needed to know and gave him a small amount of courage to voice it.

"Actually, I like you more than you know."

She cut through a small branch but said nothing.

When long, silent seconds ticked by and she *still* said nothing, he felt a trickle of sweat snake from underneath his cap and trickle down his cheek. Sweat. In twenty degree temperatures. Why couldn't he keep his stupid mouth closed?

She looked down at her hands as though to compose herself. "So do you think we'll ever get out of here?"

Jay sighed. She was an expert at avoiding topics. It was safer, he supposed, than the alternative.

"I hope so." He pushed himself off the wall and moved toward the log again. "But not if we keep sitting here." Weary of the effort, he hacked at the tree stump again.

Anna moved beside him and began to saw at a straggling branch. They worked several moments in silence, the sound of splintering wood the only noise for miles. After a few minutes, Anna's voice filled the silence. "Jay?"

"Yep?"

Her voice was soft. Timid, even. "No wonder you've been so successful at such a young age. If the way you're leading us out here is any indication, when you take over that construction company one day, it's going to soar."

His hand went still. He had no idea what to say. That was possibly the nicest, most thoughtful thing anyone had said to him. Ever. Encouraging words were hard to come by when he was growing up. He swallowed, willing his voice to work through the emotion that clogged his throat.

"Thanks, Anna. I mean it."

"So do I," she said.

For the span of another few heartbeats, all he could do was stare at his hands.

Chapter 15

With severely blistered hands and two knives that were now so dull they might be useless the rest of the trip, they had managed to make the next checkpoint on time. They stumbled upon Rain and Josiah first, kissing in some make-shift wraparound sheet draped between two trees. Bizarre for lots of reasons. First, apparently they were now a couple despite the fact that they weren't partners. Jay couldn't figure out how they'd made time for that to develop—even though he realized his feelings for Anna were really starting to take hold of his mind. Second, was the odd chanting Jay heard as the two of them belted out some Mother Earth song while they danced with their arms in the air. The sight stopped him in his tracks. He looked at them, then back at Anna, who was trying and failing to hold her laughter in check.

She didn't make it long. Laughter bubbled up before she could stop it. Jay slapped a hand over her mouth and pushed her toward a nearby tree. "What in the world was that?" he said, looking over his shoulder at the couple. He kept his hand on her shoulder, mainly because he liked it there and saw the opportunity.

"Two nut jobs having a spiritual moment, it looked like," Anna said. That set him off even more, and he howled.

He and Anna had been the first to arrive at the shelter, which made them responsible for preparing whatever dinner awaited them—a single bag of old, dried beans—so out of date that individual ones had grown moldy. They dumped them in a pile and sorted them one by one.

An hour later, Nico and Heidi showed up holding two rats and a squirrel. Jay might have been disgusted if his stomach wasn't so empty. They cooked it like a stew and tried to ignore the reality of what they consumed. His first-ever rat. From the look on Anna's pale, haunted face, it was hers as well.

Things went downhill from there, bottoming out the moment Anna spotted Heidi giving Jay a neck and shoulder rub as they sat around the campfire. He didn't ask for it—then again, it felt so good he wasn't about to stop it, either. Anna saw the exchange from her spot across from him, and went curiously silent. It both puzzled and thrilled him, and she'd barely spoken since. At first, he was flattered.

Now he was just ticked.

No matter what he tried, he was met with nothing more than grunts, sighs, and *whatevers*. It was the whatevers that tested his patience and left him wondering what it would take to snap her out of her stupor.

As if providing an instant answer, the weather took a brutal turn for the worse, determined to make them endure their agony through an ever-present veil of mind-numbing rain. Cold rain. Blistering rain. Rain that fell in thin sheets of ice, turning more vicious with each passing hour. For a solid day, it hadn't let up.

Finally, when they were looking for twigs to add to their dying fire, Jay reached his limit.

"How much longer are you going to give me the silent treatment?" he snapped. "I don't even know what I did wrong, but you're acting like I committed some sort of crime against you."

The glare she nailed him with told him he'd gone too far, but he was way past caring. He was wet, hungry, tired, cold, sticky, and sick of it. And Anna was the only person around to take the brunt of his frustration.

"Not everything is about you, Jay," she practically growled at him.

"So this has nothing to do with Heidi giving me a rub down?"

She made an unflattering noise. "Oh please. That was hardly a rub down. She was barely even scratching your neck." Dismissive words, but he saw the way her jaw clenched. Lightening cracked in the distance, as though delivering a warning.

"I think someone might be a little jealous," Jay quipped.

"Jealous? Of what, you and that life-sized Barbie doll having a public make-out session while the rest of us were forced to watch? You don't know what you're talking about." Anna outwardly seethed.

"I'm pretty sure I can spot jealousy from a mile away. But I guess if you are so happy with—what's his name, Ryan?—that you shouldn't care who I'm making out with."

"Drop it, Jay. My relationship is none of your business."

But dropping things wasn't one of Jay's spiritual gifts. Never had been. Thunder rumbled overhead, matching the churning he felt in his chest. "There are lots of single men in America, Anna. If you have to date someone like Ryan to get your parent's approval, how about finding someone a little more loyal and less friendly to the opposite sex. Not that I can blame him, I guess, but—"

He didn't see the slap coming, but the glove she wore rendered it ineffective. Jay looked straight at her without flinching, which only seemed to intensify her fire. Maybe that comment had been insensitive, and maybe he shouldn't have said it. Then again, he was mad, too. She quickly tore the glove from her hand to give it another try.

"Slap me again and you'll regret it."

Breathing heavy and waging a war with himself, he looked at her, really looked at her, his eyes following a trail of water that inched down her cheek and into her mouth. *Lucky drop*. That thought came from nowhere, but it undid him...made the decision easy. Before he could talk himself out of it, he reached for her waist and yanked her to him, lowering his head to taste her lips; wet from raindrops, open from shock. They were warm and willing under him, so he moved in deeper. A whimper escaped her throat, one that mixed uncertainty with longing. The moan she released into his mouth didn't help his self-control; the sound drove him wild.

"Jay..." She gave a halfhearted push at his chest before sinking into it, bringing her arms around his neck and tunneling her hands through his hair. Jay trailed his lips over her jaw, her earlobe, then met her gaze for a moment. In it, he saw the permission he needed and kissed her again. He felt her body tremble through the thick coat—a mix of fear, desire, cold, and trepidation. The storm raged around them, but still Jay kissed her.

It wasn't until lightning struck a few feet away that they jumped apart.

With her chest heaving, guilt took over and Anna could barely look at him. Jay knew right then she regretted the kiss, and he scrambled to undo the damage. "Anna, I shouldn't have kissed you, and I'm sorry."

He wasn't prepared for the look she gave him. But in that moment—from the fierce stillness of her expression—he remembered something his sister had cautioned him against years ago: *Whatever you do, never apologize for kissing a woman.* It was insulting, degrading, would unleash a woman's silent wrath for days...possibly years to come.

With a glare that would frighten the inhabitants of Hell, Anna slowly wiped the back of her mouth. "You're sorry? You kiss me like that and then apologize for it?

Jay wanted to stab himself with the sharp end of a stick. "I'm not sorry for kissing you, I just—"

"You know what, Jay? Forget it." And without giving him time to respond, she turned and stomped back toward the checkpoint.

***

"What do you think you're doing?" To Jay's surprise, Heidi cornered him the moment he returned from his walk with Anna. The scowl on her face matched her suddenly hostile demeanor. Unlike her normal Barbie doll appearance, she now resembled something closer to Bride of Frankenstein, complete with fangs and crazy eyes.

Jay gave her nothing more than a cursory glance. "I'm tossing these sticks on the fire, unless you'd rather do it." He handed one over. "Here, be my guest."

She flung it on top of the growing embers, then let out a sigh that would make small children hide under beds to escape overbearing mothers. As it stood, Jay wasn't intimidated in the least, not even when she crossed her arms and blew a strand of hair off her forehead.

"I'm talking about you kissing Anna in the woods." When Jay said nothing in response, she kept talking. "I saw you, so don't try to deny it."

Jay bristled, instantly annoyed. There were a lot of things he could tolerate—days without a shower, eating rats when he would rather pull up a chair at Applebee's—but being secretly followed and called out on private behavior was something he wouldn't stand for. That kiss was between Anna and him. Heidi was the proverbial third person in this crowded environment.

"You were watching me kiss Anna? What kind of person spies on a personal moment like that? Is that the only time you've watched us, or have you seen every other—"

"There have been others?" Her mouth fell open. Clearly she didn't understand that he was the only person who had the right to feel outraged here. "Do you realize you're going to ruin everything? I'm not working this hard to have you fall in love with the star of this show. What would her boyfriend think? What would the producers think if they found out what you're doing? Tell me that, Jay. Tell me that."

Tell her what?

He just looked at her, mentally counting all the ways she didn't make sense. "What are you talking about? Why would the producers care whether or not—?

She cut him off with a laugh. "Surely you're not that naïve. Shape up, Jay. Before everyone here gets as mad at you as I am right now." She pointed a finger in his face. "Starting now, no more kissing or I'll find someone who will make you stop."

And with that ridiculous threat, she turned and stomped away.

Leaving Jay completely baffled by her sudden bout of jealousy.

Chapter 16

She hadn't signed up for this.

Never never never. Not once. Not a single time since the game began had this been mentioned as part of the competition. But just like switching things up and sticking her with Jay in the first place, the producers kept changing the rules. And Anna was getting sick of it.

Besides, everyone knew she was the worst fire-builder. So this challenge was totally biased and lopsided.

"So does everyone understand the rules of this particular challenge?" the announcer asked. Dean Passmore had been inexplicably dropped by private helicopter to join them at this checkpoint ten minutes ago looking more groomed than a man should. His nails shone, his pants were perfectly pressed, and Anna could swear he was wearing eyeliner. Especially disturbing considering Anna would kill for some eyeliner right now, but instead she and all the other contestants looked homeless and filthy and pathetically unfashionable.

Except Heidi. She looked healthier than ever with a tan that had somehow deepened over the two weeks they'd been here. Come to think of it, Nico didn't look that bad either. Anna frowned at the unfairness of it all, then glanced around their group of eight. Desiree looked slightly frazzled and unkempt, as did Earth Girl—which really wasn't saying much since she *always* looked frazzled and unkempt. And drugged. But that was another issue entirely.

But overall, Jay and Anna seemed to be fairing the worst out of the whole group.

Just like she would during this challenge.

Anna had a question. "So you're telling me we have to race to the top of that hill, get some supposed red flag that I can't see but I guess will have to trust is actually there, find the two starter sticks buried underneath it, race back down here, and build a fire while you watch? That's the plan?"

Six questions, but Anna didn't see why it mattered.

"That's the plan, Miss Lloyd."

This is what mattered. This asinine, insane plot to embarrass her and assure yet another failure. On national television. For the world to document and laugh about.

"And what happens to the person who wins?"

It wasn't exactly that she wanted to know if prizes were awarded, it was more that she wanted to stall indefinitely. Until the sun went down and made this whole challenge impossible. And seeing it was only ten o'clock in the morning, she needed to come up with about seven more hours of questions to really make her plan work.

"As soon as the challenge is over, the winner gets picked up by helicopter, they get a shower and a new change of clothes, and then they get whisked off to the Taku Glacier Lodge, one of the most upscale restaurants in Juneau," Dean Passmore said. "Later tonight, the winner can eat whatever they choose...with whomever they choose. This should make for an interesting competition, don't you think?"

Anna blinked. The winner got to pick their dinner date? If she won, she would pick Jay for sure. But would he pick her? What if someone else won and picked him? What if someone else won and didn't pick her? What would she do if—

"Well, if that's it for questions," the announcer said, inconsiderately interrupting her panic attack, "what do you say we get started? There are eight red flags planted along the top of this hill, each fashioned with the same unique number currently pinned on each of your shirts. So everyone take a minute to inspect your numbers..."

***

"I hope you choke on it." Anna muttered to herself as the helicopter disappeared into the skyline, taking whatever was left of her hopes and dreams and freaking good mood with it.

Heidi won the competition in three minutes flat.

Worse, as the winner, she picked Jay to accompany her to dinner. The two of them. Showering. Changing clothes. Sharing a romantic candlelit dinner, she assumed. With wine involved and late-night expectations that exceeded the standard *Thanks for the nice time.*

She assumed.

Unless he choked on his dinner and had to be rushed to the hospital where he might or might not make it out with his life.

Which, coincidentally, is what she stood here praying for as she stood shivering, watching as he was whisked away for a night she would willingly die for.

Instead, all she had to show for the challenge was a windburn on her cheeks, a splinter on her right pinky finger, angry blisters on all other fingers, and a three inch burn mark that ran across her left wrist from a wayward ember from *Heidi's* raging fire.

Because it wasn't enough for the girl to build an intense blaze in record time. She had to make sure Anna remembered it forever by scarring her in the process. Jealousy burned through her core, challenging that blaze in sheer level of combustibility.

"Kinda sucks to see your partner leave with someone else, doesn't it?"

Nico. For the self-pitying thoughts Anna had been feeling this last few minutes, it would be worse to think your partner had intentionally left you behind. She had no doubt Jay would have chosen to take her with him if he could. But Heidi had purposefully passed over Nico despite everything they had been through over the last few weeks.

Still, Anna had to agree. "It totally sucks." They stood side-by-side, staring after a helicopter no longer visible in the sky.

Nico sighed. "Look on the bright side, maybe they'll sit down to a nice steak or lobster or eggplant parmesan and choke on it."

Anna laughed. "We can always hope, right?"

"Right." He gave her a fist bump and an amused smile before turning back toward camp.

Chapter 17

Ryan Lance slipped the laptop into his leather briefcase and stood from his chair, feeling a great deal better than he had in weeks. Finally, things seemed back on track. More importantly, he no longer felt in jeopardy of losing his rank as an up-and-coming member of the Lloyd political family.

"So just to make myself feel more at ease," he said, "you're assuring me that everything is set for tomorrow? The reports will go out? The tabloids will be notified?"

The executive producer standing in front of him nodded, though the gesture felt more curt and gratuitous than anything else. Clearly the guy wasn't concerned with the state of Ryan's feelings, but Ryan could work with that. It really made no difference as long as the situation was fixed. Then they could move forward as planned. Then everyone would stop breathing down his neck. After all, it was one indiscretion. One careless misstep.

Of course there had been others, but no one knew that and he would make sure it stayed that way.

"Everything is set," the producer said. "By this time tomorrow morning, your reputation should be in the clear. All speculation should be nothing but a laughable misunderstanding. One for the memory books, so to speak."

Ryan breathed an audible sigh and opened his mouth to respond. Before he could speak, the man spoke up again.

"But let me make myself clear, Mr. Lance. A lot of money and planning has gone into this show. We won't have you screw it up again. One more reckless decision...one more instance of imprudent behavior on your part and you'll be on your own. And if that happens, I can assure you there will be a line of people standing behind me waiting to make sure you pay for your mistakes. Am I making myself clear?"

Ryan swallowed, angry at the scrutiny. No one from his father to mother to nannies to teachers had ever been so bold as to call him out before. He had money. He had power. He had clout in this town.

But this man in the Ermenegildo Zegna black silk suit was clearly more formidable, so he said nothing but—

"Yes sir. You have my word, it won't happen again."

The man raised a well-waxed eyebrow. "That's what I like to hear." He stared at Ryan a long uncomfortable moment. "Well, son I suggest you let everyone in your circle of influence know that we're back on track. Keep it that way, understood?"

"Understood."

Ryan gripped his briefcase and left the room, bristling at the derogatory use of *son* but unable to say anything about it.

Chapter 18

"You're ridiculous."

She kept telling him that, yet Anna hadn't spent more than one second by his side since midnight. She'd spent the entire time pouting, and even though he couldn't blame her and even though he would probably be mad too, and even though it would have driven him insane to watch her fly away with some other man...he was getting ticked off.

Angry.

Irritated.

Fed up and sick of it.

He liked Anna. He liked having her nearby. All this distance was making him jittery and nervous. He needed his partner back. He needed his girl next to him, right here and right now.

His girl. Though he would never admit it out loud, that's the way he was starting to think of her. Maybe it was stupid and maybe it was a mistake that would soon come back to bite him in the butt, but he couldn't help the way he felt.

"Why am I ridiculous?"

"Because you keep asking me what's wrong. There's nothing wrong with me. I'm not in a bad mood. I'm not even upset. Why would I care that you flew off with Heidi for a nice dinner and dessert and God only knows what else? I couldn't care less. No big deal."

Six protests and a few more inches of distance—that's what her string of sentences garnered. Jay had to check himself to keep from letting loose a sarcastic burst of laughter. She was mad. She was so mad she couldn't even see through the blackness to notice what loomed in front of her.

"Anna, watch out for that—"

But too late, she smacked into the thick, low-hanging branch with her forehead and tripped over a large rock in her path, landing in a heap on her butt in what looked like a painful fall.

"Ow!"

"I tried to warn you not to hit it."

"No, I mean I cut my leg. Pretty bad, I think." She brought her knee up in front of her and swung it to the side, pulling up her pant leg a few inches. The blood was easy to spot, even through her wool sock.

"Did you scrape it on the rock or did you hit something else?" Alarmed, he knelt down beside her and peeled the sock away, cringing at the deep, inch-long gash. He couldn't be sure, but that white spot down deep sure looked an awful lot like bone.

Anna needed stitches. In any other circumstance he would drive her to the emergency room. As it stood, it was only the two of them for miles. The only hope of medical care lay inside their bag and it was questionable at best. Even the world's best doctor couldn't work a miracle with fishing line and a broken earring.

"I think it was the rock, but it felt more like a knife." Her eyes connected with his, imploring, questioning. "What should we do?"

For the first time since this trip began, Jay felt hopeless. It wasn't a good place to be, but it felt familiar, like an old college friend who'd unexpectedly returned for a visit. There was only one way to handle this; ignore the inconvenience, pull up a chair, and invite it to stay for awhile.

"I'm going to try and repair it as best I can, but first I need to get the bleeding to stop." He rummaged through his bag for a cloth and tore off a strip, then doused it with water from his canteen and pressed it against the wound. He winced at the sound of her controlled whimper but forced himself to press even harder. Within seconds, the cloth was covered in red. He ripped off another strip and began the process again.

"For the record," he said into the silence, "there wasn't anything else."

She glanced at him and quickly looked away. "What are you talking about?"

But she knew. And he knew she knew. But sometimes you had to humor a woman, and Anna was no exception. "With Heidi. We had dinner, and I'll admit we had dessert. A phenomenal chocolate cake with toasted coconut ice cream that they creatively sprinkled with—"

"Jay, spare me the painful details. I'm begging you."

He swallowed the desire to smile and dabbed at her wound with the cloth, making a conscious decision not to look at her. "But nothing else happened. I didn't kiss her, I didn't make out with her. I didn't sleep with her. Not that I would do that anyway, but I wanted you to know." He tore another strip of cloth and began to wrap the wound.

When she said nothing, he did the only thing he could think of to force her to talk. Anna was competitive; she never backed down from a challenge, not even one she couldn't win. Her pitiful attempt to start a fire yesterday proved that theory. He'd been proud of her for trying, even though he knew before the word *go* that she didn't stand a chance. She didn't back down then; he knew she wouldn't back down now.

"Spill it, Anna."

She looked him in the eye with a hard glare. "Spill what?"

"There's something on your mind, something you're unwilling to say, and I want to know what it is. So spill it. You have ten seconds. Go."

Her indignant intake of breath hardly surprised him. "There's never been a time limit on this game!"

"My game, my rules. You have eight seconds."

He mentally counted one...two...three...and started to get worried on four...five...six...

"I can't believe you went with her."

And there it was. And not to be a jerk about it, but he knew those words had been on her mind since the moment he'd accepted the invitation from Heidi yesterday. He'd seen the hurt on her face, noticed the flash of jealousy in her eyes. But he went anyway. Anyone in his position would have done the same thing. Including her.

"What was I supposed to do, say no?" He kept a firm hand on the rag pressed against her ankle, mainly to keep himself focused. Maybe then he wouldn't lose his temper the way he wanted to.

"Yes, you were supposed to say no."

"Is that what you would have done?" He was particularly proud of how calm his voice remained.

"It doesn't matter what I would have done." She tried to jerk her leg away but thought better of it and settled it in place.

"I'd say it matters a lot. Tell me, Anna, what would you have done? If Heidi had picked you, or if—say—Nico had won. If either one of them had picked you to go, would you have turned the invitation down?"

She sat staring straight ahead, silent for so long he began to wonder if she had gone mute. But as usual, Anna couldn't stay quiet for long.

"No."

He couldn't resist provoking her a little. "Excuse me, what was that?"

She sighed loudly. "I said no. I wouldn't have turned them down, but you don't have to be a jerk about it."

"I'm not trying to be a jerk, I'm just trying to point out that—"

"I wanted ice cream, too, Jay. And a shower. Not to mention that you were handed the opportunity to act like a normal human for a few hours and don't tell me you didn't at least kiss her. Because I, for one, think you did no matter what you say."

That did it. Without giving himself time to reconsider, he dropped the rag, grabbed her face in his palms, and brought his mouth down to hers. Her lips parted in shock and what sounded like the beginnings of a protest. He kissed her harder to silence it, a satisfied smile tugging the corners of his lips when he felt her respond underneath him.

And just as things started to get good, she abruptly pulled back.

"What was that for?" She scrunched up her eyebrows, looking unbearably cute.

"What?"

"That smile. It was almost like you were testing me. Like you knew I'd stop being mad the second you starting kissing me. You were testing me."

A faint alarm bell sounded in the back of his mind. "Well...did it work?"

"No, it didn't work." She pushed herself to a standing position, a determined martyr fighting through the pain she must have been feeling. "As a matter of fact, we're done here. No more games, no more questions, and definitely no more kissing. Let's just get through this trip and leave each other alone." She hobbled on one foot, and the scowl deepened on her face. Great, somehow he'd managed to make her even madder. "In fact, starting now, don't even talk to me anymore. What's mine is mine and what's yours is yours for the rest of the trip. And if you can't deal with that, then go find Heidi. Got it?"

She spun rather awkwardly on her heel while Jay watched her go. He reluctantly followed behind her. She might get killed out here, or worse. And as much as he tried not to care, he knew it was useless. He cared about Anna. Too much.

He kept an eye on her the whole way.

***

He killed a squirrel. A huge squirrel. A stupid squirrel that smelled like a giant piece of heaven. It seemed dinner with Heidi had done wonders for his hunting skills, and now he sat twenty feet away from her roasting the squirrel over a primitive–looking spit that he'd fashioned with his own hands. She watched while he searched for stones, rubbed them clean at the stream, and created a skewer made from the whittled remains of a spruce branch. The naked squirrel rested on the blistering stones as fire licked at it from all sides, searing it to perfection as Jay methodically turned it over. He never once looked in her direction.

She tried not to look at him either. After all, she'd sworn a vow of silence until the end of time. And here, a mere five hours later, she was two sniffs away from breaking it. It just figured the aroma of roasting food was all it took to weaken her resolve. The memory of his kiss didn't help either. Despite his selfish intentions, she had never enjoyed a kiss more and couldn't force the sensation from her mind. Every time she looked at Jay, she felt weak. Liquefied. A shallow puddle of want and longing. She looked at the trees, at the water, at the blades of grass in front of her, at anything to help her forget.

But then she remembered his breath on her neck.

Anna squeezed her eyes shut and stood. "I suppose I could help you if you need it." If she straightened her spine just so, maybe she could appear nonchalant.

"Nope, I'm good. Just stay over there and continue not talking to me." He turned the squirrel again. Anna watched as a bit of juice dripped and sizzled on the rocks, then slid underneath the flame. Her stomach growled painfully. Traitor.

She cleared her throat. "You sure you don't need anything?"

He barely glanced her way. "I've got everything I need right here, so...no." After a moment he turned to face her, one eyebrow raised as though he'd just thought of something. "Oh, there is one thing you can do."

Hope wiggled its way through Anna's insides. "What..." Her voice cracked with anticipation. "What is it?"

"You could find yourself something to eat before this fire dies out. Or I guess you could build your own and put that lighter to good use after all." He turned back toward the fire.

Anna wanted to pick up a rock and pummel him with it. She glared for a few seconds, then slapped her knees and leaned forward.

"Are you seriously not going to share?"

"Nope." He didn't bother to turn around. "What's yours is yours and what's mine is mine. The wisest words I ever heard." He sounded so indifferent, but Anna could swear she saw his cheek dimple from a smile.

That stupid man.

"No, they're not. You're just trying to punish me. You're trying to shove your hunting skills in my face when you know darn good and well I could look for hours and never find anything. I *haven't* found anything since the blueberries on the first day!"

"Those were awesome blueberries, too." Jay looked up the hill. "You know if you walk far enough that way, you might get lucky and find a few more."

"Jay, come on." Her voice turned pleading, weak, totally betraying her. "That squirrel is huge. There is no way you could possibly eat the whole thing, especially after that dinner last night."

His mouth tilted on a mocking smile. "Sweetheart, I could eat this and two more. But…"

Her breath caught. "What?"

"When I'm finished, if there's any left, I'll give you a bite." He removed the squirrel from the fire and transferred it into his bowl. Her own bowl stayed inside the pack, clean and unused. With a jealousy she hadn't experienced since another woman grabbed the Michael Kors bag she wanted at a New Year's Eve sale at Bloomingdale's, she looked at his bowl, unable to tear her eyes from the steam as it rose heavenward, sending a bit of its gloriousness into the air around them.

She turned away from the sight, unable to bear it.

The sting of tears pricked behind her eyes. Pressing her fingertips to them, she turned her head, unwilling to give him the satisfaction of seeing her cry. She tended to be loud about it, all sniffs and hiccups and ragged breaths. It was ugly.

She was deep into her pity party, swiping away at one tear and then another, when she felt a hand on her shoulder. Jay stood there, holding her bowl in his hand. The biggest piece of roasted squirrel she had ever seen lay inside. Not that she had ever *had* squirrel before, but still. It was the single, most beautiful gift she'd ever been given.

She blinked up at him. "I thought you said—"

"Surely you've known me long enough to know I'm not that cruel." His voice was low. Rough. "I caught this thing for you, Anna."

You need it more than I do. You're wasting away, so please eat." He waited until she grasped it, then turned to go.

"Jay," she said. He turned to face her. "Did you keep some for yourself?"

"Don't worry about me. I have what I need." He took a few steps backward, his mouth tugging up on a grin. "Now hurry up. We don't have all night."

Anna blinked at him. "Where are we going this late?"

He looked around as though noticing the impending nightfall for the first time. "Nowhere." He winked at her. "We're going nowhere."

Anna watched as he sat next to the fire. He pulled out a piece of meat from his bowl. Even from here, she could tell his meal was half the size as hers. She thought of his words... *We're going nowhere*. He was wrong. He was wrong in a hundred different ways.

She turned away to take a bite, tears beginning to burn her eyes again. There was no use denying it to herself any longer.

They were definitely going somewhere.

Chapter 19

"Jay, I'm going to do something I never thought I would do. But it's been plaguing me for four days, and I need you to be a little understanding."

They finished eating an hour ago, and while Anna couldn't exactly call herself full—she barely remembered that feeling anymore—she could call herself satisfied. A welcome improvement. Still, there was something she had to do...wouldn't be able to sleep until she made it a reality.

Jay leaned on his elbow and stretched out his legs, the easy grin she loved working its way across his face. "What's that? Break up with Ryan? Vomit up moldy beans? Give me a massage and prove once and for all you're better than Heidi?"

Stupid, arrogant smile.

"No, Jay." Anna glared at him. "You can stick with her for all I care."

He sat up, his face suddenly serious. "Okay, that was a bad joke. Please don't start a new round of the quiet game. I don't think I can take another minute of your silence..."

Aw, that was so sweet.

"...without shoving you over a cliff. Seriously, Anna. Your silent treatments suck."

"If you don't stop with the hard time," she said, "I'm going to start jabbering so much you'll wish for another quiet game. Now, do you want to know what I was going to say or not?"

"Sure. Hit me with it. Give me what you got. Spill it. And speaking of..."

"We're not playing that game right now, because I'm going to take a bath."

Jay blinked at her. "Are you nuts? Out *here*? In forty degree temperatures? That's crazy!"

"Don't hold back on my account." She made a face. "It's been a week and a half, and I feel disgusting. Pretty sure I could wring the grease out of my own hair if I tried."

"That's a mental image I don't need." He grimaced. "How are you planning to wash it? We don't have soap, unless you're hoarding some and didn't tell me. In which case I'll have to hurt you in some evil way when you're not looking..."

Anna rolled her eyes. "No, I don't have soap. I'm not sure what I'm going to use, but I'll figure it out when I get to the stream."

She reached inside her bag, digging around until she located her least dirty outfit—a black thermal tee and a pair of gray cargo pants with a mud stain on the knee. Bloomingdale's would be ashamed. She wrapped her hand around a semi-clean rag and stood up.

"Stay here. Don't come to the stream unless I scream for help. And even if I do, wait thirty seconds before you head that way."

"Anna, that's insane. You're going to freeze to death, and you know it."

"Well, at least I'll die smelling better." She tossed her clothes over her shoulder and walked toward the water. Her teeth began to chatter just thinking about how painful this was going to be. But she was filthy, more disgusting than she'd ever been in her life, and she could no longer stand the scent of herself. But mainly, she was competitive. And unfortunately, Heidi looked beautiful even without a shower. Anna was tired of feeling second-rate.

***

Jay tossed another log onto the fire and sat back down beside Anna. The sun had lowered on the horizon, painting the landscape in a grayish hue inflected with the faintest hint of orange. The colors light danced across the water, the shimmer reflecting off Anna's features, making her nearly glow in the firelight.

Not that Jay noticed.

Out of the corner of his eye, he watched as she ran a hand through her still damp hair. A powdery substance fell across her shoulder and onto the ground, dusting her black thermal shirt with flecks of brown. He frowned.

"Sand just fell out of your hair. Like, a ton of it."

She brushed it off her shoulder. "That's because I used it to scrub my hair."

"You used sand? Isn't that uncomfortable?"

She shook her head. "No. And it'll fall out eventually."

"What made you think to use that?"

He must have given her a disgusted look, because she rolled her eyes. "You are such a boy. Every woman knows that sand is an exfoliant. You rub it on your body, and the dirt comes off. They sell it at Bloomingdale's for a hundred bucks a jar."

Jay paused, trying to make himself lose the mental image of her rubbing anything anywhere. It wasn't easy, and he swallowed. "And you've spent that much? For sand?"

"Of course." She looked at him like he was the brainless one. "Of course they add a little salt and scented oil to make it smell good, but it's essentially the same. It worked well enough, at least." She ran a hand through her hair as if to prove it.

It worked. Her hair looked beautiful, and all he wanted to do was bury his hands in it. Among other things.

He forced some air into his lungs and reached into his bag, pulling out a navy sweatshirt and cargo pants. He grabbed his boots and tugged them on, leaving the laces undone, and stood up.

"Where are you going?" Anna asked.

"I'm going to take a bath. I feel disgusting, and I've had enough of it."

Her mouth dropped open. "I thought it was crazy to do that. Would make a person freeze to death."

He looked down at her. A grin stole over his face at hearing his own words being tossed up at him. "Well, are you frozen? Or dead?"

She grimaced. "Practically."

He ruffled the top of her head as he walked around her. "Well, try not to die all the way." Gathering up supplies, he held them in a bundle in front of himself and looked at her. His eyes flicked to the fire. "Keep that going for me. I have a feeling I might need to sit on top of it when I get back."

She laughed. His chest ached from the sound.

"Hurry up," she said, blinking up at him. "I don't want to be here by myself for too long."

"I'll hurry." He backed up a few steps. "But don't come looking for me if you know what's good for you. Unless you want to, in which case I'm totally down with it."

He saw her eye roll, but also the grin she tried to fight in the semi-darkness. "I will stay right here, thank you very much." She patted the ground she sat on. "Not moving. Not budging an inch. Staying put."

"Suit yourself, but I've seen the way you look at me. So don't go getting any ideas."

She narrowed her eyes. "The way I look—? I only look at you *at all* because I'm thinking about eating you for dinner if things get dire out here."

"Interesting." He winked, loving the red stain that crawled up her neck at his implication. Feeling more than a little cocky, he turned to walk away, making it only a few steps before he felt something whiz by his ear. A pinecone landed on the ground in front of him. "Your aim is off," he called to her. "You really need to practice that, maybe then you'd be better with that gun strapped to your bag. Maybe then we'd get to eat more often."

She made a disgusted sound. "Shut up, Jay!"

He laughed when a pinecone nailed him in the butt. "That's better. Not great, but better." He grinned all the way to the water, the sound of her soft laughter drifting behind him the whole way.

Chapter 20

He'd just tugged a sweatshirt over his half-frozen head when he heard a scream. It came in a short burst, as though Anna had reacted without thinking, then slammed a hand over her mouth. Jay wasn't far away, but the distance felt like miles. Desperation blasted through his insides as he grabbed his boots and took off, bare feet cutting against rock and twigs in an effort to close the gap. Heat and ice surged through him in a painful collision.

He heard her soft whimper as he rounded the last corner. Stopping with a jerk, his eyes went wide in shock, unbelief, and the tiniest bit of amusement. Anna sat rigid next to the fire, legs pulled up, mouth covered tightly, shoulders trembling.

A porcupine crouched just three feet away from her, rooting its nose into a patch of pine needles that lay under the remains of the squirrel carcass. The sound of its enthusiastic eating, combined with the sheer horror of seeing it in the first place, was nauseating, and his stomach clenched.

Anna locked eyes with him, silently begging him to do something. But he'd never dealt with a porcupine. What the heck was he supposed to do? He couldn't exactly grab it. What if the thing shot quills all over him? *Did* they shoot quills, or was that just a myth? Wishing for quick Wikipedia access, he cursed their computerless situation and gave himself a silent pep talk. *They don't shoot quills*, he decided right then and there. He took a step closer, his mind racing frantically. He needed to think of Anna.

"Okay, don't move," he said.

Her hand slipped down an inch, just under her upper lip. She leveled a look at him. "Where do you think I'm going to go?"

"Okay, fine. Just stay put," he said again, breathing in, breathing out.

She rolled her eyes. "That's pretty much my plan, Jay. Not going anywhere."

Could the woman be any more sarcastic? He needed to think. Water trickled from his hairline. From the bath or from sweat, he couldn't be sure.

And then he had an idea.

Spotting his bag a few feet away, he inched toward it, moving further away from Anna. She frowned at the distance and shifted her head to the right to look at him. "What are you doing? How is leaving going to help me?"

"I'm not leaving. Now shut up and let me think."

Jay bent low and unzipped the duffle, stopping short when the animal turned its head. It locked its gaze on Jay, two silver orbs glowing like alien eyes in the firelight. Its spine moved up, its quills out. Anna whimpered. Jay swallowed, waiting to see if it made a move, prepared to run screaming like a girl into the woods if it did, every man and woman for themselves. Bears were one thing; this was completely different.

He wasn't proud of the thought.

The animal turned back to the foliage, momentarily forgetting about everything but food, its spine settling to a more normal position. Jay exhaled and slowly reached for his bag. A few items fell out as he drew it to him—fishing net, his knife, a rumpled t-shirt, a lighter— before his hand found what it was looking for and closed around the object. With one finger he unclipped the rifle, trying to ignore the way Anna's eyes grew rounder, so round they nearly doubled in size.

"You're going to shoot it?"

He gave her a look. "I was thinking I might. Or I could play fetch with it. Or we could wait to see if it wanders off. Or climbs in your lap. Whichever you want."

Her eyes flicked from the porcupine, to him, and back. The animal took a step toward her, its rear end aligned perfectly with her face.

She froze. "Shoot it. Please...shoot it."

And he would, except Anna was too close to the animal. If she panicked or jumped the wrong way, he might accidently hurt her.

"When I say 'move,'" he whispered, "I want you to lunge backwards. Okay?"

"Okay." The single word came out breathy, frightened. "Wait! Backwards into the tree or backwards into the grass?"

His eyebrows drew together. "Does it matter? Just...backwards."

The porcupine took another step toward Anna. "Yes, it matters! Because the tree isn't very far!"

"Then lunge for the grass." He sighed and scrubbed his mouth. "Okay, ready? On your mark...get set..."

Anna blinked rapidly at him, her expression frazzling his already precarious nerves. He took a deep breath and tore his gaze from her, focusing on the porcupine. "Move!"

Anna lunged, and with a prayer sent heavenward, he pulled the trigger.

He missed.

The porcupine's needles raised high, and with a blood curdling screech, it lurched on its hind legs and headed straight for Anna. She screamed, scrambled to h

tree. Stumbling backwards,

He shot again. This t

around once, and fell into the a

for its plight and stared at it for a

thing was here just enjoying some p

business, probably thinking how long

really good squirrel, and the next it was-

Two hands shoved him from the

could you miss?" Anna yelled into his face.   again.

"Hey! A 'thank you' might be nice," h   . back at her. In hindsight, maybe he should have checked on her before he focused on the animal.

"Thank you? Are you kidding? You almost got me impaled by a thousand porcupine needles!"

Jay glanced at the animal. "I seriously don't think there's a thousand. I mean, I could be wrong, but..."

"Jay!" She stomped away and flung herself beside the fire. Grabbing a blanket, she wrapped it around her shoulders and buried her head. A tuft of hair stuck out the top, a piece of tree bark clinging to it. He scrubbed his face to wipe away a laugh, but one escaped anyway. Anna's scream. Running into the tree. The porcupine chasing her. Its hackles raised to strike. It was all too much for him.

"It's not funny!" came her muffled reply.

But it was. The funniest thing he'd seen in a very long week and a half. With a smile he thanked God she couldn't see, he lowered himself beside her, keeping his eyes on the animal in case the thing moved.

hair." He reached out to remove it, strands until it loosened completely. He

shoulder hurts," she said from underneath the blanket.

"Let me see it." He tugged on the blanket, rolling his eyes when she pulled it tighter around her arms. "Come on, Anna." He purred the words into her ear, low and breathy. "Let me see. Please?" He kept tugging, again and again, until she let go. Glancing at her shoulder, he noticed a ring of blood visible through the black material. "You hit pretty hard, didn't you?"

She nodded and sniffed, running her hand underneath her nose.

Reaching for the fabric, he hesitated. "Can I?"

Another nod. Another sniff.

Jay carefully slipped her sleeve down over her shoulder and examined the wound. It looked similar to a carpet burn—nearly two inches in diameter with a few deep scratches running across it. A sliver of wood jabbed the side, an offending splinter that didn't have the courage to plunge all the way through the skin. Jay scratched it away with a fingernail, cringing when she moaned.

"Sorry." His gaze flicked to her, then away at the sight of her sudden flush. "This needs to be cleaned up." He reached for his canteen and a strip of clean cloth, then doused it with water. Pressing it to her bare shoulder, he held the cloth in place until most of the blood soaked through, dabbing it back and forth to catch any remaining drops. When it looked clean enough, he situated her shirt around her shoulder and balled up the fabric, tossing it into the fire.

"Better?"

She nodded, her gaze locked onto the flames for a long moment. "Sorry I shoved you," she said.

He watched the way the fire danced eagerly as it devoured the strip of cotton. "Sorry I apologized for kissing you. I'm not. Sorry, I mean."

She looked at him then. Her eyes seemed bluer in the dim light. "I'm not sorry, either." She seemed to hesitate for a moment, as if trying to make a decision. Just when Jay began to consider leaning forward to kiss her again, she sighed and dragged her eyes away. "It's just...that thing," she said, breaking the mood and nodding to the unmoving porcupine. "It scared me to death. What are we going to do with it?"

Jay glanced at the animal and back at Anna, knowing the subject of "them" was closed for now. "Have you ever eaten porcupine?"

He saw her swallow. "I can't say that I have."

He stood up and slipped on a thick pair of gloves. "Well, you asked what would be the weirdest thing we would eat on this trip. I'm thinking this might be it." He picked up the carcass—much heavier than it looked—tied a rope around its body and hung it from a tree. "At least it's not a mouse," he said, smiling at the face she made.

Reaching for the knife, he began the tedious task of cleaning the animal, of separating quills and fur from the meat, meticulously stripping the animal clean. It was gross, messy. And no matter how much training Dr. Mark had given them, his stomach stayed knotted in a persistent clinch. Somehow buying food at the supermarket didn't have the same gut-wrenching effect. He wondered if he'd ever be able to shop the same way again.

He was so deep in thought that he didn't notice Anna until she stood next to him. A breeze caught the porcupine, and it swayed in a circle. Her blanket brushed his forearm as she pulled it tight around her shoulders to form a barrier from the elements. Jay wished for his coat, but he was too close to finishing to search for it now.

"Need some help?" Anna said. Her warm breath mingled with the cool air and feathered across his neck. He pulled in a shuddering breath, wondering if she had any idea the affect her closeness had on him. How she managed to smell like flowers in the middle of this mess was *not* something he needed to think about.

"No, I think I'm about done." He glanced her direction, struck by the sight of her full lips hovering just over his shoulder. He remembered those lips...wanted those lips. He stared a moment longer than he should have, then dragged his gaze away with a sigh. "Just...when this thing falls," he eyed the layer of quills dangling precariously over his foot, "please don't let it land on me."

"I won't." Anna reached out her hand, but Jay stopped her with a shake of his head.

"You'd better get some gloves. These things could cut you pretty bad."

She nodded and walked to her bag. Jay heard it unzip, heard her rummaging for the thick leather gloves stashed inside. He kept cutting. He didn't realize his mistake until it was too late.

"Anna, you might want to hurry over here," he called, looking at the meat still hanging, at the layer of skin and quills falling...falling. His voice raised a notch. "I think I'm about done, and—"

It peeled away all at once. He saw the hide slip. Tried to catch it.

It fell on his foot, still bare from his bath.

"Sweet mother of—"

"Jay!" Anna rushed to his side, a glove on one hand, nothing on the other. She dropped the remaining glove in her panic to get to him. "What did you do?"

"I didn't do anything!" He dropped to the ground and grabbed his foot, expecting to see a row of porcupine needles sticking out like switchblades on all sides. Instead, he found nothing but a few large scratches. Of those, only one of them was dotted with blood. The porcupine hide lay next to his foot on the ground. Overhead, a large slab of meat swung from the rope, dripping red and ready to be cooked. "There wasn't much visible evidence of the fiery pain that radiated through it. Maybe his foot was broken. Maybe infection was setting in. Or maybe...

"You want me to take it down and throw it away?"

"No! Don't throw it away. It sounds awful, but I'm starving." She stood and held out her hands. "Here, get up. I'll go wash it in the stream if you'll find a few logs to add to the fire. Deal?"

He stood beside her and loosened the rope from the tree, then handed it off to her.

"Deal," he said.

***

An hour later, their sleeping bags lay unrolled by the fire. They sat side-by-side on hers—it made sharing dinner easier. That's how Anna explained it, and Jay wasn't one to argue. The arrangement had worked well so far...a little too well, actually. Jay didn't want to move back to his bag just yet. Though conversation had been easy so far, after a while, Anna got quiet. Too quiet.

"Jay...I..." She tossed a twig into the flames and dusted off her hands. "Thank you for taking care of me."

He cleared his suddenly dry throat, caught off guard by her words. "I wasn't going to let you get stabbed by a porcupine, Anna."

She gave him a small smile. "I didn't mean just today. I mean for everything. Paddling us across the creek, killing the squirrel, keeping us on the right path, taking care of my shoulder." She nodded toward the tree she'd slammed into earlier. "You've done a lot for me on this trip, and I haven't said thank you." She ran a hand through her hair. "So…thank you, Jay."

He just looked at her, unable to speak. He couldn't speak because he couldn't breathe, and it's difficult to do one without the other. Eventually he managed, but first he reached for her hand and brought it to his lap.

"Then I should thank you, too, Anna. For keeping me sane out here." He gave her fingers a squeeze. "I couldn't have asked for a better partner." Sometimes the heart speaks for you, and the words were out before he could stop them. He didn't regret it.

They sat side by side for a long moment, hand in hand, the sound of their mingled breathing blending with the crackling fire. Anna grew quiet again, and just as Jay contemplated standing up to give her some space, she inched closer to his side until her blanketed arm pressed against his. His heart hammered at her nearness. When she lowered her head to his shoulder and snuggled into the space above his collarbone, it nearly exploded in his chest. At certain times in your life, you just know when something fits. When it feels right. When things almost seem meant to be.

This was one of those moments.

From underneath the blanket, he drew his arm around her waist and pulled her closer, all rational thought gone for the moment. He pressed his lips to her forehead and held them there, just the two of them against the world…at least their little corner of it.

They stayed that way for awhile, neither in a hurry to move.

Not when the wind picked up. Not when the fire dimmed to embers.

Not when a raindrop fell…followed by another.

But when the drops changed to snowflakes, Jay and Anna jumped up. Gathered their supplies.

And ran.

Chapter 21

"It would help if you would stop thinking about the weather and just focus on the question. It's basic *Spill It* philosophy, Anna. If you concentrate on the game, everything else eventually fades away."

Anna's teeth chattered, but still she managed to shoot a *You're an idiot* look in Jay's direction. "*Spill It* has a philosophy? That has to be the dumbest thing I've ever heard. Dumber than this stupid weather." On cue, a clump of snow fell from a tree branch and landed on her head. She scrubbed it off, scowling at the air above her.

Jay brushed at a spot she missed. "Says the woman who has never truly learned to embrace the spirit of the game." He reached out and dusted off her hat, which only sent more snow falling into her face. "Now, that's a nice look for you."

"Jay! That's cold!" She blew snow out of her eyes. "So now the game has a spirit, too? Give me a break."

Clouds still hovered overhead, dark and oppressive. The threat of more held steady.

"Fine," she blurted, shaking off the cold. "We would dance. It's the one thing I've always wanted to do."

"Dance? That's it?" Jay glanced up at the helicopter flying above them and gave them a salute. "I thought you would say something like sky dive. Or go rock climbing."

Anna grinned at his blatant disregard for the rules. *Don't acknowledge the cameras. Pretend they don't exist.* She could practically hear the announcer's shouts from here. "Well, Ryan actually likes to go rock climbing." She looked up and blew the camera a kiss, enjoying her little flash of rebellion. "But I have a feeling sky diving would be out of the question, and dancing is what scares him more than anything." No matter how many times Anna begged, Ryan would not dance with her. Not in public, nor in the privacy of her living room. She assumed the aversion was based on a traumatic experience. She'd never had the courage to ask.

"You realize we're going to get in trouble for that," Jay said, tilting his head toward the helicopter again. He gave them a thumbs up this time.

"I know. But I don't care. I'm so sick of thinking about nothing but sleeping, hunting, and walking that it's nice to focus on something else for a minute. Plus, the idea of the producers going a little crazy kind of makes it worth it." She waved both of her arms and did a little spin, shielding her eyes to catch their reaction. Maybe it was the movement, or the cold, or the looking up that affected her, but suddenly her vision blurred. She closed her eyes, reaching for a nearby branch to keep from swaying.

"My turn." She tried to keep her voice steady as she breathed in and out. Sweat dotted her upper lip.

"Go easy on me." Jay walked ahead of her, unaware of her struggle.

"Okay, let's see…" Her legs wobbled, and the blurriness intensified until black spots appeared. She cleared her throat and forced herself to walk steady, one foot in front of the other, blinking a few times to clear her vision. The changes started two days ago, just before the porcupine incident. Black spots, dizziness, headaches, waves of nausea. At first, she thought it was spurred on by fear. Now she knew better.

She finally examined her ankle earlier that morning. Her body was cut and scraped a dozen different ways, but her ankle was swollen...angry red with a liquid yellow center. She recognized the symptoms immediately.

A staph infection.

She'd had one as a kid, had never forgotten how sick it had made her. Raging fever, upset stomach, lack of energy.... Not the best combination, considering she had a show to finish. And doctors meant hitting the button. *She was so not pushing that button.*

If Jay found out, he would push the button. She wouldn't ruin this for him.

"You okay?" He cast a look over his shoulder and frowned at her.

"Yeah, why?" She commanded her vision to clear.

"No reason, you just got quiet there for a second."

"I'm just trying to think of a good question," she lied. She breathed in and out until the wave of nausea passed, then straightened. "Okay...here's one. If you could be anything besides a rancher...anything at all...what would it be?"

"A pilot." He said it so quickly, with so much certainty, that Anna was surprised.

She raised an eyebrow. "A pilot, really? You sound so certain. Almost like you've given this a lot of thought." What would it be like to share your dreams so freely? To not be afraid of the repercussions?

He nodded. "I have. I've wanted to fly my whole life."

"Why don't you take lessons? You don't have to give up your dream just because you're doing something else right now." She swallowed, fully aware that the words made her a hypocrite. Maybe she should learn to take her own advice.

That would never happen.

Anna's life had been mapped out since childhood. The plans had been instilled in her since she spoke her first word. During her growing up years, the phrase, *You're going to take over for me one day* had been said as often as *I love you*. Maybe more. By the time she turned eighteen, her path was so deeply etched in cement that a little thing like failing her law school entrance exam wouldn't deter her parents. It took a little creative scrambling, but they eventually found another way around the minor setback—they set her up with Ryan.

"As a matter of fact," Jay said, dragging her out of her reverie, "I'm already taking lessons. I have been for the better part of a year."

She looked at him. "You have?"

He nodded. "I figured it couldn't hurt to know how to fly myself around. As the future owner of Manhattan Construction, it might even save a little money in the long run. Besides, if the company tanks one day, it might be beneficial to know how to do something else. You know, just in case."

"Plus, it doesn't hurt to dream." Jay said staring out past the trees.

"Oh, doesn't it?" Anna replied a little quicker than she meant to.

"God is the one who puts dreams inside you. So you'd better chase them fast, before He decides to let them chase you instead." He glanced at Anna. "Because sometimes He does that, just to get your attention."

She just looked at him. "What does that mean, *before He lets them chase you?* That doesn't even make sense."

His mouth tilted on one side. "Sure it does, if you think about it."

She studied the landscape in front of them, looking for…something…anything to give her an answer. Finally, she shrugged. "I thought about it. Still nothing."

He sighed, long and slow. "Anna, Anna, Anna…" He spoke her name like she was a child. "When I was younger, my best friend's mother wanted to be an inventor. They lived down the street from me. Anyway, she sketched out designs all the time…all these ideas filled up a stack of spiral notebooks. She showed them to us one afternoon when we were in junior high. One of her ideas was for these weird pair of pantyhose. Except they weren't pantyhose. She came up with a prototype and everything. Anyway, the legs were cut off, and she had inserted some kind of binding fabric that sucked you in like a corset, except it was supposed to be comfortable. It was a great idea. Inspirational, if you will, and—"

"Wait." Anna interrupted. "Are you telling me you know the lady who invented Spanx? The lady who invented Spanx was your *neighbor*?"

He rolled his eyes. "No. I'm telling you I know the lady who *should* have invented Spanx, if she had given her dream a chance. Instead, she works at Wal-Mart, but still sketches designs in her free time. She has a pretty good one going for a lip gloss holder that clips to your car air vent…"

Anna slapped him on the arm. "That's not funny, Jay!"

He grinned. "It's a true story, and it's not supposed to be funny. It's supposed to inspire you to follow your dreams. They're inside you for a reason, you know."

The thought made Anna uncomfortable.

"I scared you a little, didn't I?" He bumped her with his elbow.

"No." She shook her head. A lie.

"Then now it's my turn to ask. If you could change one thing about your life, what would it be?"

Like Jay, Anna didn't hesitate either. Didn't even blink before the answer was out.

"Nothing. I wouldn't change a thing."

Another lie. They just kept building on top of one another.

Jay raised an eyebrow at her. "You're content with everything?"

"Yep. Couldn't be happier," she said a little too quickly.

He didn't believe her; but ever the gentleman, he didn't push.

"Well then, I'm glad you're happy." His words dripped with sarcasm and Anna had to resist glaring at him, His tone belied the opposite, but Anna couldn't argue. To argue meant to concede. That wasn't the sort of thing you did in her family. "But even though you're happy, and even though your life is perfect..." His words dripped with sarcasm and Anna had to resist glaring at him, "...I've decided it's my job to make at least one of your dreams a reality while I have a chance." Without warning, he shrugged out of his backpack and slipped hers off her shoulders. Both fell onto the snow as Jay glanced upward again. "The cameras are still up there, so what do you say we give them a show?"

Anna tilted her head to see the helicopter hovering just over the tree tops, then locked eyes with Jay in time to see him hold out his hand. She debated taking it, but he made the decision for her. He reached for her fingers and drew her to him.

"What are you doing?" Anna searched his face as her heart pounded in her ears.

"I'm making you dance with me. For the cameras, of course. If that's okay with you." She blinked at him. He had asked her to tell him the one thing she'd never done with Ryan…the one thing she wished to do…and he was offering to do it with her now.

It was more than okay.

She grinned and slid her arms over his shoulders. Linked her fingers around his neck. Rested her head on his chest. Breathed in his scent, all woodsy and musk and man. Leaning into his coat, she took him in.

It was nice to be held. Almost as nice as being kissed.

She cleared her throat.

"How exactly is this giving them a show?" She found herself lulled into submission by the thud of his heartbeat. She hadn't danced with a boy since prom.

"If nothing else, it will give them something to talk about. I figure they put us together, so maybe we should make them wonder about us." His chin rested on her head.

"Is this your way of trying to get me to kiss you again?" she asked.

"Would it work?" he whispered above her head.

"I guess only time will tell," she surprised herself by saying. She felt him smile above her. Warmth crawled up her spine despite the frigid temperatures. Everything about this felt perfect.

Until it didn't.

Without warning, a brand new wave of nausea rushed through her stomach just before lightheadedness tilted the ground. She closed her eyes and let him move with her in a dance without music, disregarding the way her pulse began to throb like a drumbeat in her temples.

When she couldn't ignore it anymore, her feet stopped moving.

"Are you okay?" Jay asked.

"Yeah, I just..." The sound of the helicopter grew louder, as though it had lowered for a better view. The noise pounded in Anna's ears like a hollow rumble of thunder.

Ignore it. Ignore it.

She tried. She tried so hard.

Anna attempted to smile up at him, but wound up doing one better. Stumbling sideways, she fell to her knees.

Threw up on Jay's shoe.

And then collapsed on top of the mess, moaning softly until the world went dark.

Chapter 22

He used his stocking cap to wipe the vomit off her face, unsure what he would use later to cover his head. The only thing that mattered now was that Anna was passed out cold and all he wanted to see were her eyes open. But at least two minutes had passed and she still hadn't moved. Jay was past the point of panic.

"Come on, Anna. Wake up." He shook her shoulders. Said her name. Tapped her cheek with the palm of his hand. Touched the side of her neck just to feel the beat of her pulse.

When her lids finally began to flutter, his heart dropped into his stomach. He'd never been more afraid in his life—not even under the weight of his father's temper, his mother's downward spiral, or his rapid rise to head of household. He expelled the breath he'd been holding and briefly closed his eyes.

Thank you God…

"So I've got to assume it was one of two things. Either you hate to dance, or you hate to dance with me," Jay quipped, trying to make light of the situation. His pulse still pounded in his ears.

She moaned and rolled her head to the side. "It wasn't either one of those. I just got a little lightheaded is all…" Her voice sounded scratchy, labored. It broke Jay's heart a little. In the last few minutes, he'd been reminded that the heart was as strong as it was fragile. Seeing Anna fall nearly shattered his to pieces.

"I think it was more than just lightheadedness," he whispered, trying not to grimace as he pushed a clump of hair off her forehead. It was filthy, smelly, and matted with vomit. She'd taken that icy bath for nothing. "Do you want to tell me about it?"

She attempted to sit, but fell into his lap with a groan and blinked up at him. "There's nothing to tell. I think the dancing just made me dizzy."

"Ah." So she was going to stick with lies, was she? "So you're telling me it doesn't have anything to do with this?" He swirled a finger around her ankle, around a particularly ugly gash that ran two inches in length on the left side. It was swollen, looked awful.

Anna was sick.

The wound on Anna's ankle wasn't just infected. It was festering. Out here in the rough terrain, she could have contracted just about anything. *It might be time to push the button.*

With a groan, Anna tried to sit up. The movement was clearly painful, but she was stubborn. Always stubborn. "Why are you undressing me, Jay?" She snatched her coat off the ground and slipped her arms inside.

"I took off your coat, Anna. You're not exactly naked."

"And my shoes and socks. And where is my hat?" She looked around, then sighed when he held it out to her. She clumsily tugged it on her head. It slipped off. She tugged again until it covered her ears. "Gloves, please?" She held out her hand, and he dropped them in her palm.

"There. Now you're all covered up again." He shook his head, anger bubbling in his gut. "Out of sight, out of mind. That'll make it better."

Her temper flared. "Except for my feet. Look Jay, it's not that big a deal. So, I have a little cut that's a teeny bit infected? In the grand scheme of things—"

"A teeny bit infected? That's like saying that porcupine back there is a little bit dead. Anna, it looks awful."

"It'll heal."

"You need to see a doctor."

"I will. When we're done here."

"We can be done right now." He glanced at the GPS hanging from his backpack. All it would take was one push.

Her gaze flew to him and she shook her head. "Please don't push the button, Jay. I'll be fine. I will." She reached for her socks. He held them away from her. It was his idea to slip them off in the first place. The least he could do was to get them back on.

He pulled her foot into his lap and slipped her toes into the fabric, first one and then the other. She flinched at the slightest movement.

Jay took his time pulling on her shoe, tying them one by one. "How long have you been feeling bad?"

Her foot still rested in his lap. She didn't seem in any hurry to move. "Since yesterday morning."

"You didn't say anything."

"I know, but—"

"Anna, we can't mess with your health out here. You need to tell me when something's wrong. And something is definitely wrong with your ankle. It was a bad cut. I'm not surprised it's infected."

"It'll be fine. I'm sure it's just—what are you doing?"

Jay unclipped the GPS from his backpack, ignoring the way Anna's eyes frantically searched his face. She was sick. They were going home. "Your ankle looks horrible. So much could go wrong out here, and we both know it. You could have a staph infection…or worse." Worry shot through him like an arrow and pinned his heart to the ground. The GPS felt like a brick balanced between his fingers, but he wasn't afraid to push the button.

He was afraid to say goodbye to Anna. But fear wouldn't keep him from doing the right thing.

"We've got to get you home." Jay went for the button, then gasped when Anna lunged at him. "Anna, you're sick. Something could be seriously wrong with your leg. Whatever it is, it's causing you to throw up. To pass out. What if I hadn't been here? What if you hadn't woken up?" His voice broke, betraying just how afraid he'd been.

"But I did wake up. And I'm fine."

"You're not fine. You need someone to look at it. It's only going to get worse out here, and back home, someone could give you the help you need."

"I can't go home, Jay."

He reached behind him for the device. "Yes, you can. I'm not happy about leaving either, but it's for your own good."

"Jay, listen to me." She reached for his hand and brought it to her lap. "I can't go home."

This was no longer about her leg. It wasn't really even about leaving.

"What's wrong, Anna?" He reached out to brush her hair off her shoulder. Cupping the back of her neck, he ran his thumb across her jaw and tilted her chin up.

"Don't make me leave, Jay, not before I'm sure. I'm not ready to add 'quit reality TV show' to the list of monumental failures I already have to live with."

Anna was no failure. He couldn't understand why she believed that lie.

What had her family done to her?

"Alright, Anna." His conscience screamed for him to stop, but he knew what he had to do. "We'll stay. But you have to promise me—"

"If it gets any worse, I'll tell you," she rushed to assure him.

He raised an eyebrow. "That isn't what I was going to say. I was going to say that we'll stay *if* you promise to tell me if you feel any more pain at all—"

"Deal," she interrupted. "I swear."

Jay shot her a look. "Would you shut up and let me finish? You might not be so quick to agree when you know all my demands."

She bit her lip. "What demands? Just because we're out here alone doesn't mean that you can just—"

His eyes narrowed.

"I'm shutting up now."

"Good. We'll see how long that lasts..." he muttered. "Anyway, I get to examine your foot any time I want, day or night. If I ask to see it, you show it to me." When her lips parted to protest, he clamped his own hand over her mouth to stop the impending rush of words. He nearly laughed at her furious expression. "And, if you start limping, we stop walking." Her eyes grew wide. He pressed harder. "And...if you get a fever—even a small one—we push the button. Got it?" He waited a moment longer, then slowly removed his hand. She started talking before his fingers completely broke free.

"I do not think I should be expected to show you my foot just because you say so. That's a little over the top, and—"

"Fine." Jay snatched up the GPS.

"Okay!" She sighed. "I'll do it. You're annoying, you know that?"

He grinned, glad to see some of her spunk coming back. "It's just part of the personality. Annoying you has become my sole reason for living."

"You're living large, then."

"Glad to hear it." He winked at her, then bit back a smile when she reached up to run a hand through her hair. She froze, a look of absolute horror twisting her mouth.

"Jay..." she slowly pulled her hand back to study it. "What is in my hair?"

"Calm down. It's just a little—"

"*What is in my hair?*"

"Well, you puked." He shrugged, fighting back the urge to laugh. "And then you landed in it. Hard, I might add."

"I have vomit in my *hair?* But I just took a bath!" Her whine reverberated across the water, so loud the other couples probably heard it. Standing up, he brushed off his pants and reached down to help her up.

"Come on. I'll wash you at the lake." When her gaze turned suspicious, he rolled his eyes. "Your hair, Anna. Only your hair."

A noise swelled over their heads, interrupting her words. They looked up at the same time. A helicopter hovered directly above them, loud and imposing, the word *Rescue* emblazoned on the side. Anna's eyes searched Jay's, concern all over her expression.

Another couple had quit, this time from somewhere nearby.

And in that moment, as they reached the lake, as Anna lay back, as Jay scooped water onto the ends of her hair, he couldn't help but wonder if he'd made the wrong decision.

Everything told him they should be heading home instead.

Chapter 23

"Do you trust me?" Jay walked away from her, toward the fire he'd assembled earlier next to the downed airplane. A downed airplane, which apparently functioned as their latest checkpoint. Anna rolled her eyes at it for what had to be the hundredth time.

Tearing her eyes away from the sad sight, Anna watched as Jay knelt down and stretched out the blade. What was he doing?

She glanced at her ankle, at the red ring that seemed to stretch wider before her eyes. Out of the corner of her eye she saw Jay stand and walk toward her, his expression grim, almost sickened. He knelt in front of her again. This was the deal though. He gently swirled the swollen area of her ankle with his fingertip, working his lower lip as he studied the spot.

"That depends on what you have in mind."

Weary eyes dragged upward to hers.

Anna sniffed and wiped her eyes, pushing the pain out of her mind. But the truth was it wasn't just the pain leaving her emotional.

So far in this game, Jay had fed her, cleaned her, held her while she slept. He had sheltered her, talked with her, made her laugh when there was nothing to laugh about. He had doctored her, sacrificed his own warmth for her safety. In two weeks' time, he had taken care of her more than anyone had in her twenty-six years. More than Ryan had in the months they'd been together.

It was a sobering thought. One that conjured up unpleasant thoughts of Ryan...comparisons between the two men. Unfair, maybe.

But painfully undeniable. She trusted him more than anyone. More than Ryan. More than her parents. Emotion tightened her throat and made speaking nearly impossible.

"What are you going to do?" she asked again. He stood and walked toward her. She worked to keep her eyes from going wide. In this instance, trust needed to equal the absence of fear.

"I just need you to trust me."

She eyed the knife. "Not sure I do, but let's get this over with anyway." At his slight smile, she took a deep breath and willed herself to calm down.

He glanced at her one more time, an eyebrow raised in permission. When she didn't stop him, he went to work. The hot edge of the blade stung when he slipped it under her skin, but strangely, she didn't scream. Instead, a sensation of relief—of emptying and draining and the release of pressure—coursed through her ankle. What seemed to weigh a hundred pounds slowly felt lighter. What felt like a raging fever burning under the surface now seemed to wane. She breathed a grateful sigh until she looked at the incision site and saw the thick mass of red and yellow streaming from it. She grew lightheaded and nearly threw up in the dirt.

"I'm sure it looks worse than it is," Jay said. She knew he was lying. Still, she wasn't prepared when he dropped the knife and pulled a strip of cloth from his bag. Dousing it with water, he pressed it to the wound.

"Oh, probably," she nodded to her leg, "Everyone knows the healthiest wounds always have what looks like ketchup and mustard running from it. Kinda makes me want a hot dog right now. How about you?"

He gave a groan and shook his head. "You have a sick sense of humor, you know that?" Holding the cloth firmly to her ankle, he reached out with his other hand to cover her own. Her hand tingled with the contact as he dipped his head to look at her. "Are you okay? Did I hurt you?"

His tender words and comforting touch did strange things to her insides, adding confusion to all the places that already felt unsure. Without second-guessing herself, she linked her fingers with his, overcome with the need to hold on. This man was kind. This man cared deeply. This man was her friend. This man was...

"What happened to you? That's the most disgusting thing I've ever seen."

...being stalked.

Anna looked up into the twisted face of Heidi and released Jay's fingers. Her temples pounded in her ears. Why was she here? And why was her voice so painfully high-pitched?

She stared at Anna's leg like it with festered with disease. Like if she got too close, she might catch whatever sprung from Anna's veins.

"I cut it."

Heidi made a face. "On what, a chainsaw? That looks awful, Anna." Her feet stayed planted, far away and unmoving. But then she smiled. "It looks like someone's going home soon. Jay, if Anny leaves, maybe we could pair up...?" She ran her index finger across his shoulder in a classic come-one move.

"I'm not leaving," Anna said.

"Jay," Heidi whined, "you need to make her leave. This is stupid. She can't keep competing with her leg like that. Push the button, Anna."

Anna bristled at Heidi's entitled tone and looked at Jay, silently pleading with him to take up for her. After a moment's hesitation, he gave a single nod.

"She wants to stay. And since we're partners, I'll have to support that decision."

"At the risk of her health?" Heidi hissed through her perfectly white teeth. Somehow she also looked perfectly flushed, like make-up and moisturizer were hidden inside her backpack. "At the risk of her *dying* out here?"

"Nobody is dying, Heidi." The veins in Jay's neck bulged.

"How do you know? She could die or…or…worse."

He frowned up at her. "If Anna leaves, I leave too."

Heidi's face fell in disappointment. Anna just studied her, dumbfounded. How could she not know this? And why did she look so pretty? It took a lot of effort not to hate her.

"That's the way the game works, Heidi," Anna explained. "Two couples have already left." When Heidi stared blankly, Anna continued. "Together."

Her mouth finally fell open. "I didn't know that was a requirement!"

Anna glanced at Jay, who was busy trying to bite back a smile. "It's a requirement," he said. "So I, for one, would like to get Anna feeling better so we can stick around a little longer."

Heidi glanced at her foot. "You probably should. Though it looks so disgusting it seems like a wasted effort."

"Hey, Heidi?" Jay asked—his patience clearly stretched thin. "Why don't you run get me some water for Anna's foot, and we'll see what we can do?"

He might have asked her on a date considering the smile that filled her face. "I'll be right back."

Anna watched her go for a long moment before she finally sighed. "Can you believe that girl? She wants me to leave just so she can have you as a partner. As if I would bow to her so easily just so she can take my place—"

"She's right, you know." Jay tossed the knife inside his pack and leaned back to look at her.

"What do you mean, she's right?" Her temper—familiar like a best friend she'd played with since kindergarten—reared its trusty head. "You think I should leave?"

"I think you're pushing yourself too hard to prove a point. I think you could wind up very sick, or worse. I think—"

At that, Anna stood. "You know what, Jay? I don't care what you think. I'm not leaving. Not for you or Heidi or your desire to be partners. I'm staying, so deal with it." With a groan of frustration she turned and hobbled off, aware that her gait made her appear pathetic. But she didn't care. She was tired of being ordered around. Sick of being trampled on. Mad at the world and her stupid situation.

But more than anything else, angry at the nagging fear that maybe he was right.

Chapter 24

She didn't know how she would possibly survive this one. The fire-building thing had been humiliating, embarrassing, not to mention impossibly unfair and a complete set up in favor of a certain busty blonde. But this.

This.

How was she supposed to balance on a twelve-inch ledge six feet high in the air with this pathetically lame leg? It just figured she would knock her head into a branch and fall to the ground and cut her ankle on a rock at the absolute wrong time. Next Thursday. Why couldn't she have contracted a staph infection next Thursday? A staph infection on a Saturday was extremely ill-timed.

The inconvenience of it all sucked the life out of her already foul mood.

"So does everyone understand how this challenge works?" the announcer asked. "Do you understand the importance of what you're about to do? Whoever stays in place the longest wins a fishing pole and fishing hooks for your team." He enunciated each syllable, then paused for drama's sake and looked each contestant in the eye. Anna squirmed under the unwelcome scrutiny. *Of course* they understood. *Of course* she wanted that pole. But she also wanted some Tylenol. Or whiskey. Whichever vise would transport her to another land where pain and trauma and festering feet were nothing but an unpleasant memory.

"As you know," the announcer continued, unconcerned with her internal pity-party, "it isn't exactly easy to catch dinner in these streams. A pole and a few worms could make all the difference in the quality of your time remaining out here in the wilderness."

Trying to distract herself from her misery, Anna focused on his beige-and-off-white ensemble that he'd uncreatively topped with a fly fishing hat. She might even laugh at it, if she found it funny. As it stood, nothing was funny aside from her long streak of bad luck. She wanted that pole. The likelihood of winning was slim at best. But more than anything else...

She wanted to sit down. Give up. Go home, pop some popcorn, and watch the rest of this stupid show from the comforts of her living room sofa.

A loud sigh escaped before she could stop it.

"I don't like this either." Jay whispered next to her. "Especially when I think of you trying to balance so high up there. You're the most accident-prone person I know, even without the bum leg."

"Thanks for the vote of confidence." She scowled at Jay.

"Mr. Maddox and Miss Lloyd, is there a problem?" The announcer sounded concerned, but his eyes communicated the opposite.

"No," Jay spoke up. "We're just ready to get started."

"Perfect." The man clasped his hands together and looked over the remaining six contestants, the oddest smile on his face. Anna suspected the man liked the idea of torture. Probably had a nasty habit of making innocent babies cry just for the sheer joy of it all. "If everyone feels the same way, then here we go. Everyone grab onto the rungs in front of you and climb up on your platform. The timer starts when everyone settles into place."

***

Forty-five minutes had passed, and Anna wanted to die. Like, chop off her legs and let her warm, pain-ridden body lie in a cesspool of mottled red liquid—*that* type of die. But she wouldn't, because she had a challenge to win. And it was right there in front of her.

So close she could almost reach out for it.

She and Heidi were the last two standing. Somehow and by some miracle she would never understand—even if someone deciphered it word by word into the plainest English that had ever been spoken—she was still in the game. Jay had stumbled and fallen twenty minutes in. Nico had drifted off to sleep five minutes later and landed hard on his left shoulder—medics were still checking to see if it was broken. Josiah needed to pee and announced it to everyone within earshot, then shrugged and hopped down as if the distance was mere inches from the ground. Desiree had voluntarily climbed down five minutes ago, citing a pain behind her left eye that wouldn't subside.

And Anna Lloyd was still in the game.

Competing against Heidi.

She would *not* lose again. Especially not to the girl who managed to do everything right, even now. Somehow Heidi looked in better shape than ever, as though the only thing she'd lost on this adventure was an extra inch of flab that she quickly replaced with five pounds of muscle.

"Are you getting tired yet, Anna?" Heidi called in a nerve-rackingly chipper voice from her perch ten yards away. Anna looked over in time to see her examining her fingernails. Her fingernails. Like she didn't have a care in the world. Like the only thing that mattered were torn cuticles and the latest shade of oxblood gel polish.

Anna went for a manicure the day before she flew here. Apparently oxblood was the latest color for summer. With a small twinge of regret, she'd settled for the clear polish with every intention of choosing the bolder shade on her next visit.

"No, I'm not tired at all," she lied, her wounded ankle halfway through the fourteenth stanza of a silent scream begging her to give up and offer it relief. Anna tried to ignore it and study her own fingernails, but the attempt made her dizzy and light-headed. Her body swayed a bit to the right, but she caught herself in time to prevent a fall. It was her first struggle since climbing up.

Worried about what her only competition had seen, Anna chanced a glance at Heidi. She wasn't prepared for the wide-eyed look of concern that stared back at her. Heidi looked genuinely bothered, like Anna's well-being was the only thing that mattered.

Anna watched in confusion while Heidi looked at the camera. At the ground. At her nails once again. Back up at her. "Well, I can't take this anymore. My feet are killing me, my back hurts, and my butt's asleep." Stunned, Anna opened her mouth to say something, unable to utter a word in time to keep Heidi from jumping off her perch. She landed with a little bounce. Brushed off her pants. And walked away.

Heidi wasn't hurt. She wasn't even tired. There was no reason to give up.

Heidi had just let her win.

***

Anna swiped her nose and slammed her body into the seat, unable to decide what ticked her off most—her throbbing ankle, Heidi's strange concession, the stupid fight she'd had earlier with Jay, or this ridiculous excuse for a bed. The airplane seat was a rusty accordion that folded into her in all the wrong places—just great considering all that ailed her. She couldn't fall asleep. She couldn't stop feeling sorry for herself.

And she was still hungry.

A tear slid down her cheek as her nose leaked onto her shirt. Gross, just gross. How much more was she going to cry, anyway? She wiped her nose with the back of her hand and turned her head to the other side. Thank goodness everyone was asleep or they would think her more pathetic than she already viewed herself.

Another tear slipped from Anna's eye. Her gaze shot upward, straight into a quarter-size lens mounted into the ceiling. As expected, the camera filmed every sordid detail of her mini-meltdown. She could see it now, the way the headline would play out on a television screen three months from now. *The Alaskan Wild—and for a poor, jilted political darling from Chicago, love gone horribly wrong.*

It was so predictable, she wanted to vomit. Again.

She closed her eyes and tried to block out the mental image of Jay sleeping behind her, tough to do since she had glanced back about a dozen times to find him curled onto his side, a dirty t-shirt balled up and tucked under his jawline like a pillow. She remembered that jawline...had felt it against her skin more than once.

Tired of remembering, she sniffed and tucked herself into her blanket, willing the memory away while catching another tear on the corner of the rough fabric. She forced sleep to come. Demanded it. After awhile, sleep nearly listened, slowly lulling her into a muddled state of awareness, until she felt movement around her feet. A hand pulled away her blanket. A finger touched her skin. She should have known Jay would bug her even now.

She just wished she wasn't quite so excited about it.

"Thanks for interrupting my beauty sleep. Just what do you think you're doing? Shouldn't you be back there in your own seat?" She gave him her best glare and leaned forward, blinking several times to clear her vision. Her eyes felt sticky, a sheen of moisture made focusing difficult. On the floor in front of her, Jay sat with a smirk on his face. His gaze flicked to her hair.

"I'm not that tired, and you need to go back to sleep. The beauty part hasn't kicked in yet."

"It requires eight full hours, but some people keep waking me up." Across from her, Nico stirred, so she dropped her voice to a whisper. "What do you want, Jay?"

"I'm checking your foot, so shut up and let me. You're going to wake the whole cabin."

"Nice to know you care about me as much as you care about them. And why is it necessary to check it now?"

"Any time, any place." He quirked an eyebrow and glanced up at her. "That's our deal, remember?"

She crumpled backward into the uncomfortable seat. "You and your stupid deals." She sighed and closed her eyes. "Fine, check away. Just leave me alone while you're doing it."

She heard the crackle of his lips as they moved on a smile. "With pleasure. I'm not exactly thrilled to have my hands all over you. Your foot is disgusting."

Anna gave him a playful kick before she remembered how much her leg hurt. The pain launched a whole new round of tears. Unbelievable.

"Be careful, Anna," Jay scolded as he peeled back the layers of the dressings he'd made for her wound. The last strip of gauze stuck, and he gave a little tug that nearly sent her cursing into the stale-smelling plane. "Sorry," he whispered. His breath feathered against the tender spot as he slowly examined the effects of his make-shift surgery. Rough fingertips roamed and explored with the slightest touch and sent a ripple of pleasure through her.

The image fell flat and did nothing to change her opinion of Jay. He'd been nothing but gentle, even now, and despite the aching throb, Anna felt slightly better.

But better didn't mean she could walk in the morning.

Especially since—because of that stupid challenge she knew Heidi threw even though the woman wouldn't own up to it—her ankle hurt even more.

They had at least fifteen miles to hike before they reached the end of this journey. The map, once a motivator to press on and keep going, now mocked her like a taunt. *You'll never make it…you'll never make it.*

Maybe it was true. With her eyes still closed, she worried her lip. She was nothing but a liability for Jay. Maybe she should end this before things got worse. Why stay here when the chances of winning were slim? Why stay when the chance of a catastrophe—death, infection, irreversible side effects—doubled every day? "I never said I wanted to be partners with Heidi," he whispered, reminding her of the allegation she leveled at him earlier.

Guilt joined her in the seat. "I know. It was a stupid accusation for me to make." Stupid and pointless, since thoughts of Jay would no longer matter the second this show was over. Sadness climbed on top of guilt and settled in for a nap.

"What else is going on in that mind of yours?" Jay whispered, interrupting her grim thoughts.

She shifted in her seat. "Nothing. Just trying to sleep."

He gave a breathy laugh. "You want to try the truth this time?" The sound of ripping fabric filled the space around them. Jay's hand slipped around her ankle as he gently wrapped the clean cloth once, twice, and finished it with a loose knot. His knees cracked as he rose from the ground and slipped into the seat beside her. She turned her head to face him, seeing that his seat managed to look even more uncomfortable than hers. He shifted to face her, his head leaning sideways against the dirty seatback. When she made no move to say anything, he spoke low enough for only the two of them to hear.

"So…nothing? You're not going to say anything?"

"Why can't you just believe me when I answer the first time?" She cracked one eye open before closing it against the sweet look he gave her.

"Well, see, I'm kind of psychic, and something tells me you're lying."

She made a face. "Psychic, or psychotic?"

He grinned "Same thing, they're both weird." He scratched the back of his neck. "Anyway, here's what I think you're thinking about."

"Enlighten me, I'm begging you." She rolled her eyes behind closed lids.

"I plan on it." Fingertips caressed her forehead, pushing back a wayward lock of hair that lay across her eyes. Anna kept her eyes closed and tried not to shiver from the contact. "I think you're sitting here feeling sorry for yourself, believing you're letting me down and buying into some crap about being a failure if you quit. I think you're worried about not delivering the money to your dad. And I think you've convinced yourself that if you *do* stay, you'll be a hindrance to me, and why bother trying because you'll probably wind up dying from some weird disease in the middle of nowhere anyway." He cleared his throat. "That's what I think. Now tell me, am I way off base?"

One eyelid cracked opened. How in the world did he do that? Maybe he really was psychic. This situation called for some good, old-fashioned lying.

"Shows how much you know. I was actually thinking about how much I love this airplane and how I hope we never leave. There's something powerful about sitting in a seat that other people probably died in. Makes me feel a little invincible, if you want to know the truth."

"That's sick, Anna."

"What? You don't agree?"

"You are the most uncoordinated person I've ever met. Invincible is hardly the word I would use to describe you."

"I won today, didn't I?"

"Yes you did. I take back what I said."

She worried her lip for a long moment. "Heidi let me win, you know."

Jay's eyebrows pushed together. "What do you mean, let you win?"

"She let me win, and it totally makes no sense. The whole time we stood up there she never looked tired. Not once." She studied Jay's face. "Until I came close to falling. Then she claimed a sudden backache and hopped down. Her back seemed fine to me. She let me win." She looked Jay in the eyes. "Why would she do that?"

"Maybe she felt bad for always beating you. Maybe she wanted you to accomplish something memorable on this trip. Maybe once, just once, she wanted you to know what it felt like *not* to lose to her." He winked at her indignant expression.

"I'm offended. I'll have you know that I could race her to the top of a mountain and win without getting short of breath," she hissed. "Which I plan on doing first thing tomorrow."

"That's your plan," he deadpanned with a raised eyebrow. "First thing tomorrow. To race her to the top of a hill. With a foot that looks like gangrene might set in at any minute."

"Erase the gangrene part and that's pretty much exactly my plan." Anna knew she sounded ridiculous. She also knew she wouldn't be running anywhere at all for at least a month, but she didn't like Jay challenging her ability to win—especially against Heidi. A girl had her pride, particularly when it came to competing against overgrown Barbie dolls with perfectly perfect white teeth and tight abs and mysteriously glowing skin. Anna's skin wasn't glowing. Anna's skin was pallid and dirty, and that was on a good day.

"When you're ready to race, let me know and I'll show up with the stopwatch." And with that, Jay pressed his lips against her forehead. "Now give me your foot."

"Again? Jay, this is stupid. What is your obsession with my ankle? Are you like that crazy guy on the news who was really into kissing women's feet? Is my ankle your weird fetish?" She sighed and dropped her leg into his lap.

"You wish." He clasped her heel and settled her foot over his thigh, keeping his hand in place, probably to make sure she didn't kick him. "I just want you to prop it up so the swelling will go down. Now shut up and go to sleep."

Oh.

Well, that was thoughtful.

She shifted to get comfortable, rolled up her jacket to use as a pillow, and closed her eyes. If he would stop running his thumb absently over her skin she might actually be able to concentrate on sleeping. As it was, she couldn't get past visions of him kissing her foot. Among other things.

She punched her jacket and settled into it. "Try to keep your obsession with my ankle in check for the next few hours, because if you wake me up again I'll kill you."

The sound of his soft laughter somehow carried her into the most pleasant dream she'd had in months.

Chapter 25

They'd walked nearly a mile over some the most treacherous terrain they'd tackled so far, but Anna barely noticed. Thoughts of a dream she'd had last night coursed through her blood like a sudden spike in fever, and Anna hadn't been able to look at Jay all day. Every time he spoke, she replied with a one-syllable answer. Sometimes her answers weren't even words, but brief sounds meant to give the impression she wasn't interested in what he had to say. So far, it hadn't worked. He kept talking, and she kept remembering. She had to stop remembering.

But she couldn't.

He had kissed her. And *not* like the first time. This kiss was the type that would've made even the most promiscuous person blush and wound up with her practically rolling on top of him, begging for more until they clutched each other in ways that shouldn't be legal. And it didn't matter that it was only a dream, because for Anna, it was as real as if they had made out inside the airplane. She ached just thinking about it.

A long sigh escaped before she thought to stop it.

"What was that for?" he asked.

Oh, I had a dream that you kissed me again...then made out with me...and I kinda want you to throw me against a tree for real right now and—

"I'm bored," she quickly said.

"You're bored. We're trekking across the Alaskan wilderness and you're bored? What would you rather be doing?"

She blushed to her hairline.

"Cleaning my apartment," she scrambled to say. Cleaning her apartment? She hated to clean, especially toilets. They're gross and stained and sticky and—

"Cleaning your apartment," he said, clearly unbelieving. "What is wrong with you today?"

"Nothing." *Everything.* She gave an exaggerated shrug, blushing as though she'd been caught spying on Jay in the shower. Which she practically had been in her stupid dream. "What makes you think there's something wrong with me? That's silly. That's crazy. That's dumb."

No, that entire sentence sounded dumb.

By the small twitch at the corner of his mouth, he obviously agreed.

"Well, based on that eloquent denial and your red face, clearly I'm the crazy one." He slipped a finger under the bandana tied around his forehead and slid it along the fold. "Spill it, Anna. What's on your mind?"

She glanced at him, her gaze instantly drawn to his mouth. The way it moved over hers. The way his arms circled her waist and pulled her close. The way his hands…

She cleared her throat, blew some air onto her overheated forehead. "You'll have to be more specific."

He shot her a sideways glance. "Alright, here's specific for you. Why is it that you can barely look at me today? And why is it, every time you do, your face heats up like a match lighting the top layer of your skin on fire? Is that specific enough?"

She faced him head on. This time she kept her focus on his eyes, tough to do when she noticed his lazy smile. "My face is not heating up. That's ridiculous."

"Anna, you look like you've spent hours on the beach with no sunscreen."

"I always wear sunscreen." Weak, but the best retort she could come up with. She turned and stomped away, or more precisely, stomped with one foot and dragged the other. In two strides, Jay caught up to her.

"Okay, the way I see it, you have two options. You can either tell me—honesty is the best policy, you know—or I can start guessing."

"There's nothing to guess, Jay."

"You've spent all day imagining me in the shower."

She stumbled. "Are you insane?"

"You finally have me alone, and you're plotting ways to take advantage of me."

"Stop it, Jay!" Her stupid face flamed brighter. That match-on-her-skin-thing was pretty much spot on. "Besides, I'm not that desperate."

"You had a dream that we made out, and you keep thinking about it. Keep wishing the dream were real. Keep thinking of ways to make it happen."

She stopped walking again and narrowed her eyes at him. "Why would you say something like that?"

"Because you talk in your sleep."

Her eyes went wide. "What are you talking about? I do *not* talk in my sleep."

"You talk in your sleep."

"No, I don't." Even she heard the doubt in her voice.

He gave her a slow wink. "You did last night."

Anna felt the blood drain from her face, then return with a raging rush. She spun on her heel, which nearly sent her into a fit of screams. But even the excruciating pain wouldn't make her stop walking. Only death would accomplish that. Fitting, since all she wanted to do was kill herself right then.

"Anna, I'm just giving you a hard time. It's not that big a deal." He shrugged. "So you said a few things. So they were slightly revealing. And interesting." That wicked smile returned. "And pretty entertaining to listen to…"

"You're enjoying this, aren't you?"

"Not as much as I enjoyed it on the airplane."

"Jay!"

"Okay, I'm sorry. I won't talk about it again." They walked a few more steps in silence. She should have known not to get too comfortable with it. "Just one question. What exactly were we doing in that dream of yours?"

She made a crude noise before glaring at him sideways. "What exactly did I say?" She didn't want to know. She *really* didn't want to know.

But then she did. Her imagination might drive her nuts until she found out.

"Well, first you said my name. Four times, I might add." He rubbed his lower lip. "And then you said *please*. And then—"

"Okay, I've heard enough." If humiliation were a fatal disease, she might have a minute left to live. "Just…did anyone hear me?"

"Besides me? No." His expression sobered a bit. "Everyone slept through the whole thing, I promise. Besides, your voice wasn't louder than a whisper. A very *interesting* whisper…"

"And you're sure they didn't hear?"

"Positive. So are you going to tell me, or not?"

"Not. And can we please not talk about this anymore?"

His smile was as soft as smoke. "I don't know…"

"Jay."

"Fine."

The silence that followed was torturous. She waited for him to say something but nothing came. Not a word. Barely even a breath. The only thing she heard was the crunching of sticks as they walked side by side. The noise grew and swelled, until the sticks sounded like hammers banging on the side of her head. When she couldn't take it anymore, she blurted out the only thing she knew to stop the sound. The only thing that might put an end to this awful, awkward moment.

"You kissed me."

"Just now? Funny, I don't remember doing it."

She made a longsuffering sound. "In my dream. You kissed me."

Jay looked up at the sky, easy as you please. "Was it better or worse than the first time?" In that instance, she saw his attitude for what it was. Supreme cockiness. Major arrogance. Of *course* it was better, and he knew it.

"Much worse."

He stretched both hands over his head and rested them there, a grin this side of legal turning up his mouth. "Sure it was."

"Believe me, it was."

His grin slipped a little. "I don't remember you moaning my name the first time."

She pressed her lips together. "It was only a dream, Jay."

His obnoxious smirk returned in full force. "You know what they say about dreams, Anna."

His immature insinuation barely warranted a response. "It isn't true."

His eyebrows shot up. "So you've heard the expression? That dreams reveal your true desires when you're wide awake?"

"So corny. Besides, I also dream about sandwiches."

"And right now, I'll bet you want one as much as you want me. Too bad I can't make either a reality for you."

That comment elicited a snort from her. "Oh give me a break. Who says I want kissing you again to be a reality?"

"You. At least four times last night." His insufferable snicker threw her over the edge.

"You're such a brat!" With a quick wave of determination, she put all her weight on her good foot and shoved him, hard. What followed was so heart-stopping, so unexpected, Anna had the sense she was floating—fear-struck and suspended in the air above them, watching the scene play out below with no way to stop it.

Jay lost his balance. Tumbled sideways. And fell over the side of the hill. The only thing Anna heard was a yell. A few choices words. And a thud.

Then everything went still.

Chapter 26

"Please wake up. Please, please wake up!" Anna slapped at Jay's face with her fingertips, then slapped it again. She scrambled down the hill several minutes ago to find him flat on his back, lying among a patch of yellow-flowered brush. So far, she'd smacked him a half-dozen times, but he still hadn't moved. Hadn't even made a sound.

"Jay, please!" With her fingers locked on both sides of his face, she rolled his head from side to side, then bent low and held her ear over his mouth. Nothing happened. "I can't tell if you're breathing!" Panic took over her voice, making her words strain in a tight squeal. "How do I do this? How do I do this? Somebody please help me!"

With a groan of frustration, she pinched his nose, tilted his head back, and locked her mouth over his.

And that's when Jay started to feel bad for faking it.

He tried to lie still as her warm breath filled his mouth, enjoying the way it traveled down his throat…filled him up with *her*. But then the woman began to pound on his chest. Once, then twice, then a third time for good measure. It hurt. This was *not* the correct way to perform CPR.

He nearly yelped, but then her mouth was on his again, and what started out as a joke on his part changed quickly as his blood started to pound. Before he had time to analyze the wisdom of it, he felt himself move. His hands reached up to cradle the sides of her face as his mouth roamed over hers. Her lips parted in shock for a moment, then softened against his as they responded. It was the kind of kiss that tipped his world upside down. The kind that took its time. The kind that felt so right that he couldn't remember whether or not it was wrong.

Nor did he care.

He came up on one elbow and tugged the front of her coat, pulling her toward him, feeling the heat of her racing heart as it pounded underneath her clothing. His skin burned at her nearness, his pulse raced with the feel of her lips moving against his. He plunged his hand through her hair and pushed himself higher, tasting her, intoxicated by her, unable to get close enough. A soft moan escaped her throat, and then...

She vaulted backward.

A dazed expression clouded her features as she slowly pressed her lips together. "Were you...? Was that...?" She blinked. The clouds in her eyes descended, replaced by a hot, burning sun. She glanced up the hillside and back at him. "Were you awake the whole time?"

Reality crashed in on him, and he was the only one to blame. Now it was time to cover, to play it cool. "Not the *whole* time. I didn't hear you slide *all* the way down the hill..."

Her gaze narrowed into slits. "You were *faking?*" She bit the words out. "I was nearly in tears, begging you to wake up, and you were pretending?"

"I was not pretending to kiss you."

Her mouth dropped open. A gorgeous mouth, a beautiful mouth. "Why would you do something so mean?"

"Because I had to know." He sunk onto an elbow, suddenly aware that his left foot hurt. That might be a problem.

"You had to know what?" She moved back another inch.

"If your dream and the reality were anything alike." He wiggled his toes. What was *up* with his foot? "So, were they?"

Her lips pressed into a hard line. "Not even close. The dream was *way* better."

Sure it was. He'd had plenty of his own private dreams in the last few days, and the reality was a thousand times better. So much better, he wanted to kiss her again, and more. Right here. Right now.

"Then that must have been some dream," he said. "Because we barely started making out and that was still…wow. Just, wow." A lazy grin lifted his mouth. He loved seeing her blush.

"At least one of us was impressed." She stuck her nose in the air to recover some dignity and stood up, slapping dirt off the back of her pants and rubbing her hands together to clear them from debris. "Are you going to sit there all day, or are you ready to start moving?" She crossed her arms. "Get up." It was cute to watch her try to keep up that ridiculous scowl.

"You sure you don't want to come back down here and join me?"

"Get up, Jay."

Knowing they were done—for now—he made a move to stand, then cried out when pain shot through his ankle. "Aw, crap!" He fell backward into the shrubbery, temporarily blinded by a crushing throb. "I think something's wrong."

Anna's scowl gave way to alarm, and she dropped to her knees in front of him. "What's the matter?" She shoved back his hair, ran her hand over his shoulder, his arm, his chest, looking for the source of the pain. Under any other circumstance, he might have enjoyed the feeling. Not this time. Finally, her gaze followed his and landed on his foot, lying sideways at a weird angle. "You've got to be kidding me."

"I think it might be broken," Jay said.

Anna fell back and dropped her head into her hands. "Because I pushed you?" She peered at him through a slit between her fingers.

Jay tilted his head, searching for the right answer. "Well, not because you *didn't* push me..."

Her hands fell away with a groan. "I pushed you down a hill and broke your ankle."

"It could just be a sprain."

"It isn't a sprain."

"It could be."

She rolled her eyes. "What are we going to do now?"

Jay wasn't sure if that was a rhetorical question, or if she wanted an answer. He thought he'd give her one, anyway. "I say we sit here for awhile and see if it gets better."

She just looked at him like he was crazy. "Sit here? In the middle of nowhere? And wait?"

He nodded. "That's the idea. Besides, in case you need a reminder, this entire trip has taken place in the middle of nowhere."

"You know what I mean. There's no water here. Or food. Or a place to build a fire. Where are we going to build a fire? It'll be cold soon, and then we'll both freeze to death!"

Jay smiled at her. She was cute when she panicked. He noticed that about her the very first day, when he witnessed her practical meltdown on the plane ride to Alaska. "Anna, I'm not proposing we build a home here and construct a swing set for the kids. Or even stay overnight. Just that you give me a few minutes to figure out how to deal with this before we take off again."

She sighed. "Oh." But then her face sagged. "I can't believe I broke your ankle."

"Sprained," he said. *Please, God, let it be sprained.* "Kind of makes that whole faking-being-knocked-out-so-I-could-kiss-you thing pale in comparison, doesn't it?"

"No." He saw the spark in her eyes just before it banked into desire. "No, it doesn't."

She was such a terrible liar.

"You're right. I'm ashamed of myself. I promise never to do it again."

She frowned before she caught herself, then lifted her chin and stared at him. "Good. And don't forget it. Both of your kisses were a disaster I'd rather not revisit." Her throat constricted on a hard swallow.

Liar. Liar.

Chapter 27

"Does this spot look okay?"

Jay turned in a circle and looked around, putting as little weight as possible on his left foot. He no longer thought it was broken, but until the competition was over, he couldn't be sure. Until then, he planned to make the best of this bad situation. His mind screamed at him to push the button, to head to the closest doctor for Valium and an X-ray, but he wouldn't do it to Anna. He'd made a promise, and he was a man of his word.

Relief coursed through him when they finally made it to the clearing. The welcome sound of rushing water nearly brought tears to his eyes. He was starving. He was tired. He was filthy from head to toe. But mainly, he wanted a drink. His thermos had run dry hours ago, and they'd long since drained the remains of Anna's.

Anna.

He couldn't believe the strength that woman displayed. His heart had swelled to twice its size today as he watched her push through the pain; he knew it had to be tearing her up inside.

"It looks good to me," she said. "So good I might sit down and cry right here." Anna dropped her pack in a heap on the dirt, sending a little puff of smoke into the air around her legs. He studied her while she unloaded supplies—a fishing net, some rope, an extra set of gloves. Even now, her mind remained focused. Her cap sat sideways on her head, a smudge of dirt trailed down her right cheek. A strand of hair lay smashed against her forehead, the crumbled remains of a dead leaf scattered inside the tattered ends.

He'd never seen anyone so beautiful in his life.

As though she read his mind, she looked his direction and smiled. His heart sputtered at the sight, turning a full loop inside his chest.

"Wanna go fishing?" she asked him, holding up her hard-won-except-not-really new fishing pole. Her pretty grin grew wider. Her enthusiasm was contagious, made him nearly forget how awful he felt.

"You're ready to fish now? Don't you want to rest for a while?"

"Yes, but resting won't feed me, and I want to eat *now*. I'll fall asleep after a few fish are gutted and cooked."

Jay arched an eyebrow. "Says the woman who couldn't handle killing a fly a few weeks ago."

She shrugged. "Things change. If a swarm of flies flew by right now, I'd catch them and eat them one by one. That's how hungry I am."

"Somehow that doesn't sound nearly as disgusting as it should. So do you want to build a fire or head to the creek? Your choice." Jay bent low and rummaged through his pack for a lighter. He dragged one out and dangled it between his fingers, tempting her to take it. At every campsite, they'd argued about whose turn it was to get the blaze going. Fishing was peaceful and refreshing, even in the chilly temperatures. Fire-building was sweaty, labor-intensive, and dirty—adding grime to the layers of mud already clinging to their skin. Anna didn't bite.

"Nice try, Sparky. You build the fire. I'm catching dinner." She moved past him, bending down for a brief moment to retrieve his empty thermos. "I'll be back in a few minutes with more fish than either of us can eat," she said over her shoulder. "I expect to see flames by then, just so you know."

"I expect to see three fish in your hands when you return," he called after her. His lips turned up at the sound of her laughter.

He had just dumped a small pile of sticks on the ground and lined them with dried leaves when he heard her footsteps. Something about the sound alarmed him. He knew she would come back soon, but this was too fast.

He turned to question her, but the words died on his lips.

Every inch of her was soaked, dripping with lake water as rivers of tears streamed from her eyes. Her cap was missing, as were her gloves. Bits of algae clung to her skin. Every inch of her body trembled. Jay rushed to her side, ignoring the explosion of pain that blasted through his leg.

"What happened to you?" He reached for her shoulders, her face, her back as he pulled her to him and held on. She smelled sour, like a strange combination of spoiled milk and dead fish, but he didn't care. She sobbed into his chest, gripping his shirt like a vise as her body heaved with each breath. Shrugging out of his coat, he slipped it around her shaking shoulders.

"I lost it," she wailed. "I don't know what happened. One minute it was propped under my arm while I went to tie in a hook, and the next minute it slipped. I tried to catch it, but the water moved too fast. Every time I reached for it, it sank deeper until it disappeared completely. I'm sorry. I'm really, really sorry." Her cries grew louder as frustration reached the breaking point.

His heart sank. Without the pole, they were back to square one. And they never caught a single fish with it. All that time standing on that ledge wasted. He rested his chin on her head and closed his eyes, thinking about what to do, coming up with nothing. Instead, he just held her until her tears began to ebb.

Once her shoulders ceased shaking, he hooked a finger under her chin and tilted her head up to meet his gaze. "We'll be okay." When she shook her head, he stopped her with a tap with his thumb. "Stop worrying. We'll go back to catching fish the old fashioned way."

"We've only caught one that way the entire time we've been here. Plus, you can barely walk. *I* can barely walk. And now because of me, neither one of us will have anything to eat." Tears sprang from her eyes all over again.

Jay ran his thumbs under her lashes and peered downward, matching his gaze to hers, eye to eye. "You have been the best partner I could have ever asked for. I was angry when the whole thing began— ticked off at the way the producers of this show paired us together. But I see now that it was meant to be.

Anna blinked at him in wide-eyed wonder. It was too much for him, those innocent blue eyes, those pink lips. She was too close, and he was only a man. With his pulse thundering in his ears and before he could change his mind, he lowered his head and whispered against her lips. "I know I said I wouldn't do it again, but…"

In the span of a breath, his mouth covered hers. Her head tilted backward as her hands moved from his chest to link around his neck. He plunged his fingers through her wet hair and pressed in close. When her hands caressed the back of his neck, his already weak body began to tremble. He took a step backward for balance, pressing his spine against a tree, pulling her with him, settling her into the space between his legs as his fingertips roamed her face, her neck, her shoulders. His hands linked around her waist as he tasted her, making up for all the tempered longing. Her drenched sweater begged to be ripped away and discarded, so he forced his hands to his side to control the screaming urge. With a frustrated groan, he kissed her harder. She misunderstood the sound and tugged at his waist. His mind nearly exploded when she lifted his shirt to expose a thin strip of skin.

The blast of cold air was just what he needed.

He dropped his mouth to her neck to try to control his breathing, linking his fingers with hers as he pressed a trail of kisses to her throat, her collarbone. Remorse tried to scratch at the back of his mind. He shouldn't be kissing her, not when she belonged to someone else.

But that didn't stop the longing.

His lips found hers once again for the briefest second before she broke away and stepped back. Desire clouded her eyes, but as they cleared he saw the unmistakable mark of guilt. She bit her swollen lip and ran a hand up her neck. "Jay, this can't keep happening. I need to work some things out with Ryan first. If I don't break it off with him, I'm no better than he is. Can you understand that?"

"Not really, no." Anger and frustration waged a battle for dominance in Jay's mind, but in the end understanding won out. Understanding, and a tiny helping of guilt. Of course she was upset. Of course she wanted to be fair. In the weeks he had spent with Anna, he'd already learned she was honorable to a fault.

"Pretend I never said that," he said. "Of course I understand."

"It's just that my parents, and Ryan—"

"You don't need to explain. I won't let it happen again, I promise." Jay couldn't stand one second of talking about that guy.

To his surprise, Anna's guilty expression gave way to a timid grin. "I think I've heard that line before."

He gave a long-suffering sigh. "And I would have kept my promise if you hadn't practically attacked me just now. What was I supposed to do, shove you away and tell you to get your ice cube lips off me? I felt sorry for you. It was a sympathy kiss, that's all."

"Oh sure, sympathy kiss. You dragged me against a tree—"

"Because I was about to faint from the smell of your hair and needed something to hold myself up. I don't think you ever got all that puke out of it."

"If anyone smells bad out here, it's you. And that beard, it's like kissing a pine cone, all rough and scratchy."

She stopped talking when they heard the sound. They looked up at the same time, and for the first moment in two days, he felt hope. *Rescue*, the red words bled across the backdrop of the gray sky.

With a wide-eyed look of surprise, she brought her gaze back down to lock with his. "Is that what I think it is?"

Jay shielded his eyes and drank in the sight, watching out of the corner of his eye as Anna did the same. "Remember that corner you were talking about earlier?" He dropped his gaze and winked at her. "I think we just turned it."

Another couple had given up. Maybe it was Nico and Heidi, or maybe the earth man and his unfortunate partner. Either way, they were now down to two. Suddenly for both of them, this game seemed winnable.

She smiled up at him. An elated smile, full of nothing but happiness, not one trace of doubt or regret. It was all the permission he needed. He reached for her coat and tugged her to him, wrapping his arms around her waist as he lifted her off the ground. He promised he wouldn't kiss her, but he never promised this. Shoving thoughts of everything but Anna straight out of his mind, he held on.

He smiled over her head when he felt her arms steal around his neck. They stood that way for a long time. And in those minutes, he lost the biggest part of himself. By the time he noticed, the empty space was already filled up with Anna.

For one brief second, he found himself wondering how he would deal with the gaping hole when this was over.

He pushed that thought away and leaned into her. She was with him now.

And maybe there was actually a chance things would stay that way.

***

After nineteen days, food mattered. Food, shelter, and a dry change of clothes *really* mattered—but for now, they couldn't get their hands on any of it. The snow began hours ago and hadn't let up for a moment. Wasn't the snow supposed to be melting in April in Alaska? They hadn't slept, they hadn't eaten—the only thing they had managed was to climb to a higher elevation.

Jay didn't regret holding her for so long—he'd do it again if he had the opportunity. But Lord have mercy, he should have been fishing. Why in the world didn't he demand they eat first? Instead, the first flake fell on their conjoined heads, followed by a rapid succession of others, and they gathered their supplies and darted uphill to wait out what they thought would be a brief flurry. That was three hours ago. Now they were stuck in the worst possible spot they could find with no idea how to find a better one.

A stick jammed into his back, and he stifled a curse.

To call this spot a shelter would be generous. More like a fort made of small rocks and shrubbery, it only offered a partial barrier from the horrendous elements. Jay pressed his back further into the sharp sticks and edged his knees up closer to his chest. The prickly limbs of a Fireweed bush jabbed into his head, his neck. His foot screamed to be relieved, to be alleviated from the harsh position, but there was no help for it. Beside him, Anna folded her legs to the side and tucked herself into his waist. Jay wrapped both arms around her, feeling her muscles jerk with violent shivers even through his thick, wet coat. He resituated the tarp to drape over their legs and remounted it over their heads. Underneath, their doubled-up sleeping bags offered minimal warmth. Their body heat would continue to lower as long as they stayed here. But the downpour made visibility nearly impossible.

Jay banged his head against the bush. Then banged it again, trying to decide what to do. If they didn't move soon, he wasn't sure how they would survive the night.

"J…Jay," Anna's teeth chattered so sharply, his name stretched to three syllables. "I…don't think…we can…do this…anymore."

He buried his face into her hair. "Yes we can." Taking a deep breath, he forced himself to speak evenly. It was so cold. Keeping his voice steady was difficult. "We've made it through too much to quit now, Anna." He searched out her hands inside the sleeping bag and brought them to his chest, covering them with both palms to warm at least that small part of her. "There's only one couple left besides you and me, and a little thing like a snowstorm isn't going to get the better of us." He pressed his forehead to hers. Their mingled breathing heated the tiny space a bit. "Are you with me? Are you listening to what I'm saying?" He felt her nod against him. "Okay, good. It's settled then, we're staying." She nodded again, her teeth keeping time to the fast-falling snowflakes.

"It's just…I want to go home." Just then, a loud crack split the night in two, and they both jerked apart. The tarp landed on both their heads. "Jay, what was that?"

"I think it was just a limb that snapped from the weight of the snow." He hoped. Snow funneled from the tarp straight down the back of Jay's neck. He sucked in a burst of air from the icy tentacle and slapped at his back. This time, a coarse word escaped before he could stop it. "Okay, I've had enough of this."

"My thoughts exactly," Anna said, burying her face into his neck. "Jay, we've got to move. Or push the button. I'm alright with either option, just so you know."

"We're not pushing the button unless we have to." He pulled the tarp down only enough to look with one eye, and cringed. Nothing but a thick sheet of white greeted him. White falling from the sky. White blanketing the ground beneath them. White walling them in at least eight inches deep.

Suddenly, black was his new favorite color.

He lifted the tarp in place again and reached for Anna's hands. "Okay, here's what I can tell you. There's zero visibility. I have no idea if we'll walk onto land or straight into the river. We could fall over a cliff for all I know. And maybe the worst part of all, the map will be completely useless."

"Please don't sugar-coat anything for my sake," she said with a groan.

In spite of his misery, he managed a smile. "Just trying to prepare you for the worst. Now, do you want to stay here or try to find a better place?"

She flipped her feet to the front and struggled to stand. "Let's go.

Jay helped her into her pack and strapped on his own, then folded the tarp and tucked it under his arm in case they needed to reach it quickly. The snow was ridiculous. He was from Texas. The most snow he'd seen in his life fell three years ago. Two inches—and school, work, and all forms of road travel were cancelled for days. Even freeways were deserted. He had no idea how to navigate in this mess. But quitting wasn't an option. Yet.

He latched onto to Anna's hand, more for his own comfort than hers. He couldn't see a dang thing out here, and in the midst of barely controlled panic, he didn't want to risk losing her, too. "Do not let go," he shouted over the howling wind. "No matter what happens, hold on to me."

"I'm not going anywhere. Just..."

He turned to look at her. He thought he saw her nose and what looked like one eyebrow. "What is it?"

She tightened her hold on his hand. "Just...please don't lead us over a cliff."

He rolled his eyes and tried to see in front of him. "I can't make any promises. Let's go." His voice was barely audible over the strong storm.

They took off walking.

Only God knew where they were headed.

Chapter 28

Finding this place had been nothing short of a miracle. This cave was dank, small, and drippy. And for the first time in life, Anna felt claustrophobic.

"How much longer do you think we'll need to stay here?"

She ran a finger under her collar and pressed her back against the wall, the coolness of the stones seeping through her sweatshirt. Somehow, the pressure and the temperature eased her anxiety. Her shoes, coat, and gloves encircled the small fire in front of her, sitting side by side with Jay's. All their clothes were nearly dry. Soon, they would be able to leave again. But even though the walls were literally closing in, she didn't want to go. This was the warmest she'd been in days, but the only way out of this wilderness was to keep walking to the edge of it, and with two wounded feet between them and more snow falling than even Chicago could manage to dump in so little time, the entire task sounded about as pleasant as a root canal. Performed on her. By Jay. Out here with no anesthetic.

They had found the cave the day before, but since arriving, they hadn't been able to do much else but unload supplies, lie down, and wait. Snow continued to fall at a steady pace, stopping every few hours merely to gather power and begin again. It didn't escape her notice that as the snow built its strength, Jay's and Anna's waned from lack of nourishment.

At least twelve inches of snow covered the ground as far as the eye could see, and judging from the gray clouds suspended like thick billows of smoke directly overhead, snow seemed to be the only weather pattern in the foreseeable future. Not one break...not one ray of sun gave any hope for it to end.

For the first time since this adventure began, Anna was depressed. Depressed and emotional. Depressed and feeling completely isolated. Depressed about staying here, and depressed about leaving. She looked at Jay and sighed, watching as he flipped over first her coat and then his, trying to dry them completely.

Truthfully, she was even depressed about him.

He'd shown her nothing but kindness and compassion, offered her more encouragement and support than she'd been shown in a lifetime. Had been exactly what she dreamed of in a man, in all the ways that mattered.

Except that he wasn't in her parent's plans, and she didn't know what to do about it.

Instead, Ryan was tied to every goal her parents had groomed her for from birth—it didn't matter that her dreams were different. She never wanted a high-profile life in Illinois politics. She had no desire to see her name in headlines or her comings and goings analyzed in the Style section of the Tribune. That was her mother's dream, her father's ambition. And it was their expectation that Anna would follow suit. Until three weeks ago, when she boarded a plane to spend what she thought would be an adventurous getaway—one last shot at fun before pressures and responsibilities and burdensome demands kicked in.

But Jay had changed everything for her. And so did catching Ryan kissing another woman in that magazine.

But, what was she going to do? Leave Ryan—abandon the tiny amount of respect she had gained from her parents? She wasn't so sure they didn't love Ryan more than they actually loved her. She saw no way to depart from her parent's long-held plan without severe repercussions.

She wasn't dumb—she knew the fallout would be bad. Could see it in slow-motion, like watching a movie with a plot so predictable she could recite the lines along with the actors. She was more confused than she'd ever been about anything in her life. In three weeks' time, Jay had worked his way into her heart until his presence filled up all the corners. When he kissed her yesterday, she'd pushed him away out of obligation, nothing else. If left up to her, she would have kissed him and more, to heck with the consequences. Other than normal teenage rebellion, never in her life had she defied her parents.

Jay might not realize it, but the rest of the country did.

He moved behind her to string up their socks, using a bit of fishing line to hang them close to the fire to dry.

"That's a terrible habit of yours, you know."

Anna blinked—as confused as if she'd just been yanked from an unpleasant dream. He stood in front of her, toe to toe, looking down at her with his hands on his hips. He looked thinner, weak from the pain from his foot, but his muscles still showcased his fit physique. She swallowed, her pulse racing in her throat. He indicated for her to move over, then sat down beside her on her sleeping bag, so close their legs touched knee to ankle. A sense of safety traveled through her at his nearness. If she could find a way to scoot closer, she would.

"What is?" She frowned at him.

He leaned his head against the wall and closed his eyes. They were both so tired. "Asking questions, but not listening to the answer. You do it all the time."

"No, I don't." She bumped his shoulder and made a face.

"Then tell me what I said." Without opening his eyes, he readjusted his bandana, pulling it low on his forehead.

"Said about what?" She tilted her head so that it rested against his.

"You just proved my point. You asked how long we would need to say here, and I said probably another week, at least. But of course you didn't hear me."

Her head snapped up. "Another week? There is no way I'm going to stay here—"

"Kidding." Jay smiled. "Only kidding. I'm hoping to leave here by morning." He slanted one eye open to peer at her. "If you think you're up for it."

"I'm up for it. Though suddenly another week here doesn't seem so bad." She sighed. "I can't believe this storm. There's literally nothing but white for miles. I don't even know how we're going to begin to find food in this mess."

Jay cleared his throat. "That's why we've got to move. If we don't find something soon, I think we might be out of options. I don't want to quit, but it's starting to sound like the smarter idea."

Anna couldn't respond around the lump in her throat. To quit meant to leave. To leave meant to return to Ryan. To return to Ryan meant to say goodbye to Jay.

To say goodbye to him meant to die inside.

She closed her eyes and leaned into him, her skin growing warm at the feel of his hand closing over hers. She'd drawn the line at kissing, but she was more than fine with this. He smelled like sweat and grass and firewood—odd in a snowstorm, but uniquely comforting. Tears pricked at her eyes, but she forced them back. Years of hiding genuine emotion made her an expert. Jay brought her hand to his lap. Before long, she felt herself drift, wrapped in the security of his closeness.

As reality faded, as the sweet escape of slumber closed around her, she had only one thought, like her mind was stuck on replay.

For now, she had Jay.

***

A short while later, the earsplitting blast of a gunshot ripped her from her sleep. "My ears are still ringing, you know. They probably will be until tomorrow." Jay rolled his eyes and took another bite. That woman was so ungrateful. Good thing she was so hot.

"Would you have preferred I let it hop on by?" He closed his eyes for a moment and swallowed, determined to enjoy the taste of his meal as it made its way down his throat. He picked up Anna's thermos—now filled with melted snow—and took a drink. With no river for miles and no other source of water, at least all that white stuff had been good for something.

"No. But some cotton balls might have been nice. A little warning, maybe." She licked her fingers one by one. He had to force himself not to stare. If the woman had any idea what seeing that did to him...

He focused on his dinner, small as it was, and took a deep breath.

A squirrel. One minute, the sound of Anna's deep breathing had lulled him into a semi-unconscious state. The next minute he heard a movement at the entrance of the cave. Out of nowhere a squirrel had scampered toward them, probably foraging for food itself. Thank God his gun was nearby. With trembling fingers, Jay said a little prayer, latched onto it with his right hand, cocked it slowly so as not to startle the animal, and pulled the trigger. It fell over immediately, shot straight through the eyes. Guilt pricked his conscience for a moment. The poor thing was just innocently looking for something to eat, after all. But that only lasted for a minute. Okay, maybe a second. Out here, it was every man, woman—and squirrel—for himself.

"Yes, because cottons balls are just overflowing in your backpack." When the last of the bone was picked clean, Jay tossed it out the entrance of the cave. He watched as it sunk into the snow and disappeared under the layers. "Next time, I'll pack your ears with snow."

"Don't you dare," she said. She held out the remains of her meal and studied it, as though wishing for more to magically appear. When nothing happened her arm reared back, and she let the bone fly. It landed next to Jay's, burying itself underneath the snow. She stared after it, a deep longing etched all over her face.

"I'm sorry there isn't more." Jay reached for a long stick and stirred the fire. Sparks shot toward the roof of the cave and billowed out into the cool air at the cave's opening. They needed more firewood. The thought of searching for more out in this mess made his shoulders heavy with dread.

"You have nothing to apologize for." She came up beside him and crouched low to the flames. "Finding our dinner has officially made you my hero."

Jay looked over at her. Her eyes shone in the firelight. Her hair was both matted in places and poking wildly in different directions. Her face was smudged with dirt, the undersides of her fingernails were caked with it. She was in desperate need of a shower, not to mention a decent meal.

She was heartbreakingly beautiful. More beautiful than any woman he'd ever seen. And the realization completely ticked him off. He wanted her to end things with Ryan so they could be together. But that day felt like an eternity from now...like a wishful moment in the future that may or may not ever happen.

He ran a hand over the back of his neck and tried to shake off his melancholy mood. Deflecting, pushing it way down under the surface…that normally worked. He cleared his tight throat.

"Just now? After I've rowed you across a river, bandaged your severely disgusting foot—more than once, I might add. After I've forgiven you for sending that fishing pole to a watery grave, and a whole lot of other stuff?" He raised an eyebrow at her then, trying to mask the insecurity. *Keep it light. Keep it nice and light.* "A *lot* of other stuff, Anna. I should've been wearing a cape in your mind weeks ago."

He expected a witty comeback, a dig at his over-inflated ego, but Anna didn't bite. Instead, she offered him a sad smile, seeing right through him. "In my mind, you've been wearing one since the day we met. Since you pulled my bag out of that overhead bin and treated me like a real person."

They stared at each other as firelight played across their features. Her breathing changed, as did his. He knew he should look away, but he couldn't. He hadn't liked her at all that day, but things had definitely changed. He knew he should keep his mouth shut, but since when did his mouth ever listen to him? "Anna, when this is over and we return to real life, what happens then?"

Just as he feared, the spell was instantly broken. She looked away and reached for a small stick. Tossing it into the fire, she scooted back onto her sleeping bag and brought her knees to her chest, leaning on her arms to look up at him.

"I don't know. Really, I just don't know."

He inched back onto his own bag, feeling like he needed to tread carefully to avoid spooking her. The fearful look in her eyes tugged at his chest, but he felt hopeless to ease it. Besides, he knew enough about her to understand that she wasn't afraid of him. She was terrified of her family's reaction. He'd be lying if he said her hesitation didn't cut a little.

"Fair enough," he said. "I won't bring it up again."

"Jay, I—"

"I mean it, Anna. As far as I'm concerned, the subject is closed." He leaned back against the wall and pulled his legs up in front of him. "Come here. Sit with me for a minute." He pushed down the foreboding sense of the inevitable and held out his arms, beckoning her to come toward him. She offered a hesitant smile and eased his direction, settling herself between his legs and leaning back into his chest. Her head rested against his chin, and she sighed. Jay wrapped his arms around her waist and leaned his cheek into her hair. They were friends, and he could live with that. He sat there, doing his best to convince himself, but there was just one problem with that little scenario.

He'd never met a friend who fit against him so perfectly.

Thinking this, he closed his eyes and gave in to the urge to pull her closer. He ran his fingers through the ends of her hair, easing out the tangles as best he could. After several moments her breathing slowed, soft and steady and pulling her under. He kept working on her hair, enjoying the way it gradually smoothed out and slipped through his fingers, like silk. After awhile, his eyes grew heavy with exhaustion.

He needed to get up. He needed to gather firewood to keep them warm for the night. He needed to get busy, to find food.

He needed to...

He jerked awake a few hours later, surrounded by a heavy blanket of blackness. The fire was out. The temperature inside the cave had plummeted. He shivered, searched around with his hand, flicked on the first lighter he found, and felt panic rise until it nearly burst out of his lungs.

Anna was gone.

Chapter 29

Jumping up was his first mistake. As Anna walked back inside, Jay rubbed his newly smashed head with a gloved hand and shot her a killer glare.

"Where the heck have you been? Are you trying to get yourself killed? Because I can take care of that at the nearest lake if you'd prefer. Right now, I might enjoy shoving you in it and watching you sink."

"Oh, quit being so dramatic." She dumped a pile of small sticks on the ground in front of him. One landed on his fractured foot. He could swear he heard the bone crack a little more. He stifled a long string of curses and watched as Anna arranged the sticks just so. "We needed firewood, and you were too busy snoring to be of much help." She brushed her hands on her pants and looked up at him. All he could make out was the glow of one of her stupid eyes. It reminded him of a raccoon. A rabid one. He wanted to tame it…by kissing it long and slow, then trailing his lips down her cheek, her lips, her neck…

Thoughts like that only made him madder.

"You should have told me you were leaving. I'm not that hard to wake up."

She curled her lip at him. "How would you know? Have you ever tried sleeping with yourself? It isn't pleasant, let me tell you." If she was trying to elicit a smile, it wouldn't work. He was too mad. Until she stood and walked toward him, then reached out to poke at the corners of his mouth, first one side, then the other. Darn woman.

"Lighten up and stop at glaring at me," she said. "I'm a big girl, and I was freezing, so I found some sticks. You're welcome, by the way."

"I didn't say thank you." He flicked her hand away and sighed, silently commanding his racing heart to calm down. She was fine, she was here. She wasn't hurt or lost or dead. And maybe he was being dramatic, but the thought of her not with him, *alone* out there in these harsh conditions had terrified him more than he'd ever been afraid before. "You scared the crap out me, Anna. Don't do that again."

For the first time, she seemed truly puzzled. "I did? Why?" Her eyebrows pushed together as she studied him. "I was only a few steps away. It isn't my fault that you woke up before I got back." She pulled a few leaves out of her coat and leaned down to push them underneath the pile of sticks. "Hand me that."

Jay raked a hand across his eyebrows and pushed the lighter into her outstretched hand. Her fingers closed around it and she flicked it on, holding it close to an impossibly dry leaf. He watched her, her mouth tucked under while she concentrated on getting a flame started.

She had no idea. The woman seriously had no idea. And suddenly he felt like he needed to clue her in. "If something happened to you, I wouldn't be able to live with myself, that's why." His voice broke. "Just, don't go off without me again. Alright?" Flames licked the leaves, incinerating them in seconds as they latched on to the pile of sticks. Anna watched them climb, blinking furiously into the blazing swath of color. If he didn't know better, he'd think she was crying. But he had seen her cry, and it wasn't this pretty to look at. Finally, she stood and turned to face him, all kinds of unspoken questions in her eyes. Questions...mixed with a fair amount of fierce determination. They were separated by a half-dozen inches. She blew into her hands to warm them, then wrapped her arms around his waist.

"If something were to happen to me, it wouldn't be because of you. You've taken better care of me than anyone in my life. And I mean *anyone*." She dropped her forehead onto his chest and tightened her hold on him. His hand drifted up to the nape of her neck. The other rested at the curve of her spine. The blue wool of her hat scraped against his chin, brushing like sandpaper across his jawline. They stood that way for a few moments, both of them weak and hungry, tired and practically propping one another up. The fire grew behind them, filling the small space with a nice warmth that had been absent minutes ago.

"If this is the best care you've had for thirty years, I feel sorry for you. You're dirty and hungry and a couple weeks away from becoming a walking skeleton. My care is severely lacking, I'd say." He gently kneaded her neck muscles.

A soft moan of pleasure sounded from the back of her throat. "I'm not thirty." Her voice sounded muffled against his coat. He knew she would zero in on that part of his statement.

"Thirty, twenty-six." He smiled over her head. "Same thing."

Without moving, she slapped his back. "It is *not* the same thing." She moaned again. She seriously had to stop doing that. He searched for a snarky comment to distract his over-stimulated self.

"Give or take a few wrinkles."

At that her head snapped up. "I do not have wrinkles." She gaped at him and pointed to the space between her eyebrows. "Those are frown lines, and something tells me you've singlehandedly managed to make them a whole lot deeper these last three weeks. I'm gonna need Botox to repair the damage hanging out with you has caused."

He pursed his lips to the side in fake consideration. "Frown lines, sure. Let me see you smile. I'll bet you a hundred bucks you have wrinkles on the sides of yours eyes, too."

With a hard smack on the arm, she flashed the widest, ugliest, most exaggerated smile he had ever seen. Only clowns and crazy women with dentures smiled that way. His grandmother had been dead more than fifteen years, and he still remembered the frightening way she came at him with those yellow teeth, the way they clicked together when she talked. Looking at Anna now, he shuddered.

She still turned him on, though.

He still wanted to kiss her, still wanted to bring her to him, rake his hands over her hair and body and pretend they were the only two people in the world. But just before falling asleep earlier, he'd made a decision—until the game was over and they had a real talk, he was done kissing her. He wouldn't play that way anymore. Though he wasn't exactly the purest of the pure when it came to relationships, he believed in the whole one man, one woman concept the Bible talked about. Unless Anna made whatever peace she needed to make with Ryan, he wouldn't try to worm his way into the guy's place. Ryan might be a first class jerk, but Jay didn't want to wind up a clone. He wasn't a thief. He didn't steal other people's women.

He unwound his hand from Anna's hair and bent to inspect the fire. He had grown warm without the need for flames, but it was time to move on. To think about something else. "Not bad." He nodded toward the blaze, then looked at her. "For a girl. A girl with a festering, rancid-looking foot, no less."

"My foot is not rancid, Jay. That's disgusting. And as for being female, women do almost everything better than men. It's a known fact. I read about it in—"

"Cosmopolitan? Along with twelve fail-proof tips to seduce your date Friday night?"

It was the wrong thing to say. Anna laughed, low and amused. Jay, however, eyed the snow, debating whether or not to throw himself face-first in it to cool off. When you didn't have cold showers readily available, sometimes a guy had to improvise.

As he geared up to jump, he realized something neither one of them had noticed. Sometime in the last ten minutes, the landscape had changed. And instead of an endless wall of gray, a hint of sun poked through the clouds. Even the trees seemed to stand taller, thankful for the depressing reprieve. That made two of them.

"Anna, it stopped snowing. Maybe now we can pack up and get out of here, if you think you're up for it."

***

The snow might have let up, but Anna's uneasy sense of foreboding, dread, and panic had piled high inside her mind. It built by the hour, nearly burying her, at times, in a weighted mass of despair. She wasn't stupid. They were on their last leg of the journey. According to the map, they had ten miles to go. According to the announcer, the map couldn't always be trusted.

She got her first hint that civilization was close by about an hour ago, when Jay spotted a cluster of trees that were recently chopped down, leaving nothing but six-inch stumps behind. It matched the one Anna had seen before they reached the last checkpoint, but back then, she hadn't given it more than a passing thought. Now, she knew the end was near. The reality sent her into freak-out mode.

What was she going to do? How could she leave Jay? How could she stay with Ryan? How could she live with herself if she made the wrong decision?

But then, the decision just might be made for her. Bit by bit, Jay already seemed to be pulling away. Not in any tangible way. If asked, she wouldn't be able to explain it. He still pulled her close, he still joked, he still kept her laughing without trying. But she could see it in his eyes, in the way they turned down at the corners when he thought she wasn't looking, as if he dreaded the end as much as she did.

Anxiety settled like a hot volcanic rock in her stomach every time she thought of it.

She was so rooted in her thoughts that she didn't notice the crater in front of her. Without warning, her foot landed in the sunken pile of snow and she fell deep. She wound up on her butt again, with a buried tree limb breaking her fall. Like a steak knife poised to cut all the wrong parts, it jabbed straight into her most uncomfortable area, and she yelped. If only she had screamed loud enough to cover up the sound of Jay's obnoxious laughter.

"If this were *Dancing with the Stars*, I'd give you a four. You really need to stick that landing a little better if you want to earn a higher mark." He reached out a hand, which she swiftly swatted away.

"You couldn't be more wrong." She tried to push herself to a standing position, but succeeded only in burying her arms to her elbows. Great. Now everything was cold and wet, and just when the fire had finally gotten them dry. "That's the best fall I've had so far. Should earn me at least a six.

She grunted and groaned, and finally after an exhausting amount of effort, she managed to find her feet. Although "find" was generous. In total, the snow had accumulated to at least thirteen inches, and not one bit of melting had occurred. Her feet were somewhere under there. She began the tedious task of clomping through the layers to catch up to Jay.

It wasn't until she went to toss him a glare that she spotted it.

"Jay, what is that?" She pointed through the trees to a thin, black strand of what appeared to be cable suspended in the air. A clump of snow fell off her glove.

"Where?" He squinted in the direction of her hand, his neck moving up and down trying to spot it. "I can't find what you're—" He stopped. His eyes went wide. "Are you kidding me? That's a power line, Anna. It's a power line."

She blinked rapidly at it, then at him, then back, unable to process what it all meant. "Do you think there's a house around here, then?" She could barely force out the words. A power line meant people lived around here, right? Because only people used power, right? Anna's gaze swept the area around them, searching. She didn't see a house. She certainly didn't see another human. Could this all be a cruel joke?

"I don't know. I can't imagine someone living this far away from anything."

"What does it mean, Jay?" She slammed a hand to her forehead, trying to make sense of things. They'd been out here so long that she was a tiny bit certain the power line was an illusion. A figment of two very overactive, underfed imaginations. Next, they'd be stumbling upon a Wal-Mart, overjoyed at the prospect of a nearby bag of powdered donuts. Still, she couldn't give up the fantasy, such a nice fantasy it was. She clutched his arm with her sopping glove and repeated the question. "What does a power line mean, Jay?"

He faced her, wild hope dancing across his eyes. "It means we're close Anna. This thing is almost over." He picked her up and swung her around, backpack, bulk, and all. He laughed, threw his head back and shouted. She laughed with him. She shouted with him.

All the while, a small part of her died inside.

Why did it feel like she was only going through the motions?

And why, two minutes later, when a red Rescue helicopter flew overhead, sending a fine dusting of snow swirling across the landscape around them, did she lose the ability to even fake a smile? Anna swiped the mist of snow from her eyes, thinking the same grim thought, over and over and over.

They were the only contestants left. The virtual guaranteed winners. Which meant the second they made it out of here, they would be declared the victors. They would celebrate. They would head their separate directions, go back to where they came from, and get back to normal.

Game over.

Chapter 30

Ryan Lance leaned over his Gucci bag and sifted through the contents inside. Three Italian silk ties, two Prada button downs, and a ridiculously expensive pair of black leather lace-ups that cost nearly as much as his top floor Michigan Avenue apartment. Nothing practical at all, which meant a complete overhaul in his wardrobe in record time before he needed to race back to the airport. Not that it mattered. The only thing he cared about now was the small item in his pocket that only he and two others knew about. But if things went as planned, the whole world would hear about it soon.

It was the *if* in that sentence—the unknown—that placed everything in question. That's why he needed to get to Alaska fast, make amends with Anna, and put this entire ordeal behind him. He knew she'd seen the photos. He wasn't naïve enough to think thirty days in the wilderness would keep her away from the news, not when television cameras were trained on her twenty-four-seven.

No, he was certain she knew about the affair. He just hoped she hadn't learned about anything else. Nothing would ruin his plans to join Alexander Lloyd's family. And definitely not his latest fling with that ridiculous Hollywood actress everyone in the media was so eager to talk about.

Because of her, Anna might dump him. And that couldn't happen. He would do just about anything to keep her around…whatever it took to keep his future from unraveling completely. He hadn't spent the last year being groomed for political life to let it slip away.

Ryan powered on his phone and scrolled through messages until he found the one he needed. He had a plan, one he'd set in motion long before he threw down that foolish challenge to Anna about auditioning for *The Alaskan Wild*.

Ryan checked his watch and mentally calculated the time. Three days, nine hours, and seventeen minutes. According to the producers, he had that much time to fly back to Chicago from his business trip, make arrangements, grab Anna's parents, and get to Alaska.

Anna wanted to know he was committed, so be it.

In three days she would get exactly what she'd been waiting for.

Chapter 31

"Well, you were right. Now let's see if we can find anything worthwhile inside," Jay said.

Anna reached for his arm. "Wait, you're just going to walk in there? What if someone's home? What if they call the police for breaking and entering?"

He barely looked at her as he grasped the door handle and gave it a little shake. "We're in the middle of the frozen tundra, Anna. I seriously doubt any cop cars could make it out here in time to arrest us." He rattled the knob harder, unable to make it turn. "But if they do, I'm counting on you to sacrifice yourself while I find something to eat. Do that for me, would you?"

"If anyone's getting arrested, it's you. This is your idea. And if there's any food inside this house, it's mine." She shoved him out of the way. "Move over and let me try. Seriously, do I have to do everything all the time?" With an upside down whack to the metal, the knob gave and the door creaked open.

She seared him with a look and led the way through the cabin's weather-beaten front door. Her first break-in. Her parents would be so proud. That thought alone sent a pleasant rush of adrenaline through her, quickly followed by a sharp slap of guilt. Even here, her upbringing wouldn't give her a break. Bits of the door's leftover stained finish fell from the door like flecks of dandruff and scattered over the entryway. The home smelled like must, mold, and—oddest of all—paint thinner.

"I think this place is haunted," she said. Cobwebs clung to every corner, the wood floor bore a dull gray pallor that appeared to come from a good half-inch of dirt, and a strange whistling skirted through the rooms like a muted whisper.

"It's isn't haunted, but listen to that wind," Jay commented.

"It probably isn't wind at all. More like the spirit of a woman murdered by her crazy son and left decomposing in a wooden rocking chair in front of the dreary attic window."

Jay rolled his eyes. "You watch too many movies." He stepped around her and headed for the kitchen as if he held the deed to the place. Just like that, he began opening cabinet doors. He slammed one closed, and then the other before starting on the drawers. The room whistled again, pebbling her skin. She shivered.

"Oh, really? I dare you to get in the shower and see if Norman comes at you with a knife." Anna opened a drawer; empty.

"You'd like to get me in the shower, wouldn't you?"

Anna laughed. "Oh, we're back there again? Please. If I wanted to get you in the shower—" She opened an upper cabinet door and gasped. "Jay, I found something!" Reaching up on tiptoes, she grasped onto a burlap bag that looked like it came from the nineteen-fifties and pulled it down. "What do you think is inside?"

Jay pulled on an old-fashioned drawstring sewn into the material. "Well, it's either rice—since it says *rice* on the label here..." He was a kindergartener teacher trying to teach a girl to read her first words. "...Or it's the bones of Janet Leigh stuffed inside real tight. In that case, we can finally give her a proper burial."

Anna glared at him until the bag gave way and nearly unraveled her emotions. With a cautious glance in her direction, Jay reached his hand inside and pulled out the contents. Tears welled in her eyes as a thousand grains of brown rice waterfalled through his fingers.

"Let's cook it!" She opened a cabinet door in search of a pan. Finding nothing but a rusty metal rolling pin and a roll of chalky, disintegrating paper towels, she headed outside to retrieve the pan clipped to her backpack. "I've got a pot to cook it in," she said when she walked back inside. She flipped on the faucet over the kitchen sink and was greeted by the sound of nothingness. The pipes didn't even groan in protest. "Okay, new idea," she muttered. "Let's fill the pan with snow and build a fire." She stopped in her tracks when she saw Jay's long face. "What's wrong? Why aren't you helping me?"

"Because I don't think we should eat it."

She slammed a hand on her hip. "Look, I get that you're an honest guy, I really do. And I understand that I was the one who didn't want to break in here in the first place, but now is not the time to worry about helping ourselves to—"

"Half the rice is moving," he said without looking up.

Her mouth fell. For once in her life, she had no words. She swallowed, wishing she could unhear what he had just told her, longing for the days when the strangest thing she'd ever eaten was a porcupine. Had that only been last week?

Anna stared at the burlap bag, imagining all sorts of unpleasant things buried inside. She swore she saw it give a little. Her stomach lurched, because the only thing she could imagine squirming around in that much rice was...

"What color are the moving things?"

"White," he answered, his face a little pale. Wiggly white things. So much worse than worms.

She palmed her stomach and took a shuddering breath. One of these days, she would learn to leave well enough alone and become more of a *yes* girl. *Wouldn't you rather stay home instead of needing one last shot of adventure?* Yes, Dad. *Don't you think you should spend more time worrying about Ryan and less time chasing these ridiculous dreams?* Yes, Mom. Instead, she had told them both no, hopped on the first plane to Alaska, and now faced the prospect of dining on a bag full of maggots. This was where that foolish independent streak had gotten her.

"What should we do?" The question was barely a whisper, laced with equal amounts of hope and fear.

Jay stood up and brushed his hands together. "The way I see it, we have two options. But you're not going to like either one."

His confidence in her was touching. "Well, if you're so certain I'm going to hate both, then just pick one and be done with it."

"Then search in the cabinets for two bowls, because we're getting ready to do some separating."

***

"I can't believe I let you talk me into this."

"I believe your exact words were "just pick one and be done with it." Jay flipped through the rice in his palm, plucked one offending creature, and emptied both hands into their respective bowls. The white side wiggled erratically, welcoming their new guest. Anna shuddered all over again.

"And you pick *now* to listen to me? After three weeks off doing your own thing no matter what I've said. That's awfully chivalrous of you, but your timing stinks."

"Sweetheart, I gave up chivalry with you a long time ago." He reached in the bag for more rice and bugs. "And as for the timing, if I waited on you to make a decision, we'd still be sawing the limbs off the tree, more likely dead inside that cave."

Resisting the urge to squeal like a girl, she dropped a nasty worm into the bowl and wiped off her hand. "*You'd* be dead. I'd still be alive, because I would've feasted on your leftover body parts until someone came along to rescue me." She adopted a threatening glare, all the while loving the way he called her sweetheart. Of all the things she would miss, his endearment would top the list. Along with his smile, his wavy hair as it fell over one eyebrow, his smoldering eyes, the way his muscles moved under his sweater while he built a fire...

"Leftover body parts?" He dropped another worm into a bowl and eyed her with amusement. "As if you would be able to stomach that. Do you realize your skin is half-green just thinking about this rice?"

She picked up a few grains of rice and threw it as him, saying nothing when what looked like a tiny white grain slipped down the front of his collar. She would miss this, too. The bickering. The teasing. All of it.

Against her better judgment, Anna's mind flashed to their last kiss, to the promise he'd made to never let it happen again. She studied her hands for a moment before locking eyes with Jay's.

They sat that way for several minutes, neither of them able to look away.

Chapter 32

"My best guess is that we'll be finished in the next three days or so, assuming the map is correct." Anna just looked at him, the stirrings of boldness beginning to inch up her spine. One of them needed to be honest, and frankly, she was exhausted by her own thoughts. She shook her head. "You know, I'm not ready for this game to be over. If I had it my way, I wouldn't ever leave. And as far as putting it behind me, I'm not sure I'll ever be able to do that. Because the way I see it, forgetting about this trip means forgetting about you. And I'm not going to be able to do that, Jay."

She felt his eyes on her, golden flecks of summer sun burning like hot rays on her persistently frigid head. Though she tried to ignore him by focusing painstaking attention on her hands, it didn't take long to realize he wouldn't give up staring until she acknowledged him. Finally, she looked up. His eyes were nearly her unraveling. She expected understanding. A little tenderness, maybe. What she got was the jagged points of anger aimed straight for her head.

"What do you want, Anna? Because I know what I want. I've known it for awhile. But something tells me I'm not going to come out a winner in this adventure." He wasn't talking about the reality show, and they both knew it. With a frustrated groan, he shoved aside his bowl. It wobbled to the left before it banked right and settled again. From his spot sitting cross-legged on the dusty floor in front of her, Jay clasped his hands together and delivered a well-placed glower. She felt the demand coming before he issued it, and like everything else in her life, she was unprepared and completely unsure.

"So tell me, Anna, when this is all over, who is going to lose?" He gave a rough gesture across the space between them. "Me, you, or both of us? Because from my viewpoint, the answer to that question lies completely with you." He usually liked his women a little less predictable, but there Anna sat, blinking at him wide-eyed like a deer caught on the wrong end of a hunter's rifle. A bad metaphor out here, but that was beside the point. And somehow in spite of it, he was completely, inexplicably turned on. What red-blooded American male wouldn't be? He was alone with this hottest woman he'd ever laid eyes on.

He rolled his eyes, convinced this entire situation was nothing more than God's big joke on his personal life. If only the man upstairs had kept him home, none of this would have happened. But He had other plans. And Jay was mad. Because of all the women in the universe, he had to go and fall for Anna freaking Lloyd. A woman shackled to her overbearing parents like a disease with no cure.

Maybe that sentiment wasn't fair. Maybe he didn't care.

Looking at her now, his heart gave a hopeless thud as the reality of his situation crashed over him like a storm. He loved her. Oh, dear God, he loved her. He was in love with Anna Lloyd. And she belonged to someone else. And in a few short days, it would all be over. His foolish indulgence in chasing a little fun had led to this moment where his whole life was falling apart. When he started this, he'd wanted a thrill. Well, Anna had given him one, and he was headed home without her.

Why, God? Even he knew his prayer was more ticked off and self-pitying than anything else. *What have I done to deserve this?*

"You know what, Anna? Don't answer that." He stood and made a dismissive gesture. "I'm going to start a fire." He limped off in a pathetic attempt to show indignation. Dang foot.

And dang Anna for giving him this dang foot.

He reached for the door handle, sticky from old gas fumes and long stretches of dormancy, and flung it open, satisfied with the way it bounced back and hit the wall, as if it were as angry as him. A blast of arctic air slammed into his face, but even that didn't temper his frustration. He nearly made it outside before the sound of her voice stopped him cold.

"Jay, wait."

And just like that, his anger deflated. For a moment, he thought about ignoring her, stoking his anger a little more, and searching for sticks. He turned in the doorway to face her. Sunlight from the afternoon sun speared her with a direct hit, bathing her in a glow that made her look almost ethereal. An angel. His angel. Except like a real heavenly host, he had no tangible grasp on her and likely never would.

"What, Anna?" His voice was hoarse with emotion. "I get that you don't want to talk about this right now, so just...just let me build a fire." He slapped the doorframe and started to turn.

"Jay, wait," she said again, setting the bowl down in front of her. She stood and walked toward him, stopping an arm's length away, hugging her arms to her chest. Self-preservation. He recognized the gesture. "It just...there are plans for me, Jay. So much more involved here than a simple breakup. I need more time. Please don't be upset with me."

"Too late." With his emotions suffering from a rough case of whiplash, he turned and whirled on her. "The way I see it, we have about fifty-two hours until we make it out of this wasteland. Then one of two things happens. You go your way, I go mine. Or we stick together and see if we can make something of...." He moved his finger back and forth in the space between them, "...this. Of us. Which is it going to be?" A bird chose that moment to squawk overhead. They both scowled up at it. Of course *now* they would see one, when neither of them was holding a rifle.

Turning her attention back to Jay, she nailed him with an icy glare. "So you're saying I have five minutes to figure this out? You need to know now, before I even *talk* to Ryan?"

"Yes, that's what I'm saying." Finally, a branch he could grab.

"You are out of your mind." She turned to stalk away, but could only manage a limp. He might have laughed if it were one bit funny.

"Well, that makes two of us," he said. "You're a friggin' head case, and I must be completely crazy to be attracted to you." He broke the limb in half over his knee.

Her head snapped around. "Whose fault is that? I look like crap, I feel worse, and we both know I'll need at least three showers to look human again. If you have feelings for me, one look at Heidi's perfect perfectness at the finish line will cure you like that." She snapped her fingers and yanked two pine cones off the ground.

"Would you stop bringing up Heidi?" He tossed his sticks down. Perfect spot for a fire. "I don't even like that girl, and you act like we have some secret fling happening behind the scenes."

"And you would if she had anything to say about it." She glared at him. "Besides, the only reason you feel anything for me at all is because I'm the only one here. Give it five minutes after we're done and you'll get over it. *Then* you can date Heidi."

"Would you leave her out of this? And besides, do you really think so little of me? Of *yourself*?" He raised his arms out and practically shouted at her. "Do you have any idea how beautiful you are?"

He hadn't expected her laugh. "Oh, that's rich. One minute I'm a head case, and the next minute I'm beautiful? Make up your mind, Jay. You can't have it both ways."

"I *want* it both ways. That's what I'm trying to tell you, but you're too pig-headed to listen!" He yelled at the sky. "The most pig-headed woman I've ever met!"

"Yet you want me to dump Ryan without even talking to him and move on with you," she deadpanned.

He rubbed the back of his neck and took a deep breath. No one had ever accused him of being sane.

He studied the ground for another moment, then dragged his gaze up to hers. "Tell me you're happy, Anna. Tell me you're happy, that you're in love with your boyfriend, and I won't say another word."

"You don't know how *not* to say another word." A non-answer if he ever heard one.

He waited, knowing he was asking a lot. He also knew that he couldn't go home without knowing…without saying it.

He'd lived with too much regret in his life to pile on more.

"I love you. Do you know that?" The words should have rattled him or made him question being so impulsive, but they were exactly right. He'd never been more certain about anything. "Maybe I'm crazy. Maybe I expect too much. Maybe…" He looked up at the sky and dragged in a slow breath. "Maybe a lot of things. But life's too short to keep things inside, and you deserve someone who loves you. I just thought you should know." He turned to seek out the lighter, to do anything but stand here.

"Jay, don't…" She touched his arm, and he stopped. "Please don't walk away. Not when I haven't told you how I feel."

He turned to face her. "Well, you got me to stop," Jay said. "Is there anything you want to say, or am I just supposed to stand here all day?"

"No...there's something I want to say."

Silence stretched. His eyebrow went up. "Need more time? Fine. I'm going to make a fire." Jay turned to leave.

Anna shot forward and grabbed his arm. "Why do you always do that?"

"Do what?" He shoved a hand across his bandana before he ripped it off and fisted it. His hair stuck up in all directions. "Enlighten me please, on my personality flaws."

"Well, first of all there's the seriously questionable taste in hairstyles..."

He smashed his hands to his head and pressed down, then sent a pinecone flying with a swift kick at the snow. Miraculously, it landed on top of the firewood. Perfect kindling.

"Then there's the sunny disposition and hostility toward nature," she continued.

He scowled at her. "Cut the crap, Anna."

Anna sucked in a breath. Confrontation wasn't her favorite thing.

Her mouth opened on a retort, but she slowly closed it.

Standing here now, she grew uncomfortably aware that there was something pathetic about a twenty-six year old woman still trying to win her parent's approval. When she was younger, she dreamed of fairytales and princes and happily ever after. Now, she believed in nothing but disappointment. And there Jay stood, her partner in this adventure she didn't want to end, transferring his own disappointment straight at her.

"You have no idea what I deserve," she said. She wrapped her arms around her waist, chilled more from the look in his eyes than the weather. "You've known me for, like, four weeks. You can't possibly know much about a person in that short of time."

"I'm great at reading people," he said. "You're like an open book, some pages scribbled on, some pages ripped, some torn out altogether—all kinds of missing pieces scattered everywhere." The words sounded harsh, but they were delivered with the gentlest caress. "But I'm pretty sure I know your whole story anyway."

"Then tell me what I'm thinking about right now." Her voice wobbled on the last word. She didn't want to know. Based on recent history, she had no doubt Jay would guess everything spot on.

He took in her eyes, her lips, her neck, gathering up answers before his gaze locked with hers again.

"You're thinking you allowed yourself to fall in love with Ryan, and since then he's trampled all over you. You're thinking your parents have heaped all kinds of unfair expectations on you, but being the dutiful *only* child you've always been—a girl, no less, instead of the boy they dreamed of to carry on your father's legacy—you've let them dictate your life because it's your job to make them happy." He tilted his head to the side and looked straight into her soul, most likely unaware he was doing it. She hugged herself tighter, uncomfortable with the scrutiny "You're thinking that if you were a braver person, you'd put a stop to it now. And you're thinking you're not brave, so you're stuck."

Unable to speak around the weight constraining her lungs, she merely shook her head in agreement.

Jay bit his lower lip, dragged his eyes toward her mouth and held them there as her pulse throbbed, every part of her on edge. She didn't know how he managed to do it, but once again he'd read her mind. It had happened so often these last weeks that she gave up trying to count. Jay understood her in ways no one ever had. He sparred with her, met her insult for insult and accepted her fully. Because of it, this man had worked his way into her heart in every way that mattered, and all at once she knew. Tears filled her eyes because she knew.

She loved him. In under four weeks' time and completely unexpected, she had fallen for him. For his obnoxious sense of humor and his sometimes crass behavior. For his boyish charm and verging-on-cocky self-confidence. For his gentle demeanor and caring spirit.

"I'm not trying to make you cry." He reached up and caught her first tear, then rubbed it away between his gloved fingertips.

"You always manage to do it anyway." Her breathy laugh fell flat.

For awhile they studied each other, and when she couldn't take it any longer, she reached for his coat and fingered the hem, lingering on a button as her pulse pounded in her throat. She didn't know what to say to him, but she knew how she felt. And despite illness and hunger and broken-down bodies, she wanted him to kiss her. She wanted to kiss him back. She wanted to know, just once, what it felt like to be so completely understood and cherished. The heat radiating off his coat told her he wanted the same thing, so she took a step forward, her hand stealing up his chest, his neck. Her heart soared when his fingers closed around her wrist.

And plummeted when he pulled it back down to her side.

"I promised I wouldn't kiss you again, and I always keep my word." His gaze was like a smoldering ember. She swallowed, thrown off by the words she hadn't expected. In another world, she might have been embarrassed. As it stood now, she was too stunned to consider it.

"After everything you just said? After you basically just opened up my mind and dissected it piece by piece?" Her shock fell away as anger slid in its place. "I'm not going to tell anyone if you break that moral code of yours." Did she sound desperate? She was *not* desperate. But she wanted him to kiss her.

He knew it, too. A corner of his mouth turned up on a smirk. "I get that you're having trouble controlling yourself right now. I mean," he used his hand to give an obnoxious sweep down his own body, "look at me. I'm irresistible. Eye candy for the romantically bereft…"

"Candy makes you fat, and I'm hardly bereft." She turned to stalk away, for no real reason except the jerk was making fun of her and she didn't know what else to do. Standing there while he laughed at her wasn't an option. She'd waited her whole life for someone to love her back without strings or expectations or a whole plethora of pressure behind it. Before she could separate or process any of them, he hit her with a half-lidded stare that made her knees go weak. "Fine, you want me to kiss you? I'll kiss you."

His head dipped, her chin lifted, and before she could remember to blink, his mouth crushed hers in the craziest kiss she'd ever experienced. The softest threads of pleasure unraveled inside her as he moved in closer, dug his fingers into her hair and slid them over her earlobes, her jaw, her neck. She nearly melted, struck that somehow in the midst of the coldest Alaskan snowstorm, she'd been swept away on the warmest ocean wave.

And then without warning, the wave dragged her under when he unwound himself from her, stepped away, and brushed a piece of bark off his coat. Her mouth remained open with unfulfilled desire.

"There. I did what you wanted," he said, stretching his arms behind him. "At least we got that out of the way."

She blinked, waited for her eyes to focus, and saw red.

Had he just—?

And then she just——?

She slammed a hand on her hip. "Was that supposed to be some kind of test?"

"Yep. And judging by your reaction, I'm giving myself a big, fat A-plus. On the mind reading and the make-out session. You, on the other hand, could use a little work."

"I wasn't even trying. In fact, had I realized earlier your skills were so lacking, I never would have kissed you in the first place." She dragged a hand over her still-burning lips. That kiss had been so good, so soft, so...so...wrong on every single level. She wanted to take it back, rewind time and punch herself for falling under his romantic spell.

"I don't seem to recall you feeling that way the first time." His mouth cocked on a lazy smile. "Or the second. Or just now, on the third..."

"Well, there won't be a fourth!"

"So I've heard, over and over and over." He hesitated, then took a slow step forward until they were eye to eye. "And I've decided you're right. Enough is enough." All humor left, and his voice dropped to a hoarse whisper. His fingers came up to graze her face, a touch lighter than a sigh. "We might as well end this now."

Anna blinked, baffled and confused, pulse throbbing from his soft caress. *End it? How could they end something that hadn't even started? How could they——?* And then she understood. At that moment, she realized he wasn't the only mind-reader among them. It was as if a film had been yanked from her eyes, unveiling with perfect clarity the last ten minutes.

Jay Maddox had bared his soul and looked straight into hers. He'd told her he loved her and sliced up her life. He'd been vulnerable and kissed her without pretense. Jay Maddox had shown her a glimpse of his deepest feelings; now, Jay Maddox was giving her an out.

Now the fate of their relationship was up to her.

Chapter 33

Jay rattled the lock to make sure it was secure and stepped back from the cabin, feeling like he was leaving the only source of stability they'd seen in weeks.

"Need help with your pack?" he asked her.

"No, I've got it."

He ignored her and picked it up, then held it open while she shoved first one arm through a strap, then the other. He turned her around and clipped the straps together, then, before he could risk glancing into those ocean eyes and giving in to the pull of her again, he turned away to kick snow on the fire's remaining embers.

"Alright, let's go."

She glanced backward for a long moment before settling her gaze on him. "I don't want to leave this cabin."

"Think you might miss all the cobwebs and maggots, do you?" The top layer of icy, melted snow crunched beneath Jay's feet, then double-timed when she caught up to him.

"Especially the cobwebs. And old plaid sofas. I think I might buy one when I get home." Anna pulled her hat lower across her forehead.

He nodded. "You should, and I just might put myself on a rice-only diet for the rest of the year." She smiled over at him.

"Okay, so…movies," Jay said. "We've already established that your favorites are the worst of all time." He gave her a sidelong glance, grinning when her sad expression turned into a soft smile. "With the exception of Monty Python, of course. So now, onto music. Who's your favorite singer? Spill it."

She sniffed. "That's easy. Adam—"

"Do *not* say Adam Levine," he said before she could finish. As he knew would happen, she actually attempted to look outraged.

"I wasn't going to say him."

He made a disgusted noise. "Yes, you were."

"No, I wasn't. I was going to say Adam…Ant."

He raised an eyebrow. "Adam Ant, sure. Quick, right now, sing me a line from your favorite song. Ready, go." He held out his hand like a microphone and waited. Nothing. Nothing but sputtering lips.

"I don't have to sing for you." She swatted his hand away from her face. "Besides, what's so wrong with Adam Levine? What'd he ever do to you?"

He rolled his eyes. "Nothing but look perfect and have every woman in America swooning for him, that's all. Besides, he sings like a girl."

She raised an eyebrow. "Jealous, much? And he does not sing like a girl. And…swooning? Seriously, are you a sixty-year-old man from nineteen-fifty?"

"There is nothing wrong with the word *swooning*."

"Sure there isn't. If you're a woman." She raised her foot behind her and kicked his rear. They walked a few steps in comfortable silence. "So tell me yours."

He looked up at the sky and took a deep breath. Maybe it was his imagination, but the tree line seemed to be thinning out. A clearing of sorts appeared to be up ahead. Different than all the other clearings they had stumbled on so far, in that there didn't appear to be anything beyond it. His pulse tripped a little with dread, but he said nothing.

"I don't have a favorite singer, but I do have a favorite style of music."

She slipped a finger under her hat and ran it along her hairline. These caps were getting on both their nerves, and even though he didn't want to be, he was hyper-aware of all her movements today. "Which is?"

He cleared his throat. "Some would call it hardcore. Others would call it metal. Back in the eighties they called it punk rock."

When she said nothing for a long moment, he glanced over and nearly laughed. She looked at him like he'd dropped out of the sky from Mars, complete with horns made of crystals and a rainbow-colored body. Totally and inexplicably baffled.

"You've got to be kidding me."

"No, I'm not kidding. Why is that so hard to believe?"

She continued to stare at him. "Because you're...you. I figured you were into ballads or...or... boy bands."

He shot her a death glare and decided to avoid that attack on his musical tastes. "It isn't like I'm into the whole biting-the-head-off-the-bat thing. I just like my music loud."

He didn't know why, but something about that statement appealed to her. For the next five minutes, she didn't stop smiling.

***He was a mass of tangled contradictions. A web of layers she could no longer decipher. A puzzle missing corners and a few middle pieces. She liked it that way. Liked *him* that way. Just when she thought she had him figured out, he threw her a new one.

The guy liked hardcore. *She* liked hardcore, but outside the confines of her car, she hadn't listened to it in years. Instead, she divided her time between old Elvis Costello and the occasional Rod

Stewart—the newer bluesy stuff, none of the seventies crap, as Ryan so often referred to it.

This latest revelation was just the next thing in a series that left her confused. Jay both cussed and prayed. He was young and wise beyond his years. He was gentle and he had a temper. He was kind and sarcastic. Happy and sad. Tender and strong. Filthy and so dang good looking. But what really threw her—what really kept her shaking her head—was that he believed in her—as is, no strings attached. For the first time in her life, Anna felt understood.

She reflected on it for a few moments, until Jay tripped over something in their path. Something metal. Something that sent her adrenaline pumping and plunging at the same time, an uncomfortable side-effect of being both elated and crushed in a single heartbeat. Of all the things she expected to see out here—another cabin, a hunter, an Eskimo pointing them to the nearest exit—this wasn't it. She couldn't explain why she was so surprised, she just was.

An hour later they sat side by side on another sawed-off tree stump, both staring down a long strip of white and gray, trying to decide what to do.

"Should we wait to see what happens, or follow this and see where it leads?" Anna asked again. She looked to the right, then all the way to the left as far as she could see. But there was nothing. Nothing but that blasted strip of metal.

"The first thing we're going to do is check out your foot. I haven't seen it today, and I want to know what we're working with."

She nearly protested, came close to telling him once again how ridiculous he was being. That just because he snapped his fingers didn't mean she should have to remove her shoe in all this snow. She resented it because it made her even colder than she already was. She turned to tell him as much. But then she saw his face.

She knew what he was doing. Could read his mind the same way he often read hers. Their journey was nearly over, made painfully real by this unexpected strip of railroad track they both stared at now. In very little time—an hour? a day? two? however long it took for a train to pass—their journey would be complete. Glancing at him now, she could see the relief, but also the regret. She didn't need to see her reflection to know it was mirrored in her own eyes. His expression cut like a wound she couldn't soothe, bone deep and aching.

She slid her hands up and down her thighs a few times to try anyway.

When that didn't work, she reluctantly began to remove her hiking boot, aware of his eyes on her every move.

"Here," Jay said, "let me do it." He patted her thigh and held out his hand, wagging his fingers until she deposited her foot in his lap. She could have told him it was better and saved him the trouble of checking, but she wanted to be fussed over. Years of being raised to be independent to a fault, and in less than a month she'd grown to depend on someone else's care. There was no way to fix this, no way to forget what it felt like.

He slipped off her boot, then gently pulled away her sock. The intimacy in those two simple acts made the blast of cold air feel like nothing but a soft breeze.

"See? It's fine." She wiggled her toes to mask the strain in her voice. If Jay noticed, he didn't say anything.

"It looks better, I'll give you that much. But it's hardly fine." His strong hand glided over her ankle and up her lower calf with the gentlest touch. A tingling started at the back of her neck and worked its way downward. She barely controlled a shiver that had nothing to do with the weather. "See this?" He tapped at a spot just above her big toe. "The swelling has gone down, but only because it's beginning to spread out. The area wasn't this large yesterday."

"But I can walk now, and that's really all that matters."

"Said the wheelchair bound man right before he lost his legs."

Anna gave him a reproachful look that quickly faded into submission when he began to knead her calf muscles. "I'm not going to lose my leg." Not that she cared. She closed her eyes and leaned back, barely suppressing a moan. "I would, however, like to lose this coat. And this thing on my head." She pointed to her hat. "And the hair currently growing on my legs. I swear, I look like a guy."

She heard him smile. "Trust me, you look nothing like a guy. In fact, you're more beautiful than ever." She blushed, feeling his eyes on her, but didn't dare look at him. She couldn't, not when she knew what she would find. Love…all over his expression.

"Thank you, Jay," she said.

For everything.

And with sadness pressing in around her, she turned her head away and stared numbly down the long stretch of abandoned railroad, knowing that same track would eventually carry them away from here.

Chapter 34

They made it less than a mile before they heard the whistle. Jay looked up to see a plume of smoke heading straight for them and waited for the elation to take over. The relief he should feel at having this torturous journey over. Any minute now he would have only his second decent meal in a month. But even that didn't conjure up any enthusiasm. Instead, he felt nothing but a consuming wave of anger and more than a little panic. Forget his resolve to pressure her; the woman might want to ruin her own life, but that didn't mean she had to ruin his.

"So you're good with this?" he asked, stepping on yet another ice-slicked railroad tie. They'd walked over thousands in the past couple hours, having left the tree stump in search of civilization. He didn't even try to mask the accusation in his voice. "Because it's over now, this little game." His voice rose an octave, the occasional word echoing off the cotton-topped mountains.

"What do you want me to do, Jay? Leave Ryan and tell my family to forget their plans? You keep dancing around it, keep telling me you're not going to pressure me. You keep telling me to make my own decisions, but you don't like the ones I've made. Like everyone else, you want me to do what you want."

"That isn't fair, and you know it."

"It is fair. You want me to choose you. Just say it. You want me to leave everyone else and choose you. That's why you told me you love me, right?"

Her insinuation ticked him off. "I didn't lie, if that\s what you're asking. But that isn't the point. That's never been the point." Her inability to see the obvious truth drove him nuts.

"Then what's the point?" She took a step closer and yelled in his face. "What's the point?"

"What do you want, Anna? Stop thinking about what everyone else wants. Your parents with their ridiculous expectations that no one, *no one*, should put on their kid, no matter how old she is—"

"I'm not that old!"

"Shut up and let me finish!" He raked a hand through his hair and looked down, trying to catch his breath. When he was calm enough to speak without yelling, he looked up. The train bellowed in the distance, closer this time.

"What do you want?" he finally asked. "Forget about expectations. Forget about your parents, forget about Ryan. For the love of God in heaven, forget about me." He slammed a hand to his chest. "What do you want, Anna? Even if it isn't what I want to hear. I can handle it, whatever you have to say." Another whistle. Coming closer.

He watched as her eyes darted left, then right, then back again. She gnawed her lip, swallowed once, then twice. Glanced at the train, at the mountain beside them. A woman trapped. The bravest woman he'd ever met, afraid of her own desires. When he couldn't take it anymore, he reached out his hand and trailed it down her arm. The simple touch snapped her eyes up to him.

She didn't have to speak for him to see the panic in her eyes. "I want to stay here, with you."

He tried a dull smile and ran a thumb across her cheek. "We both know staying in Alaska isn't an option." The sound of squealing brakes caused his pulse to pick up speed. The pressure in his chest made breathing nearly impossible. "So I'm going to ask you one last time, the choice is yours." He wouldn't beg. He hadn't begged since the week his father died and his mother hadn't bothered coming to the funeral. He tipped her chin up to meet his gaze.

"Who's it gonna be, Anna? Me or Ryan?"

Begging. Had it really come to this? Jay swallowed his pride.

"Spill it, Anna."

***

He hadn't stopped kissing her since they hopped on the train. They started before it pulled to a stop beside them, breaking apart for a moment to toss their backpacks onto the wooden floor, thank the conductor, and heave themselves up. They collapsed in a heap side by side, not knowing where they were headed. Away from the wilderness, that was all that mattered. Anna tucked herself into the space between his legs. Exhausted, they leaned back against the wall. It took only a few seconds for her head to turn and find him again. It took even less time for him to respond. He still couldn't get over the fact that she had chosen him, that in the time it took her to answer, their adventure had gone from ending to just getting started.

Spill it, Anna.

And with one step forward, one glance up into his face, and one tug on his shirt—she chose him. A wave of relief nearly sent him fist-pumping into the frigid Alaskan air. Instead, he grinned and crushed his mouth with hers before the train slowed to a stop beside them. The ten minutes they sat locked together since only confirmed her choice, and he'd never been happier.

Jay's hands came up to frame her face again as a heady rush of desire came over him. Even the overpowering scent of sawdust, the faint hint of manure, and the filminess of two people who hadn't showered in weeks couldn't break through the headiness. She tasted like an earthy mix of dirt and sunshine, and she was with him. No matter what they faced at the end of this line, he wouldn't have to tell her goodbye.

He shifted, and a sliver of weathered wood from the train's wall jabbed into his back, slashing through his muddled senses. It wasn't enough of a stab to fully distract him. He simply nudged the offensive plank away with a flick of a finger and pulled her closer. Nothing broke his hold, not exhaustion, not uncertainty, not worry about what waited for them when the train stopped moving. Certainly not a splinter. Nothing except the lurch of the train as it finally pressed on the brakes and announced their arrival back in civilization. For the first time in awhile, he was thrilled with the idea of this journey ending.

Anna dragged her mouth from his, her full lips all puffy and pink. "We're here already?" The blue centers of her eyes searched his before she broke contact and scanned the area around them. Other than a fine layer of straw, a few dead bugs, and piles of wood shavings, there wasn't much to see.

He tucked her hair behind her ear, recognizing raw nerves when he saw it and doing his best to ease her fears. "I would think you of all people would be ready to be here. Back to civilization, back to a doctor, back to McDonalds."

That earned a smile, and her stomach growled on cue. But still, she didn't say anything, just sat staring at the ground, a tell-tale crease between her eyebrows that sent his gut spiraling downward.

"Anna, I have no idea what waits for us when we step off this car." He heard the faint sound of helicopter blades even before he said the words. "But you've got to face everyone eventually. And I'll be right beside you the whole time."

She glanced upward, listening as the knives chopped through the air, appearing worried they might slice into her. A shadowed smile tried to reach her eyes at the same time an ocean began to fill them. "Thank you, Jay. For all of this. You have no idea how much it means to—"

He pressed a finger to her lips. "I know exactly how much it means. So enough with the thank you's, or we'll be here all day." He palmed her face with both hands and brushed his thumbs under her eyes to catch the wetness, then stood to help her up. They might as well face this now, whatever firestorm awaited them. With any luck, they wouldn't get burned in the process.

For the first time, some of Anna's apprehension rubbed off on him. Neither of them knew what awaited them on the other side of this car, and he didn't exactly relish the idea of finding out. He was sweaty, exhausted, and completely changed from the man who began this adventure. The thought of going backwards ushered in the first pang of a headache.

"Let's get this over with." He reached for the door handle and gave it a tug. "This must be what a cow feel likes right before it goes off to slaughter."

"Or what a criminal feels like just before she faces the noose."

Jay paused, caught off guard by the look on her face. She no longer looked worried, she looked sick. Terrified. "Stick with me, kid. Today's the first day of the rest of your life," he said, wondering if she would get the reference.

She didn't disappoint him. "I hated *American Beauty*. Stupid men and their mid-life crises." She looked away and didn't say anything for a minute, mulling something over in her mind before she finally sighed and nodded toward the door. "Alright, open it up."

He did as she asked, unable to shake the feeling he was making a mistake.

Chapter 35

Sunlight sent pricks of pain into their eyes as Jay pulled the door open the rest of the way. Standing in the shadows, they both blinked into the brightness, the aroma of winter and cologne hitting them from their spot on the old car.

"Hey, I might find myself in the middle of a crisis one day," Jay said over his shoulder. "And as far as your questionable taste in movies goes..." The rest of the words died on his lips as his vision cleared to reveal the sight in front of them. Anna may have been the one worried, but Jay found himself skirting the edges of a nervous breakdown. People. Dozens—no, hundreds. All with cameras trained on them. Big, industrial cameras with labels mounted atop like red flags issuing a warning: *Take another step, and face the consequences.* He squinted through blinding flashes to read the familiar, though incomprehensible words. ABC...CBS...Fox News...CNN. People everywhere. People in jeans. People in coats. People in suits.

He scanned the crowd, overwhelmed by the size, overwhelmed by the lights, needing something to focus on. He found it in the form of two curious onlookers staring straight at them from their spot front and center. They stood hand in hand and looked exactly like he remembered from news clippings—polished, well-groomed, confident, and dripping with money. The woman wore a Burberry coat buttoned to her chin. The man's Louis Vuitton boots were easy for even a hick from Texas to make out. Anna's resemblance to both her parent's was unmistakable. For only the second time since they began this journey, he felt way out of her league.

Jay's gaze shifted to Ryan, standing next to Anna's father like a puppy ready and waiting to play fetch. Eager. Twitchy. His tail practically wagging between his legs. Yet somehow he still managed to appear incredibly confident, like nothing...no one...could unravel his carefully crafted life in spite of the poor choices he'd recently made.

Jay suddenly felt inferior; unsure. Maybe Ryan was right.

He slowly hopped off the train and reached up to help Anna down, linking her hands in his and depositing her next to him. Turning back for their bags, he shouldered both to spare her the effort. Questions began firing at them before they turned around.

"Anna, how do you feel on your big day?"

Her big day?

"Are you nervous to be back?"

Nervous about these cameras aimed at our faces.

"What did you do for food? You look like you haven't eaten in days."

Because we haven't.

"How did you manage to cross the terrain when you were obviously so ill prepared?"

Wait just a second.

But before he could respond Dean Passmore, the show's announcer, appeared freshly spray tanned and highlighted, and held up his hand to stop the commotion. Cameras from various news stations swung his direction as he attempted to control the situation. With a glance toward Anna's family, he pushed past Jay and headed straight for her.

"Anna, how does it feel to be back with your family?" Despite bringing a shaking hand to her hairline, Anna held it together. "They've been here for two days, anxiously awaiting your return."

"Two days?" Anna said. "Why?"

The announcer blinked at her and looked around, a glimmer of amusement tweaking the corners of his mouth. "Because you're late." His eyebrows worked against artificial gravity and pushed together in mock contemplation. "Were you not aware of this? Ms. Lloyd, according to the cameras that were following you the whole time— until you dropped off the radar, that is—most of America thought you would be here forty-eight hours ago. Your family is here to surprise you, though hopefully it hasn't been ruined by the poor timing of you and your companion."

Her companion? Confused, Jay focused on that bit of crappiness for a moment. After everything he'd gone through for this show, and now he was nothing more than Anna Lloyd's companion? He tried to get angry, but then remembered the second part of Dean Passmore's sentence.

A surprise? What kind of surprise could her family possibly have planned for a television show? He couldn't process why, but something in his gut began to stir. Why were so many news cameras here? There had never been national news channels at this show's finale before.

Something else hit him. Jay spotted all the other contestants in the crowd, all looking surprisingly healthy and...camera-ready. Even Earth Girl and Boy no longer looked quite so...earthy. Not one of them looked as though they'd just roughed it in the wilderness.

Not a single one.

But the announcer wasn't finished talking. "...after all, it isn't every day that the daughter of a presidential candidate wins a survival show, especially the week before a primary. Some might say the timing couldn't be better." Laughing, the announcer turned to Anna's father, now approaching them with a confident swagger and his own out-of-place smile. He stretched a hand out with the self-assuredness of a candidate giving a victory speech and shook the announcer's hand, then straightened his jacket and waited expectantly for the inevitable questions to start. He spared Anna a brief nod, but quickly got back to the more important task of facing the media.

Jay couldn't deny a bit of awe at seeing the man up close and personal. Still, he frowned at Alexander Lloyd's less-than-passing interest in his daughter. And for some reason, he couldn't shake the feeling that—

"Mr. Lloyd," the announcer interrupted his thoughts, "how does it feel to finally have your daughter back? You and Mrs. Lloyd must be incredibly grateful."

On cue, her mother came sauntering forward, fluffing her hair and seemingly recharged by the spotlight. "I was sick with worry," she gasped, air kissing first one side of Anna's face, and then the other. "What took you so long to get back? The last two contestants were rescued nearly a week ago. We've been waiting here with Ryan for two days now." She smiled into the camera lens before motioning behind her to wave Anna's boyfriend over. "Aren't you just so happy to have our Anna back?"

Ryan snaked an arm around Anna's shoulder. "Deliriously happy." Something sparked in his eye at the same time he planted a kiss on her forehead. She flinched but didn't pull away, and that bothered Jay more than all the media attention. "But not as happy as I hope to be soon."

Jay didn't know what that meant, but he didn't like it. And it only took one glance at Anna's pale face, at her mother's shared wink with the announcer, at her father's jutted chin, and at Dean Passmore's expectant smile to know he was suddenly the only one in the dark.

Jay felt sick.

Something wasn't right. Nothing added up.

Anna's parents weren't worried. Worried people didn't show up in full make-up and designer boots. Worried people didn't half-heartedly kiss children just finishing up a reality show. Worried people didn't check their reflections during off-camera breaks and share knowing looks with the producers of reality shows.

He studied Heidi again. Nico. Desiree and everyone else.

Contestants who braved the Alaskan elements for a month didn't recover this fast, no matter how top-notch their medical care had been.

It took another minute, but a dozen scenarios collided in his brain at the same moment Ryan reached into his back pocket and extracted a little black box.

Everything exploded when he went down on one knee.

Beside him, Anna stood rigid, a frozen block of ice to blend in with the atmosphere.

"Ryan, what are you doing?" She whispered the words and glanced at Jay, but she knew exactly what was happening.

Anna was a smart woman; smarter than people gave her credit for.

Jay was the only idiot out here.

"I'm doing what this show has helped me to do. I'm doing what I should have done months ago." Ryan opened the box. "I love you, and I'm certain you love me. Give me a chance to prove how much, Anna."

Jay eyed the massive stone, pretty sure the thing could cut more than glass. Things like skin. Beating hearts. New relationships.

"You cheated on me. I saw the tabloids. How can I marry someone who can't be faithful?"

A collective gasp went through the crowd at her bold words. Her mother pressed well-lined lips together. Her father loosened his collar. Ryan paled, then blushed, a remorseful look on his face.

"Anna, those pictures were taken five years ago. They were published now just to discredit me and make your father's campaign look bad. This sort of thing happens in politics all the time. Surely you know that by now."

Jay saw the way she hesitated. Saw the flicker of doubt that maybe...just maybe...she'd been wrong about her boyfriend for a month now. He saw the worry, the sadness, the disbelief that she'd spent so much time questioning his integrity.

Jay could relate. He didn't believe a word of Ryan's all-too-convenient story.

"Ryan, I..." *Don't love you. Want to be with Jay. Want you to leave us alone.* He mentally finished the sentence for her, silently prompting her to repeat any of those phrases or come up with some creative ones of her own. "...don't know what to say."

That wasn't what he had in mind.

"Say yes, Anna. Please make me the happiest person in the world, and say yes."

Through his blinding anger, Jay swore he heard Anna's parents take a collective breath and hold it. The microphone inched a little closer, the camera's lens zoomed and refocused, the announcer raised up on tiptoe to catch her response. The daughter of America's most famous politician was being proposed to by what was surely JKF's long lost son, they looked so much alike. Who would've thought it?

Not him. Certainly not him.

Jay glanced at her, too mad to care about her response. And that's when it happened. Anna began to twist her thumb, rotating it around with her other hand in a grip so tight he thought she might break it at the joint. He glanced from her to the ring and then the spectators around them. If anyone else noticed, they gave no indication. Just waited with expectant smiles. It seemed to Jay that when it came to Anna, no one noticed much of anything.

But he noticed. She seemed to sense it, sliding a gaze heavy with dread toward him for the briefest second before turning back to Ryan.

"Okay." The word was a whisper, a breath that latched on the tails of despair. No one recognized it but Jay. "I will. I'll marry you." Everyone squealed and offered one another congratulatory hugs. Anna pasted on a smile, but it wasn't genuine. Through it all, he stared at her, feeling like too much of a sucker to do much else.

Spill it, Anna.

He'd never pictured himself as a stupid person. Not really. He'd taken on too much in life to go at it blindly, had way too much heartache behind him not to know better. But it took until that moment for it to occur to him that she had never really answered the question before they stepped on the train. She'd taken a step forward. She'd pulled him in for a kiss. She'd made all sorts of silent promises that he assumed meant something real. Believing in promises was his first mistake. His second, the one that really mattered, was getting too distracted by her nearness to focus on her response…a response that now slammed into his gut like a back-alley ambush.

She hadn't answered him. But in every way that counted—in the one way he didn't see coming—she had.

She agreed to marry Ryan…a man she didn't love.

And in that moment, the bravest woman he had ever met in his life crumbled into the weakest.

Chapter 36

One week later, Anna let herself inside the apartment and dropped her purse on the entryway table. Switching on a lamp, she took in the room and the loneliness it represented. The leather sofa that no one ever sat on. The crystal goblets that had never held a drop of wine. The fifty-inch television that had only seen the color black since the day they hung it on the wall. She kicked off her shoes and curled up on the only piece of furniture she liked—an old rose-covered chair she inherited from her great-grandmother. It smelled like must and perfume, a perfect combination of comfort and stability in a life spun out of control.

She blinked at the wall as loneliness crashed around her. Before...in the days prior to leaving for Alaska, she'd at least been content. Accepting. Her way of life didn't seem all that odd until Jay shone a spotlight on the strangeness of it all. Until she met him and discovered the potential for so much more.

Who's it gonna be, Anna? Me or Ryan?

Like always, Jay's words came to her unbidden. She never went more than two minutes without remembering all of them.

She wasn't proud of what she'd done, choosing Ryan while Jay stood by completely blindsided. But the choice wasn't really hers to make; she'd known that sad fact her entire life. Not that it made things easier. A blind man lived without sight. An elderly person lived with forgetfulness. A grown daughter lived under the thumb of her ambitious parents. That didn't mean any of them liked it. I mean, what was she supposed to do, say no on national television?

She thought of Jay all week, longed to see him, wanted to tell him her foot was better, wished to tell him she was sorry, prayed for a redo of their last five minutes, replayed every second they spent together in her mind.

Her list of regrets grew by the minute, keeping her mind busy even when she did nothing but sit and stare. So she sat. Switched positions. Tossed out scenarios in her head and tried to imagine better endings. She composed texts to Jay, then deleted them. She thought about calling, then changed her mind. Every urge to contact him needed to be suppressed, every thought extinguished. Not easy, since she had spent the last month happier than she'd ever been before, despite their awful circumstances. When a man makes you happy in spite of grime, cold, and weeks without bathing, you've found a man to hang onto.

And for that, she spent the past week trying to forget he existed.

She hadn't laughed once since she returned home. In seven days, from the moment she climbed on the plane bound for Chicago, there hadn't been a reason to.

She didn't know why she'd treated Jay so badly on the train, but she had. She'd taken the coward's way out. By moving toward him. By pulling him in for one last kiss. By trying to convince herself she deserved one more shot at happiness. By playing his game of *Spill It* without actually spilling anything at all. The memory hurt.

But not as much as the pain of marrying a man she didn't love.

Why hadn't Anna seen the on-air proposal coming? And more importantly, why hadn't she done something to stop it? And why couldn't she shake the nauseating feeling that the engagement had been planned in advance? The show's producers *had* to have known about such an outlandish surprise.

She dropped her head in her hands and grieved quietly for her new life. For the loss of her old one, brief one. For everything she would never have. And for the man who offered it all to her, whose gift she had tossed away next to a rusty set of tracks in an Alaskan wilderness.

She cried into her fingers…begged a God she wasn't sure she believed in for a way out…and eventually drifted off to sleep.

Chapter 37

Two weeks. Enough time to know that wishing for Anna to materialize wouldn't make it happen. Enough time for Jay to tell himself that even if she did, he would tell her to leave. Enough time to convince himself that the disastrous ending to their trip was actually for the best, that he wanted nothing to do with liars. Enough time to know that he was better off without her.

But not nearly enough time to believe that load of crap.

He unplugged his iPod and turned into the parking lot, the cold shock of high-rises and concrete nearly taking his breath away. After a month of living among trees, mud, and wildlife, then following it with recovery time spent locked inside his home, the harsh ugliness of progress slammed him in the gut. He threw the gear in park and stepped out of his black Land Rover, then propped his arm on the door and looked up, not ready to face his first meeting at Manhattan Construction. He studied the gray granite tiles that headquartered his future way of life—progress, structure, development, growth.

Destruction.

A heaviness settled inside him, joining the melancholy mood already residing there. None of this was natural. Beauty manufactured. But it was safe. It was all he knew. And if asking Anna that last question, if knowing for certain she would choose him, if that were any indication...

He didn't know much of anything.

Jay grabbed his briefcase and shut the car door, then made his way inside the building. Back to reality. Back to trying to navigate through a life he no longer wanted. Then again, maybe it wasn't the job he doubted. Maybe it was the prospect of facing life without the one person he wanted to do life with.

His phone buzzed inside his pocket. Pulling it out, he checked the screen, rolled his eyes, and dropped it back inside without answering. Heidi. He'd made the mistake of giving her his number, and she hadn't stopped calling since he returned to Texas.

Turned out she wanted to come for a visit.

Chapter 38

Anna's foot was completely healed, save for a small scar that ran just below her ankle bone. Her weight was almost back to normal, and her nails were no longer chipped. Her hair had been highlighted, trimmed, and styled to erase all evidence of dirt, grime, and weeks without washing. She'd been scrubbed clean and polished to perfection.

Anna had never felt dirtier.

Forty-seven days, and she still hadn't laughed, not one single time. She knew this because she'd counted every day since she stepped off that train, meticulously checking them off in the box inside her brain that held her memories. The box she revisited every night at bedtime, every morning at sunrise, and all the breathable seconds in between when she could, in fact, breathe. Sometimes the memories got so real, so raw, that she found herself holding her breath, hoping any minute Jay would materialize and she could release it on a relieved sigh.

She would give anything to go back. To the dirt, filth, and food deprivation, even if it meant eating porcupine every day of for the rest of her life. Even if it meant letting the thing attack her, shoot quills into her thigh and run right over her while she lay flat on her back. She missed Jay. She missed the snow. She missed it all. Yet here she sat, reaching out to taste yet another cake sample and listening to jokes about table settings. She didn't care about table settings. She would shove the table over and shatter all the priceless china and roll around on the shards of broken glass if she could just go back. But, she still couldn't bring herself to call things off with Ryan. And she hated herself for it.

She hated herself for being so freaking weak and for what she'd done to Jay. She deserved the pain she would feel when she faced him at next month's premiere. The hiding would be over...the regret would not. But for now, she faked her way through life the way she'd been trained to do.

"The chocolate. Definitely the chocolate." Anna closed her eyes and fake moaned around a bite as though that cake held all the keys to happiness on an edible ring. "I can't figure out why anyone bothers with anything but chocolate." She pushed away the platter of red velvet, banana, and almond concoctions and effectively ended the tedious selection process. Her mother would be thrilled. Laura the wedding planner could check another item off her to-do list. They could move on to important things like flowers and paper stock and the benefits of bubbles over birdseed and a hundred other things she didn't give two flips about because all she really wanted was to lay in a pile of snow somewhere on an Alaskan mountainside. Or, truthfully, on a wide-open Texas grassland. She had never been to Texas. Not that it mattered. Texas probably didn't want her to visit, anyway.

"Anna, don't talk with your mouth full." Colleen Lloyd, Anna's mother, cleared her throat and slid her gaze between the wedding planner and her, as though every ounce of embarrassment the woman possessed lay on the inside of her daughter's mouth.

Anna licked her fingers one by one, well aware she was acting like a two-year-old. "People shouldn't ask me questions and serve me cake at the same time. You know me, mother. That's never been a good combination." She gave her fingers another lick, and a childish smack of her lips for good measure. It earned her a sharp kick under the table. She deserved it. It wasn't her mother's fault she was a coward. She pushed her legs underneath her to avoid getting kicked again. A twenty-six year-old woman afraid of her own mother.

Coward.

Her mother picked up a Champaign flute and took a sip, swiping off the lipstick mark she left behind with a long, pink fingernail before setting the glass back down. Every movement the woman made was graceful, elegant, all the things Anna would never be.

"…and so that's the one I would choose. What do you think, Anna?

She stared at her mother and blinked, all at once aware of her wide-open mouth and saucer-shaped eyes. She closed both and straightened in her seat. "The chocolate…right?" She reached for a napkin, stealing a look at Laura, who sat with her pen poised over a creamy linen binder. Anna frowned at the look on her face. "I thought we already decided…" She rolled the napkin between her fingers, a poor substitute for her thumb but slightly more refined. Both women stared at her with something akin to distain.

Her mother gave a barely audible sigh and slipped the napkin out of her hand. "Anna, you have got to focus. The wedding is in three weeks and there is still so much to cover. Why you wanted to get married so quickly is beyond me, but we're doing this at your insistence, so please make a more concerted effort to engage." The napkin landed in a wad on the table. Anna eyed it like a child who'd lost a favorite toy. "Now, we were discussing the menu. I was telling Laura that a roasted beef tenderloin would be in order. Unless you would prefer to try something different, like an upscale seafood buffet or something along those lines, though I'm not sure it's sophisticated enough. But I suppose the decision is up to you."

Anna took a sip of water and peered at her mother over the glass, then, feeling especially feisty, set it back slowly back down.

"What about porcupine or squirrel? I've somehow come to acquire a taste for those lately."

Her mother finally cracked. "Anna, stop it. You've been back in Chicago for nearly two months, and you've done nothing but sulk and complain." She fixed Laura with a pointed stare. The woman carefully eased herself from the table, leaving her notebook and briefcase behind. Smart woman. Obedient. She knew who was paying the bill. "I knew letting you go was a bad idea from the moment Ryan asked us to, but we agreed. But you've got to put it behind you and move on. Your father's future is riding on so much right now, and like it or not, it's your job to make sure—"

"What do you mean, Ryan asked you to?" Was it her imagination, or had her mother's face paled a few shades? "Auditioning for the show was my idea, Mother."

Colleen cleared her throat. "Right. But we're talking about your future, young lady, and I for one—"

"What about my future?" The words were soft, but delivered with an edge. Here she was—independent, earned a good living, had a respectable degree, albeit not the coveted law one. But on the issue of how to live her life, she would forever remain a child. "What about mine?"

Her mother sat back, her expression a mix of exasperation and…something else. Anna couldn't decipher it. "Anna, it's normal to have second thoughts, to experience a sudden bout of cold feet associated with even the most confident marriages. I had them myself, right before I married your father." She tilted her head and let out a wistful sigh, a flicker of something Anna wasn't supposed to see crossing her features for the briefest second. Longing. Regret? But just as quickly, it was gone, replaced by her mother's trademark composure. She rested a manicured hand on the table between them, tapping her fingernail on the cloth to emphasize her points. "But you've got to push through those doubts, see them for what they are—distractions designed to take your eyes off everything you've worked for. Think about the future, Anna. And above all, never lose sight of the goal."

"My goal, or yours?" Anna whispered. A mistake, painfully evident the second her mother's face changed from sympathetic to steely, all in one ragged breath. Whatever boldness Anna felt was as fleeting as the triple chocolate cake sample, which lay in leftover crumbles on the creamy Wedgewood china in front of her.

Her mother didn't say anything right away, staring long enough to make sure Anna felt the full brunt of her displeasure. Finally, she raised an eyebrow. "I think you've lived in this family long enough to know those will forever be one and the same."

Anna sighed, knowing all too well that her mother spoke the truth. So she did the only thing she could do…the predictable, the expected, the familiar. She pulled that napkin across the table and balled it in her lap, twisting, turning, mutilating.

"Let's go with the tenderloin. A seafood buffet sounds like too much trouble." But even as she said the words, she couldn't let go of something her mother had said.

Ryan's idea?

Chapter 39

Jay dumped another load of manure on the pile and reached up with an aching hand to wipe his brow. He loosened his tie and rolled up his shirt sleeves, having come here straight from work, needing something to take his frustration out on. This pile of crap was as handy as anything, and someone had to clean up the area. *Do you shovel manure?* The memory tore through him...mocking...and he hissed a breath at no one. *No*, he'd answered. *No freakin' way.* Yet here he stood, shoveling dung like an idiot just because he was ticked. Well, he was sick of being angry. Sick of wishing for something he couldn't have. Sick of pining away for someone who had tossed him away like yesterday's dinner.

With a growl of frustration, he let the shovel fall and turned to stomp away, slamming into Heidi. She'd arrived a half-hour ago—his fault since he had texted her the stupid address—and she hadn't left his side since. She appeared in front of him when he closed his car door. Bumped into him when he walked toward the barn. Smacked into his back when he stopped to pick up a shovel. Clearly personal space wasn't a term she understood *at all*. All he wanted was as few minutes alone, but Heidi was determined not to give him the option.

"I'm sorry." He caught her arm and bit back his anger. "You should probably stand back a little more so that doesn't happen again." She might have said yes, she might have said no. All Jay knew for sure was that she stood there in her oversized button-up shirt that showed a little too much skin up top and her short, short cutoffs that showed even more down low. A month of hiking and living off the land had done her all kinds of favors. And even though he tried not to notice, tried not to ache, he did both, which only added fire to the frustration that flared every time she came near. "What are you wearing?"

She grinned. "Why the bad mood?" Her voice practically purred, all warm and concerned and innocent. "I'm wearing cutoffs. Like them?" She gave a slow spin and tried to reach for his hand again. He crossed his arms to make the move impossible. "I'm trying to break them in before an audition next week."

"They're fine, but I need to work." Jay tried to maneuver around her, but she stepped sideways to block him. He hesitated mid-stride. "An audition? For what?" His eyebrows pushed together as he looked at her.

"For a television pilot, of course."

"A television—wait, what? Are you suddenly an actress?"

To his surprise, Heidi laughed. Really laughed. Like they were sharing a joke he was supposed to be a part of. Except he didn't get the punch line.

"Of course I'm an actress. Just like you're an actor." She touched his arm, ran her fingers down the length of it. "We're all just trying to make a living here, Jay."

He didn't return her smile. "I'm not an actor. I work in construction. Just like I said the first day of the competition."

Heidi laughed again, but it slowly died on her lips when she realized he wasn't kidding. "You work in construction? Like, you build things?"

Jay let loose a breathy laugh. "Generally not with my own hands, but yes. I oversee building projects."

Heidi's deepening frown was making him feel better. She tilted her head in thought. "Is that why—?

She didn't finish. Jay didn't appreciate all the layers of disbelief currently stacking up in his mind. "Is that why what?"

Heidi tucked her lip between her teeth. "You really fell for her, didn't you? It wasn't an act?" He said nothing. Her face went slack. He couldn't tell if she looked frightened or ashamed, but the combination of both made her look vulnerable. "That day you came out of the woods...when I told you to stop kissing Anna...that you were going to ruin everything. You had no idea what I was talking about, did you?"

"I still don't have much of an idea." His words carried an angry edge. "Are you telling me you're an actress, not a nineteen-year-old college student from Texas A&M?"

Heidi looked away and swallowed. "I don't even know where that college is. Jay, I'm a twenty-seven-year-old actress who just happens to look young. As far as I knew, everyone on that show was acting." She looked at him then. The corners of her eyes creased in thought.

"Everyone, that is, but Anna."

Jay couldn't believe what he was hearing. He looked at the sky, the dry ground, the pile of manure that seemed so therapeutic just a few short minutes ago. Finally he settled back on Heidi.

"I want the whole story, and I want it now." He pointed at her. "You've got five minutes to tell your version. Start talking."

Chapter 40

Anna dabbed a layer of shimmery gloss across her lower lip the way her mother taught her years ago, concentrating on the plumpest spot to make her lip pop. Of the few memories she recalled of her childhood, the most vivid involved her mother at the bathroom counter, meticulously highlighting and darkening as she readied her face for another benefit. Colleen Lloyd lived for nights on the town, thrived on any excuse to wear her best gowns and hobnob with local celebrities. As Anna grew older and her father grew more famous, the celebrities became bigger. More famous. Clooney. DeNiro. Winslet. Her mother dropped names as often as she dropped cash. Gowns became more expensive, make-up more elaborate, usually professionally applied.

Anna tucked her Cover Girl gloss inside her department store clutch, both of which were chosen just to make her mother crazy. Plus, she hated public gatherings even more than she hated fashion, although she had to admit the on-sale Dillard's ensemble she picked up for ninety-five bucks back home made her look good. The short coral strapless dress made her blue eyes bluer, and combined with her new highlights and tousled curls, she was a far cry from the woman who left Alaska nearly three months ago.

Her hands shook just thinking about seeing Jay again.

She didn't know if she could go through with it, if she could act normal and pretend his presence didn't affect her. She reminded herself that it was just a premiere—two hours of fake-smiling and waving to photographers, then back to the hotel and home on the first flight tomorrow. And Ryan would be by her side. That should help a little, at least that's what she told herself.

The limo arrived on time to whisk them to Nobu—a swanky club in the heart of downtown that boasted a one-year waiting list, though clearly exceptions were made for Hollywood premieres, even reality shows. One final turn onto La Cienega Boulevard made it obvious this premiere was anything but unimportant.

Anna clutched her waist, suddenly feeling underdressed in a sea of glitter and diamonds. For a moment, she felt as vulnerable as the child Ryan often made her feel like.

He'd explained the tabloid pictures. The magazines had even printed a retraction apologizing for the five-year-old mix-up. But something about the entire situation felt...off. More importantly, Anna no longer felt settled. Or sure. She shifted in her seat, feeling increasingly uncomfortable in her skin.

"Stop worrying about what you're wearing. You look fine, although a new necklace might have been in order." Ryan glanced at her bare neck and sat back to take in their surroundings. "Just stay by my side and remember, the goal is to make your father look good." He slipped his hand through hers and gave a little squeeze just as his cell phone buzzed in his pocket. Pulling it out, his lips tilted in a soft smile before he tucked it away again.

"Who was that?" It was just a question. A simple one meant to sound innocent. But once nerves got ahold of her, sarcasm tended to alter her tone in ways even Novocain couldn't numb. Jay found it funny, even challenged her with wisecracks and rebuttals. Judging from the look Ryan leveled in her direction, her humor wasn't on his radar.

"No one you know." He turned away to peer out the window, his not-so-subtle way of dismissing her. Maybe it was the anticipation of seeing Jay or the tension that wound her tight, but his casual rebuff wasn't going to work. Not tonight.

"Try me. Maybe we've met at a fundraiser or a watch party. Maybe we know each other from high school or college, or maybe even work. Who knows, maybe I've met her at the grocery store." Her thoughts were met with silence—turned out the rebuff worked after all. Anna twisted her thumb, then remembered her new French manicure and moved on to her engagement ring.

The car slowed and pulled to the curb. "We're here," Ryan said with a sigh. "If we're lucky, we'll be out of here in an hour. Remember to smile, wave, and adore me." He gave her a brief smile, one more laced with manufactured tolerance than genuine affection. Had he always smiled at her like this? Was she just now noticing that his eyes didn't light up in the center or crease in the corners the way...the way she remembered someone else's doing?

Anna pulled herself together and stepped out of the car. This wasn't the time for lost memories or unpleasant comparisons.

It was time to work. She had a job to do, and Anna Lloyd knew how to get it done.

Chapter 41

He knew the minute she spotted him. Not because she actually looked his direction. To a casual observer, he might have been invisible, just another fixture meant to accent the scenery like the lighted topiaries or the flickering candles set in clusters at each round table.

But then, a casual observer didn't know that when Anna panicked, she pulled at her thumb, stupidly twisting it until he was certain it would pop out of socket. He couldn't believe she had never broken it, should have the way she forced it six different ways from normal.

In two minutes, she had pulled away, busied herself by attacking her engagement ring, fisting it so tightly against her palm he expected to see it burst through the back of her hand.

She was definitely panicked. Quite possibly a couple of heartbeats away from an all-out meltdown. Jay was in danger of it himself, but for completely different reasons than Anna. But someone had to make the first move. And since the only person he saw when he looked for other options was Heidi, Anna's fiancé, and the obnoxious, fresh-off-the-Botox-line announcer, he seemed to be the only candidate for the job.

He took a deep breath, thought about knocking back a few Rum and Cokes just to make the encounter halfway bearable, decided against it in favor of water, and headed her direction. His feet couldn't have moved slower if they'd fallen off behind him.

She looked beautiful. Heartbreakingly, bone-achingly beautiful. His chest hurt just staring at her, so he concentrated on his glass, the swirling ice cubes, the parquet floor. He was so focused on staying calm that he nearly ran into her, stopping abruptly before colliding with her foot. Squaring his shoulders, he assumed a casual demeanor and forced a grin.

"Nice shoes," he said. "I can barely see your scar from that nasty infection." Slowly, he locked eyes with her. Oh boy, he was in trouble. So much for casual.

She swallowed, but her chin came up a notch. "You mean the scar you gave me when you stabbed my ankle without asking?"

"If I'd waited for your permission, you'd probably be sporting a wooden leg right now. Then those stilettos you're wearing wouldn't look so nice." He hadn't meant to be so quick with a compliment, but his mouth had other ideas.

"You're only saying that because you've never seen me wear anything but hiking boots."

He looked her straight in the eye. "No, I think they look nice because they do. Then again, something tells me you would look good in anything." Another compliment, and this time he wasn't sorry.

Her chest rose and fell on a shaky breath. "Thank you, Jay."

"Except maybe algae." He winked. "I don't seem to remember that being your best look."

She surprised him by laughing, then slapped her hand over her mouth to prevent the sound. It was the Anna he remembered. The Anna he missed. The Anna he still apparently loved.

His life had gone to crap.

Jay almost forgot about Ryan standing there. Then the guy ruined that blissful state by coughing, forcing Jay to look at him. Anger sparked inside him the second they locked eyes.

"Good to see you again. Jay, isn't it?" Anna's fiancé said, though his tone suggested he was less than happy about it. Especially with his narrowed eyes and thin smile, which pretty much communicated that as far as Ryan was concerned, Jay could dive-bomb himself into Hades and stay there forever.

Based on everything he now knew about the show and Ryan's involvement with it, Jay seconded that motion. Except Ryan would wear the cape, horns, and carry the pitchfork. The man was slime in the worst possible form. Totally deceptive.

And Jay had decided not to say a word to Anna.

Jay nodded. "Nice to see you, too." Five words. Five syllables. The most he could manage without telling a complete lie.

They stood as a threesome without talking, Jay looking at Anna and Anna looking at Ryan and Ryan glaring at Jay—the three of them linked inside a hula hoop that spun in place and went absolutely nowhere. Thankfully, or not so thankfully, Heidi appeared and broke the ring of awkwardness while managing to add to it in her own unique way.

"So, is everyone having fun? It's so good to see you again, Anna. And what a handsome fiancé you have. Ryan, right?" She held out her hand and Ryan took it.

It took only seconds for Ryan's stare to morph into a captivated smile.

Clearly he agreed with her assessment.

***

As far as a premiere party went, this one was surprisingly subdued. Not that Anna had ever been to a party like this before, but she had her imagination, and everything she conjured up before tonight didn't measure up to this.

Only a smattering of camera flashes filled the crowded room, though the celebrity list was impressive. Anna spotted one of the Kardashians early on. She nearly fell over herself when that singing show host walked through the front door, so star struck that it took her nearly an hour to notice how short he was in person. He was about a thousand times more handsome, so that made up for it. Then last year's Bachelor arrived and she could barely think, let alone speak. Though she would never admit it out loud, she watched every single episode of that series, sometimes rewinding her DVR when she missed an especially crucial part. Like the kissing.

But as celebrity-enamored as she was, she rarely took her eyes off Jay, even as they roamed the room separately, even as she tried to hide it from everyone. After awhile she got tired of all the pretending and found a remote bar stool in the corner of the room. It offered a clear view of the guests, but sat far enough away for her to escape for a moment. The evening had been thrilling, but she felt tired.

She scanned the room until she found him.

He was better looking than she remembered, which created all kinds of problems for her. First of all, there was his clean-shaven face. Then his perfectly mussed hair that looked designed by a pricey stylist....his well-rested expression that no longer looked strained from worry about their next meal...his suit that accented a trim physique the way flannel shirts and bulky coats never could.

But it wasn't his appearance that drew her in and gripped her in a fist of longing. It was his voice. Particularly the way he had so easily slipped into his old role, taking none of her crap and not expecting her to take any of his. Like always, it was that last part that had her despairing the most. She took a sip of seltzer to soothe her dry throat.

She'd made a mistake. A monumental one she saw no way out of. Her wedding to Ryan was two weeks away. Invitations were sent.

Reservations were made. The dress was altered to perfection and guests had responded. Their picture had already graced the front page of the Chicago Tribune's society section, earning the kind of reaction from her mother that let Anna know she'd finally, *finally*, done something right.

Yet she'd done everything wrong. Starting with agreeing to marry a man she didn't love when the one she was crazy about stood only a dining room's length away from her. She couldn't reconcile the two…not when her wedding to Ryan was in full swing.

"You know, something tells me we made the wrong decision."

"What?" Startled, Anna whipped her head around as Jay lowered himself onto the chair next to her. Somehow he'd read her mind all over again. She would never, *never*, understand his ability to do it. "What are you talking about?" Just because she'd made the wrong decision didn't mean he needed to point it out here. At the premiere. In front of everyone. She leaned back, hopefully removing herself from any mind-reading force field he had sucked her into.

"I'm not going to bite you, Anna." Like the pain in the butt he was, he closed the distance between them and grabbed her drink, taking a long sip as he gazed at her over the rim. "I'm talking about this show. We willingly signed up for it, but being here is weird. Not sure I could ever get used to being in the spotlight."

As if his words carried an invitation, a camera flashed in their direction. Anna didn't even try to smile. "Me either. I like my life private, without all the pomp and circumstance." Across the room, Ryan talked to a supermodel she recognized but couldn't name, famous for her lingerie ads. Tonight at least, an angel wing wasn't in sight. "Everyone here seems to enjoy it, though."

Jay titled his head. "You'd think you would be used to it by now. Being in your family, and all."

"I'm not." They just looked at each other before Jay finally turned away and reached for a cocktail napkin.

"Ryan seems to be having a nice time. The limelight suits him."

Anna studied the way Jay folded and unfolded the corners. "He thrives on it. Always has."

He gave a sarcastic laugh. "You're prepared enough for it, too. You'll probably wind up being perfect for each other." He drained her glass and set it down in front of her.

"Thanks a lot," she said. "It took me ten minutes to order that drink. Good thing I didn't want any of it." She stared at the melting ice cubes.

"I'll get you another." Jay raised his hand and motioned to the girl behind the counter, blonde and built and coming right toward him with a big smile on her face. Figured. "Can she have another…" He glanced at her. "…what were you drinking?"

"I wasn't," she deadpanned, then rolled her eyes and focused on the bartender. "Seltzer, please."

Jay repeated the order as though she hadn't just done it herself and faced her again. He had that serious look in his eyes, so she thought it best to keep the conversation rolling. But, stopped short when an interesting spectacle appeared in front of them. Josiah and Rain—otherwise known as Earth Thing One and Two—chose that moment to walk into the club. They were an hour late, but what's time when you live on nothing but love, harmony, and the very occasional shower? Anna's jaw fell, but it wasn't their late arrival that confounded her. It was their clothing.

Both wore business suits.

His from Prada—Anna knew this because Ryan had one just like it in his closet. And hers from Max Azria. Anna knew *this* because she'd been saving for months to buy one just like it except in animal print, because animal print was still in style and currently she didn't own anything like it.

Anna couldn't tear her eyes away from the sight. She had spent nearly a month with the couple, should be used to their ability to shock by now.

She wasn't.

"Why do they look like that? They're...normal." she said to Jay as he sat beside her. "The way they looked in Alaska...this doesn't make any sense." When he didn't respond right away, she glanced over to see him staring at them, an almost angry set to his lips. He watched, transfixed, for a moment longer before finally swinging his eyes to her. Without saying a word, he rolled his eyes, stood up, and set the glass down on the counter. In that moment Anna knew there was something he wasn't telling her, but someone chose that moment to bump her from behind and knock her into the corner of the bar.

"Ow!" She rubbed the top of her ribs.

Jay scowled and turned to chastise the person who had hit her, but the area was packed with people so it was hard to tell. His hand gripped her shoulder. "Are you okay?"

"I think so. This place is too crowded."

"Do you want to get out of here for a few minutes?"

She looked up at him, and her heart tripped at the hope on his face. Still, uncertainty toyed with her emotions. "I don't know. The show is getting ready to start, and I'm not sure we should—"

"Just a walk around the block, Anna. I'm not asking you to fly to Vegas with me. We'll be gone five minutes." With one hand, he pushed in the bar stool. He held out his other hand to her.

She reluctantly took it, then scanned the bar, wondering what Ryan would say if he discovered her missing. She spotted him talking with the same supermodel, only now they stood a little closer, grinned a little wider, touched a little more.

Anna tried to work up some anger, but nothing surfaced. Nothing but resignation.

Lately the emotion had become her best friend.

With a sigh, she nodded. "Let's go. I don't think anyone will even notice we're gone."

Chapter 42

"Are you cold?" Seeing her shiver, he shrugged out of his jacket and draped it over her shoulders, while behind them, the fading tones of slow reggae music hummed in the background. He could imagine the Earth children holding a séance in the middle of the Alaskan wilderness. He almost missed it.

Too bad the whole thing was fake.

"Thank you. I'm not sure I've been warm since I got home from Alaska, like the snow got stuck inside my bones and hasn't melted yet."

Jay smiled. "Give it time. I think my body finally thawed last week." At the sound of her breathy laughter, he jammed his hands into his pockets and slowed his step to match hers. A man on a bike held out an arm on a left turn, and they stopped to let him pass. While they waited, Jay looked up at the night sky, most of it blocked by the tall buildings that marred the Los Angeles skyline. For the hundredth night since they'd been back, he missed Alaska and its unobstructed views.

For the thousandth time since talking with Heidi, he questioned his decision to keep Anna in the dark.

"The view just isn't the same here, is it?" Anna surprised him by saying. Somehow the woman managed to read his mind, so often it sometimes unnerved him. He didn't think she was even aware of it.

As long as she couldn't read all of it.

He shook his head. "Sometimes I wish I could go back, just to see all those stars one more time." There wasn't much he missed about Alaska, just a couple of things, really.

"So do I," Anna said. "There's nothing prettier than seeing the land for what it's supposed to be. God made something perfect with one sweep of His hand, and man just seems to be messing it up."

He remembered his own similar thoughts only a few days ago, when he was in a particularly bad mood. His outlook had improved markedly since then, mostly in the last hour.

"Oh, apartments and shopping centers aren't *all* bad—" His head whipped to hers. Finally, Jay couldn't take it anymore. "Everything set for the wedding? I saw the write-up online. Nice picture of the two of you."

Anna gave no response. Curious, Jay glanced her direction, watching as she rubbed her eyebrow, scratched behind her ear, sniffed a couple times.

"It was just a question, Anna. Am I going to have to wait until you go through all your nervous habits before you answer?" They crossed a side street, the road desolate and dark.

Her eyebrows slammed together. "What nervous habits? I don't have any nervous habits." She cleared her throat. Twice. Went for her thumb again.

Jay reached for it and laughed. "Sweetheart, you have more nervous habits than a cornered jackrabbit." He linked their hands together, palm to palm, and smiled to himself when she didn't pull away.

"Like you would know anything about that, seeing as you've never actually *cornered* one before." An underhanded blow to his lackluster hunting skills. He suppressed a comeback at her feistiness, tough to do since it itched to get out.

"Touché. Now, tell me about the wedding?"

She shrugged, sucked on her lower lip. "Everything is ready to go. My mother has made sure of it. All we need now is a bride and groom." She tried to laugh. It didn't work that well.

Jay stopped in the middle of the road to face her, his heart picking up speed. The pace had nothing to do with oncoming headlights. "I guess you have both of those, so you're right on schedule." His voice cracked, so he tried again. "Two weeks, huh? That's not much time."

"No, it isn't." Anna's gaze flicked to the side. "Jay, let's get out of the street." She pulled on his arm, but he just stared at her for a moment. She pulled harder and finally got his attention. His feet moved, even though they felt like lead. Anna was getting married. The reality gripped his chest and wouldn't let go. A thousand unspoken words hung between them, and tension filled the space. The swish of their steps mingled with the hum of city traffic as the only sounds within blocks. After awhile, Jay couldn't take the silence. "Anna…"

"Please don't start." She pulled her hand away from his arm and buried it inside her coat. "I'm marrying Ryan, and that's the way things have to be."

He shoved his hand into his pocket. "Even though he cheated on you?"

"Those pictures were five years old. Even the tabloids backed his story up."

The doubt in her voice practically shouted in his ear.

"You're right. Everything is good, then. This should be the start of a very happy life for you."

A light turned off beside them, a local store closing for the night. "Yes it should. Besides, marriage is about forgiveness and commitment more than anything else."

"True. You've got the forgiveness thing down, so score one for you. The commitment thing ought to be easy."

"Yes it should," she repeated. She sounded like a freaking robot.

That did it. He'd had enough of her induction into Stepford-Wifery. "Are you going to keep repeating those three words until you believe them? Because you sound like a girl who can't think for herself."

Finally, he looked at her. "It's just that I'm having a hard time accepting the fact that you think I'm not good enough for you. And that you'd trade real love just to keep up appearances. He felt like screaming but couldn't manage more than a harsh whisper. "You're willing to marry some guy you don't love—who doesn't love *you*, for heaven's sake—when I'm standing right here. I've told you before, and I'll tell you again. I love you, Anna. Still. And something tells me you feel the same way. But you're willing to toss that aside and ruin your whole life. And I don't get it. I'll never get it." He shook his head. "What kind of person is willing to do that?"

"The kind of person that has no other choice!" She yelled, startling them both. "The kind of person who will be hated by everyone she knows if she doesn't go through with it! So what am I supposed to do?" Finally, her control broke and washed away in a long stream of tears. Streaks of muted black trailed down her cheeks and over her lips. Jay pulled her to him and wrapped his arms around her shaking shoulders, resting his chin on top of her head as she cried. The sound of her muffled voice nearly broke his heart.

He nearly told her. But to unload now would be selfish, and he knew it.

"What do you want me to do?" she asked into his jacket.

He choked back his own ragged emotions. "I want you to choose me. I promise I won't hurt you, and I'll work my whole life to make you happy." He took a deep breath and tipped her chin. They met eye to eye, hers watery, his stinging. "Choose me, Anna."

There it was. On the line. This was about him. This was about her. This was about knowing what she wanted without Ryan's warped character and poor decisions becoming a factor. Right now, he needed to know where he stood.

She looked at him, her breaths coming in ragged gasps. "And if I can't? If I go through with my wedding to Ryan, what then?"

He just looked at her. "Then I guess that's it. Show's over, sweetheart." His words were sharp, but barely audible. "Don't let that be how this ends. I won't ask again."

He didn't have to. She lowered her head and tucked it against his chest while he held onto to her, hoping like he'd never hoped for anything in his life. He wanted her, but he wanted her to want him more. And it was the uncertainty that nearly killed him.

Twenty minutes had passed when they walked back into the restaurant, but nothing much had changed. People still danced. Ryan still chatted with the blonde, only this time in front of the giant television screen that began to roll the show's opening credits. Guests still mingled as they made their way toward chairs to watch the premiere.

And Jay still waited for her answer. And for once in his life, begged God to just let Anna choose him.

But it wasn't until she kissed his cheek and looked up at him that he knew his bargaining chips had run out. She slowly wiped her eyes, and with a final sigh, dragged herself over to Ryan's side. Jay watched as she pulled up a chair and lowered herself into it. He watched as Ryan shot her an impatient look, as the blonde stood up to leave, and as they both grew resigned—side by side—watching a show on the screen that was nothing but a lie.

The Alaskan Wild...all that work for no reason at all.

Jay watched his own smiling face fill the screen as they disembarked the plane that first time in Alaska. Watched Anna as she worried her lip, then followed him down the steps, out of her element and fresh out of confidence. What a difference a month had made. He barely remembered that girl.

Sadly appropriate since, starting today, he needed to forget her. So with a sad sigh, he stood. He'd told her he wouldn't ask again, and he meant every word. With one last look around the room, Jay walked out of the club and into the night.

Leaving reality shows and Hollywood and the only girl he'd ever loved behind him.

Chapter 43

Something about her dress didn't feel right, and Anna tugged on the waist again. No matter how many times it had been altered, the seamstress never got it perfect, and now Anna was paying for the lady's shabby work. She squirmed inside the fabric, but her skin still felt prickly. Itchy.

Restless.

Jay left her. He wasn't coming back.

Grief surfaced for one uncomfortable moment, but Anna forced back the tears and reached for her veil, which was draped over a white velvet chair. The intricate scattering of diamonds and pearls made the veil even more valuable than the Carolina Herrera dress, and Anna didn't want to ruin it. She might not love the dress, but she knew how to respect something so beautiful. Years of schooling had taught her well.

As she turned, she caught sight of her reflection and stilled.

She couldn't breathe.

All alone in the bridal room, she stared at the woman looking back at her, mesmerized by what she saw. Her hair lay in perfect ringlets across her bare shoulders, tanned from the airbrushing session her mother insisted on yesterday. *White makes you look pale,* Colleen had explained, sucking her teeth at Anna's sarcastic offer to dye the dress black. *This isn't a joke, Anna. Do you know how much this dress cost?* Anna did. Of course she did. She'd only been reminded a million times.

Expertly applied lashes swept dramatically across her upper lids, making her eyes stand out like rounded orbs of coal. Her nude lips gave an Angelina Jolie-type pout, full and luscious and supermodel-worthy, complimenting her slender neck and the single diamond pendant that draped elegantly around it. Her shapely nails glimmered at the tips from a pale-pink French bridal manicure, a perfect way to showcase the large diamond residing there and the wedding band that would follow shortly. She looked great. Better than she ever had in her life. Gorgeous, really. Perfectly perfect.

She was miserable, and had no one to tell.

A knock sounded on the white paneled door, and it cracked open an inch. Anna turned, barely making out the outline of someone's nose. An eyeball blinked at her, and Anna worked to contain a sigh.

"Can we come in?" Without waiting for an answer, five bridesmaids burst into the room—made up of one high school friend Anna hadn't seen since graduation, three cousins she couldn't stand, and one Great Aunt on her mother's side she met for the first time last year. Her mother had made the choices herself and notified Anna later. Anna hadn't argued. So much about this wedding was a production, anyway. It was easy to relinquish the bridesmaid selection as well.

"Sure, come in," Anna muttered to the group of women already fussing over her hair, her veil. One busied herself trying to jam a foot into the shoes Anna hadn't yet slipped on. With thoughts of athlete's foot and contagious bunions floating through her mind, she tore her eyes away from the sight and swatted her mother's hand away.

"Mom, please don't play with my fingernails! It feels like you're trying to pull them off." She jerked her hand back and pushed against her cuticle.

"Well, you have a chip on one corner..." Colleen clasped her hands together and scanned the room, forgetting all about Anna's manicure. "It looks like everything is ready. You should see the crowd in the auditorium. The entire city has come out for this." She gave a little bounce on her heel—the most excitement Anna had seen from her since her father made his first television appearance nearly a decade ago. "Even the governor is in attendance, making good on his promise to give an endorsement when this is over.

Her mother, forever in campaign mode. Anna scratched her waist as she eyed an unopened can of Diet Coke sitting on the table in front of her.

"Anna, stop messing with your dress." Colleen scolded. "You're going to rip it, and after we spent all that time having it fitted just right."

"Your mother's right," her aunt spoke up, shaking her foot out of Anna's shoe. It flipped once and landed on its side. "It would be a shame to ruin it. Just think of how much you can sell it for later." The woman eyed Anna's dress. "Maybe I could try it on after the wedding...?"

Anna sighed at the tactless question just as the door opened again. All the taffeta-adorned bodies in the room swung to greet it.

"It's almost time," her father said, popping his head in. "I'll meet you down the hallway in five minutes, Anna. Make me proud. Didn't send you to Alaska just for the fun of it." He gave a little laugh, then closed the door with a firm tug, leaving Anna standing in a room full of skittering, giggling people. She snatched the Diet Coke, opened it, and downed half, feeling two seconds away from suffocating.

Five minutes. Five minutes until she walked toward her new life as Mrs. Ryan Lance. Five minutes until she fulfilled the duty her family had anticipated for months now. Five minutes until settling for second best would become a permanent way of life. Five minutes until she made a decision she could never reverse...would never reverse, because no matter how much she didn't want to do this, she believed that marriage should last forever. She took another sip.

Wait.

What had her father just said?

Anna pulled the can from her lips and looked at her mother. "What did Dad mean, you didn't send me to Alaska for the fun of it? No one sent me there. Going to Alaska was my idea."

Her mother never paled. Never paled.

She stood in front of Anna, every ounce of blood draining from her carefully made-up face.

"I'm sure he just meant that we knew how rough the trip would be for you."

Her mother never fidgeted. *Never fidgeted.*

She busied herself gathering up soda cans, picking up bits of paper, straightening her jacket and straightening it again. Anything to keep her eyes off Anna. Anything from exposing more of the guilt currently stacking up like a pyramid in between them.

Her mother finally met her gaze, impatience beginning to situate its familiar self around her mother's demeanor.

"Anna, I really don't see—"

"The truth, Mother."

Colleen Lloyd's exasperated sigh could have provided a cushion if anyone in the room had craved a nap.

She clicked her tongue and checked her watch. "Well, you might as well know. It's not like you won't find out eventually anyway. Your trip to Alaska was your father's idea. One that Ryan agreed to, of course." Her mother smiled, seeming to think it was the best way to deal with the situation. "Looking back it was so easy to get you to agree. Then again, you've never liked to have your stamina challenged. Ever since you were a little girl you—"

"I'm not in the mood for a stroll down memory lane. Why did he want me to go to Alaska? I don't see what he could possibly gain from it."

Her mother rolled her eyes. A childish gesture Anna had never seen from her before. "Exposure, Anna. Media attention. Especially when it was leaked that you were doing the show for charity's sake." She fluffed the ends of her hair. "Of course, it didn't hurt that the show's executive producer is one of your father's biggest supporters. Thank goodness, since we would end up needing him to clean up the mess Ryan made—"

Her mother caught herself, but the damage was done.

"The photos?" They weren't old. Down deep, Anna had known it all along.

Colleen gave her a dismissive wave. "We can talk about this over cake. Right now, we have guests to greet and a wedding to attend. Are you ready?"

Was she ready?

Shards of glass exploded in her stomach, so Anna upended her soda to repair the damage. She gasped when the can slipped from her fingers. The oxygen left the room as everyone held a collective breath and waited for the liquid to land. Then all at once, all seven women jumped into action.

"Don't spill it on your dress, Anna!" Her mother shrieked.

"Jump back!"

"Someone grab a towel!"

"Do you think it can be saved?"

But Anna didn't move. Just watched the can bounce, the contents pool around her dress and rush for that lone sideways shoe. Brown fluid disappeared as the silk fabric slurped it up, but Anna remained frozen. It was hard to react. She just didn't care.

Don't spill it, Anna! her mother had said.

Don't.

Spill it.

And all at once, Jay's words came rushing back to her.

What's your worst allergy, Anna?

When was your first kiss, Anna?

What's your favorite movie, Anna?

If you could do anything with your life, what would it be, Anna?

His questions zoomed like arrows desperately searching for a target as they intertwined with everything she'd just discovered about Ryan.

A cheat.

A liar.

And above all...

A manipulator who played games with other people's lives.

One by one, she replayed Jay's questions in her mind. Her answers...his challenges...her reluctance to keep playing...his insistence she do it anyway. She successfully dodged all the arrows her memories tossed at her, dismissing them as nothing more than meaningless inquiries that no longer mattered.

"Who's it going to be, Anna? Me or Ryan?"

People talk about the moment of truth as being a harsh reality that requires a split-second decision, but Anna had never experienced one for herself. Until now.

"Can I have a minute alone?" she asked, more to herself than anyone else.

"Anna, don't do anything rash."

"I just need a minute, Mother, I promise I'll be right out."

With what seemed to be a satisfied glance at her, Colleen ushered everyone out of the dressing room, leaving Anna alone in the middle of it. The silence was suffocating. Deafening. Liberating. With a hand to her stomach, Anna looked around, looking for…something.

Something.

She spotted her shoe, still lying there with a brown stain marring one side of it. Once beautiful, it was now covered in ugliness. So ugly, she no longer wanted to wear it. And right then, for a reason that really made no sense at all, she found what she was looking for.

She'd had her fun, lived her last wild adventure, gotten her bit of rebellion out of the way in the woods of Alaska. She had fallen in love, learned about loss, and somehow managed to make it through. Now, it was time to grow up. Be responsible. Face her future, and do the right thing.

Anna's gaze burned into the door. The window. She looked longingly toward it, wanting with everything in her to find some of that courage Jay so often talked about. But she'd never been one for bravery, no matter what he said about her. She imagined herself climbing onto the sill, shimmying down the fire escape the way she had seen it done in movies, and fleeing toward another life entirely. Leaving her family behind and running toward Jay…into the future she wanted more than anything.

You're the bravest person I've ever met.

Jay's words, back to haunt her. Climbing out the window seemed the most cowardly scenario of all.

Anna took a deep breath, wiped her eyes with the back of her hand—being careful not to ruin her makeup—and started for the door. Her bare feet propelled her forward even as part of her heart died behind her.

But she had made her decision. She wasn't thrilled with it. Not even close. But maybe she would be. Eventually.

But eventually didn't make now easier, and this was definitely not easy.

This was just something she had to make herself live with.

***

Once Jay had been happy. Once, despite heavy pressure and responsibilities he'd been too young to mess with, his life had been good. So good that he thought he deserved an adventure…a little getaway to test his ability to live off the land.

It had. And now his life sucked because of it.

His toothbrush had just begun to work its magic when he heard a knock. Straining to hear the squeak of the front door opening, he held it in his mouth waited. Instead, he heard a soft rap again. He rinsed and turned off the faucet, then dragged himself back toward the living room, trying his hardest not to cuss under his breath. Considering his purely foul mood, only prayer and self-control made it possible.

He walked to the front door and stole a glance into the peep hole of his front door. And what he saw made his heart drop into his feet.

Anna stood on the other side of the door, pacing back and forth.

***

He stood in the open doorway and looked at her, heart pounding and bewildered. He couldn't believe she'd shown up here—was elated by it, in fact—but that didn't mean he would just let her walk inside; not until she begged for forgiveness for tormenting his soul and clarified the stupid statement she'd just made.

"You want to try again?" He just looked at her. "Because that was the dumbest thing I've ever heard."

"It was not! I said I'm sorry!"

"No you didn't. You said, and I quote 'Love means never having to say you're sorry, but I'll say it anyway.' It doesn't matter how many times you've seen *Love Story*—that line is lame and categorically untrue. I want a better apology or you're staying out there on my porch." He moved to close the door. He should have known she'd do something as childish as plant her foot against the doorframe, making it impossible for him to do it.

"I'm sorry, Jay," Anna said, her voice barely above a whisper. "And maybe you haven't noticed, but I didn't go through with the wedding. I couldn't."

He'd noticed. The first thing he had done upon seeing her was glance at her bare ring finger. The sight of nothing but skin gave him all kinds of hope. But that hope made him a little mad, and a whole lot stubborn. No way he would let her off without a hard time. He deserved the entertainment.

"That's good about the wedding, but apology not accepted. Not until you can quote a better movie line." The glare she leveled his way was cute. He caught his grin before she noticed it. "I'm waiting, and hurry up. I don't have all day." Behind Anna, Jay's sister pulled into the driveway. She was as devilish as him. This could make things fun.

"You've made that clear since the day we met." Anna glanced behind her at the approaching car, then turned to face Jay with scrunched eyebrows. At least she was actually thinking. "Fine, you want another line? How about, frankly my dear—"

"Try another." He rolled his eyes.

She rolled hers back before pressing a fingertip to her forehead. "What we've got here is a failure to communicate?"

"Nope. *Cool Hand Luke* was a favorite of my dad's. Not mine.

"You're being ridiculous."

"Don't recognize that one."

She made a disgusted noise. "That wasn't a movie line."

"Then you still have work to do," he said. "Hey, sis, come meet Anna," he called. He didn't miss the way both women's eyes widened, though Anna's expression mixed in a little fear to make things fun.

His sister, Jessica, walked up onto the porch. Anna eyed the ground, deep in thought. Her head snapped up. "I think this is the beginning of a beautiful friendship?"

"Gross. *Casablanca* sucked. Try again."

"It did not! It was worth it for that kissing scene alone!"

"On the beach? In the sand?" He shook his head, enjoying the lie. "Talk about uncomfortable."

"Uncomfort—?" She threw him a disgusted look. "Talk about having no taste in movies.

His sister smiled behind Anna's head. "He's completely classless when it comes to movies. But if you want to get on his good side, start quoting *The Godfather*. He's pretty stereotypical in that way." Jay glared at her at the same time Anna's face lit up.

"The Godfather, huh? Fine." She took a step toward him, either oblivious or uncaring that his sister was taking in every movement. "Jay, I'm sorry. It took me awhile to come to my senses, but you need to know that I love you." She picked up his hand. "That I'm done with Ryan and family obligations and things that don't matter." And circled his palm. "Because of that, I'm here to make you an offer you can't refuse." And linked her fingers with his.

But it wasn't until she took another step in his direction and tugged on his shirt that he lost all sense of everything. His pulse pounded so loud he could barely remember what they were talking about. He swallowed and moved in closer, so close he could bend down and kiss her if he wanted to.

"An offer I can't refuse, huh?" He remembered that look in her eyes, the way his fingers felt when tangled in her hair, the way her lips tasted under his mouth. He could totally kiss her if he wanted to. "Which is?"

She smiled up at him and told him what she had in mind.

And right then, more than anything...

He wanted to.

Chapter 44

One year later

It was an anniversary of sorts, and Anna wasn't happy. Things hadn't gotten easier like she hoped. Not even a little. But maybe they would.

Eventually.

She pressed a hand to her eyes to stop the tears that threatened to escape, not wanting her husband to see her crying. Again. He had witnessed more tears in the past few days than any man should be forced to endure, managing to stem each emotional outburst with a hug, a shoulder rub, a kind word...like the supportive guy he was. Anna had to admit, this marriage had surprised her. Despite her earliest reservations, they were good together.

She loved him. Once she realized it, she had told him so a thousand times. She really, really loved him.

It was this place that she hated.

She sniffed, caught another tear on her glove before he had the chance to see it fall. Or so she thought. His boots appeared in front of her, just close enough that they nearly touched the tips of hers.

"You're crying? Again?" He sighed, loud and long. "Anna, what is wrong with you this time?"

She flung the water droplet off her hand and glared up at him. Supportive, her butt. "I hate camping! And even more than camping, I hate this place!"

"What do you mean, you hate this place?" Jay looked around, taking in the trees, the sky, the towering snow-topped mountains. Beautiful to most people, but nothing more than torture to her. "This place is gorgeous. It's perfect. And it holds ninety-nine percent of all of our good memories. How can you hate it?"

She vaulted to her feet and got right in his face. "Good memories? You call nearly starving to death a good memory? You call being attacked by a rabid porcupine a good memory?" She pointed a finger in his face. "You call doing a fake reality show with a bunch of actors who got to sleep in a hotel every night and never roughed it for a second while we busted our butts trying to survive out here a good memory? Are you crazy?"

Instead of swatting her hand away like she expected, he latched onto it, sliding each of his fingers around hers, one by one until they were all conjoined, pressed against each other base to tip...five on five...a tough connection to break.

From the moment they met, they were meant to be linked together. It had just taken Anna awhile to admit it.

"I might be, because I say yes to all your questions." His voice was as gentle as a whisper.

"I still can't believe you didn't tell me right after you found out." She inched closer to him.

"I didn't want your decision to stay with Ryan, or not stay with him, to be based on my revenge."

Her lips were close to his, but she wouldn't allow them to touch. Not yet.

And in that moment, her mind went back to the dressing room. The doorway. The decision that changed everything and nothing in the span of five long minutes.

You're the bravest person I've ever met.

Except a brave person didn't shimmy down a fire escape and away from their own wedding. Brave people used doorways, walked down rose-strewn aisles, confronted domineering parents, and broke up with indifferent, cheating grooms.

But…a brave person knew when they were wrong. And then they picked themselves up, swallowed their pride, drove straight to Texas, and admitted it.

So that's what she did, exactly one year ago today, her quivering limbs carried by Jay's words the whole way.

As she drove, she thought of her parents, of their anger that only intensified with each word she spoke. When they finally admitted everyone involved with the show had been hired actors—including Heidi, which explained her healthy appearance and inexplicable deepening tan—she lost it. When she then explained her unwillingness to accommodate their plans, they offered no tears. They didn't beg. They didn't break down and ask her to reconsider.

They simply called her selfish. Told her to get out. And maybe she had…maybe everything that happened was indeed her fault. After all, her father lost several huge financial supporters after Anna "embarrassed the family" and ran out on her own wedding. Support that possibly cost her dad the title of Mr. President when the money for his campaign ran out two months before the elections.

So maybe she was to blame. But secretly, she felt like a winner.

She had Jay. She had her dignity. She had a job she loved in Dallas. And most importantly, she had a firsthand example that marriage could be great. When the pastor mentioned that marriage shouldn't be entered into lightly at their wedding six months ago, for the first time in her life, she believed the words.

As for Ryan, it turned out that the supermodel at *The Alaskan Wild* premiere was an actual Kennedy—real life political royalty. A real-life American sweetheart who drove a Bentley and resided in Los Angeles. With her platinum blonde locks and his jet black tresses, they looked good together. Like Ken and Barbie on a Malibu beach. They had been dating since Anna called off the wedding, and she wished them nothing but the best.

Mostly the best. And maybe a bad case of poison ivy in places too private to talk about.

But whatever.

With a breathtaking smile, Jay wrapped his arms around her waist, her fingers still locked in his, her arms trapped behind her back. She felt like a prisoner in the best kind of jail.

"Maybe I am crazy," he said, "but yes. The best memories in my life were made right here. And I don't know about you, but I think we ought to try to make a few more while we have the chance." His smile morphed into that wicked grin she loved.

But still. "Why Alaska? Of all the places you could have chosen for a romantic getaway, you had to pick Alaska? When you said it was a surprise, I expected someplace warm. I've never even been to Hawaii…"

He rolled his eyes. "Hawaii is overrated. Besides, who needs it when we have all this?" He looked up to the sky. "It's beautiful out here. Come on Anna, admit I'm right."

She tracked his gaze upward and took in the view, a hint of a smile working its way across her lips. Jay told her early on that her parents would come around, and her father had called just yesterday. It was the first time they had spoken since she walked out of the church.

Not a long conversation, strained in every way that counted, but it was a start. If history had any bearing on today, it wouldn't be long until her mother followed in her father's footsteps. She just might get her family back one day, but this time she would join them as a whole, independent woman. The way she should have been all along.

Anna grinned and slowly locked eyes with Jay. "If you recall, I said I would never admit it again. But I guess it *is* beautiful." With a sigh, she squeezed his fingers, her hands still firmly secured behind her back. "You know," she said, biting her lower lip. "Last time we were out here, you kissed me a couple of times. But now, we're out here all alone…no cameras around…and we *are* married…"

Jay raised an eyebrow. "Well, Mrs. Maddox, are you thinking what I'm thinking?" He moved in closer, every inch of their bodies pressed together. "Out here? In the cold?"

She grinned. "Why not?"

He unwound their fingers and brought his hands behind her neck. With the gentlest touch, the pads of his thumbs caressed her face as he brought his lips to hers. She kissed him back. Of course she kissed him back. And then she let go.

"Well?" she said, prompting him.

Jay bit back a smile and shook his head. "Okay, here's one for you. When did you first know you had the hots for me? Spill it, Anna." They linked fingers and resumed the hike they'd begun an hour ago, playing the game they had started exactly a year earlier. Since then, as Anna searched for a job in Dallas and moved into an apartment and then into Jay's Texas home, they'd tossed out a couple of questions each day, determined to know all they could about each other for as long as they could.

She squeezed his hand. "You want the truth, or the nice, politically correct lie?"

"I hate politics, so the truth, of course. This game always requires the truth."

She mulled over her answer, a little embarrassed to admit it. "Okay, when we landed in Alaska and I couldn't get my luggage out of the bin. You came over to help and walked up looking ticked off, but then you smiled and said hello." She looked over at him, an impish gleam taking over her face as something occurred to her. "So you know what that means, don't you?"

He whipped her around and met her eye to eye, forehead to forehead. "Do not say it, Anna. Do. Not. Say. It."

She knew he would hate her next words, but she didn't care. She slowly opened her mouth to speak, enjoying the pained look on his face.

He gripped her shoulders. "I'm warning you…"

"It means…" She smiled wide and wiggled out of his grasp, then spoke in the sultriest voice she could deliver.

"…You had me at hello."

Jay let out a groan that echoed through the mountains, then jerked her to him. "Only a sap would fall for that stupid *Jerry Maguire* line. It's gonna cost you more than just a kiss this time."

She giggled. "I'm so scared. Whatever will I—"

Her words were cut short when he locked his mouth over hers. She fought to get away for a second, but then sighed and gave up, falling into the kiss as she gave into her husband's demands. Because this past year she had learned that sometimes…sometimes…

You just had to do what you were told.

The End

Also from Amy Matayo:

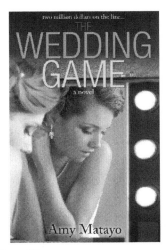

Cannon James has a plan: Sign on as a contestant for his father's new reality show, marry a blonde hand-picked by the producers, and walk away two million dollars richer. It's all been arranged. Easy. Clean. No regrets. Until Ellie McAllister ruins everything by winning the viewer's vote. Now he has to convince America that he's head over heels in love with her. Not easy to do since she's a walking disaster.

Ellie McAllister has her own problems. She needs money, and she needs it now. Despite her parent's objections and her belief that marriage is sacred, she signs on to The Wedding Game...and wins. Now she's married to a guy she can't stand, and if she wants her hands on the money, she has six months to make voters believe she loves him. Not easy to do since he's the most arrogant man in America.

It doesn't take long for Ellie and Cannon to realize they've made a mess of things…even less time for their feelings for one another to change. But is it too late for them? More importantly, can the worst decision they've ever made actually be one of the best?

Made in the USA
Charleston, SC
30 November 2014